W9-BRN-481

Ex-Library Friends of
Lake County Public Library

The Mother-in-Law

Also by Sally Hepworth

The Family Next Door

The Mother's Promise

The Things We Keep

The Secrets of Midwives

Wenn du an meiner Seite bist

The Mother-in-Law

Sally Hepworth

St. Martin's Press
New York

LAKE COUNTY PUBLIC LIBRARY

3 3113 03529 6716

This is a work of fiction. All of the characters, organizations, and events portrayed in this novel are either products of the author's imagination or are used fictitiously.

THE MOTHER-IN-LAW. Copyright © 2019 by Sally Hepworth. All rights reserved. Printed in the United States of America. For information, address St. Martin's Press, 175 Fifth Avenue, New York, N.Y. 10010.

www.stmartins.com

Library of Congress Cataloging-in-Publication Data

Names: Hepworth, Sally, author.
Title: The mother-in-law / Sally Hepworth.
Description: First edition. | New York, N.Y.: St. Martin's Press, 2019.
Identifiers: LCCN 2018046838| ISBN 9781250120922 (hardcover) |
    ISBN 9781250225177 (international, sold outside the U.S., subject to rights
    availability) | ISBN 9781250120946 (ebook)
Subjects: LCSH: Domestic fiction. | GSAFD: Mystery fiction.
Classification: LCC PR9619.4.H48 M679 2019 | DDC 823/.92—dc23
LC record available at https://lccn.loc.gov/2018046838

Our books may be purchased in bulk for promotional, educational, or business use. Please contact your local bookseller or the Macmillan Corporate and Premium Sales Department at 1-800-221-7945, extension 5442, or by email at MacmillanSpecialMarkets@macmillan.com.

First Edition: April 2019

10 9 8 7 6 5 4 3 2 1

LAKE COUNTY PUBLIC LIBRARY

For my mother-in-law, Anne,
who I would never dream of murdering.

And for my father-in-law, Peter,
who, on the odd occasion, I have.

Acknowledgments

Here we are again, another set of acknowledgements—my fifth to date. Fifth! I can't quite believe it.

I'd like to start by pointing out that while I have had fleeting murderous thoughts about many people in my life (you know who you are!), I have never once fantasized about murdering my mother-in-law. I suspect this is the reason I was able to write this book without blowing the entire family apart. So thank you, Anne, for being astoundingly good humored through this whole process. I'm not sure all mothers-in-law would have been so gracious upon hearing the title of her daughter-in-law's upcoming book.

To my amazing crew of police who fielded my unorthodox questions—Megan MacInnes, Andria Richardson, and Kerryn Merrett. Thank you for answering my emails, reading the manuscript, and even helping me brainstorm murder techniques (reminding me that if my mother-in-law were to suddenly die of unknown causes, it would all be on the record). Ladies, I am forever in your debt.

And where would I be without my incredible editor, Jennifer Enderlin? Thank you for trusting my instincts and helping me regain control of my manuscript when I stop trusting them. You embody what a good editor is. Thank you also to the team at St. Martin's, many of whom I had the pleasure of meeting in New York last year. I look forward to many more meetings.

I'd like to extend my thanks to my publishers around the world. Special thanks to Cate Paterson and Alex Lloyd at Pan Macmillan Australia for your keen editorial eye . . . and for taking me out for lunch occasionally. I love lunch.

To my publicists—the irreplaceable Katie Bassel and the incredible Lucy Inglis—if I could bottle the two of you, I would. If anyone knows a way to do this, please let me know.

To my gorgeous Rob Weisbach. How did I get so lucky? You are the best in the business and a true gentleman. I'm so grateful for all that you do. (Also thank you for starting to use emojis—you know how I love them.)

To my writing squad aka The Bellotta Girls (it has a nice ring to it, doesn't it?), thank you for sharing the joys and indignities of being a published author with me. As far as I know I'm still the only one who has had a book shoplifted during a signing, and I'll wear that badge with honor. Special thanks to Jane Cockram and Lisa Ireland for reading this book in draft form and giving me feedback. Also special thanks to Meredith Jaeger, my critique partner and friend.

To my family and friends who live in terror of being cast as a villain in one of my books. It's a valid fear. Be nice to me.

And finally, to my readers—thank you for allowing me to share these characters with you. I hope they touch you, move you or entertain you in some way. If they do, my job here is done.

The Mother-in-Law

Lucy

I am folding laundry at my kitchen table when the police car pulls up. There's no fanfare—no sirens or flashing lights—yet that little niggle starts in the pit of my stomach, Mother Nature's warning that all is not well. It's getting dark out, early evening, and the neighbors' porch lights are starting to come on. It's *dinnertime*. Police don't arrive on your doorstep at dinnertime unless something is wrong.

I glance through the archway to the living room where my slothful children are stretched across different pieces of furniture, angled toward their respective devices. Alive. Unharmed. In good health apart from, perhaps, a mild screen addiction. Seven-year-old Archie is watching a family play Wii games on the big iPad; four-year-old Harriet is watching little girls in America unwrap toys on the little iPad. Even two-year-old Edie is staring, slack-jawed, at the television. I feel some measure of comfort that my family is all under this roof. At least most of them are. *Dad*, I think suddenly. *Oh no, please not Dad.*

I look back at the police car. The headlights illuminate a light mist of rain.

At least it's not the children, a guilty little voice in my head whispers. *At least it isn't Ollie.* Ollie is on the back deck, grilling burgers. Safe. He came home from work early today, not feeling well apparently, though he doesn't seem particularly unwell. In any case, he's alive and I'm wholeheartedly grateful for that.

The rain has picked up a little now, turning the mist into distinct, precise raindrops. The police kill the engine, but don't get out right away. I ball up a pair of Ollie's socks and place them on top of his pile and then reach for another pair. I should stand up, go to the door, but my hands continue to fold on autopilot, as if by continuing to act normally the police car will cease to exist and all will be right in the world again. But it doesn't work. Instead, a uniformed policeman emerges from the driver's seat.

"Muuuuum!" Harriet calls. "Edie is watching the TV!"

Two weeks ago, a prominent news journalist had spoken out publicly about her "revulsion" that children under the age of three were exposed to TV, actually going so far as to call it "child abuse." Like most Australian mothers, I'd been incensed about this and followed with the predictable diatribe of, "What would she know? She probably has a team of nannies and hasn't looked after her children for a day in her life!" before swiftly instating the "no screens for Edie rule" which lasted until twenty minutes ago when I was on the phone with the energy company, and Edie decided to try the old "Mum, muuuum, MUUUUUM . . ." trick until I relented, popping on an episode of *Play School* and retreating to the bedroom to finish my phone call.

"It's all right, Harriet," I say, my eyes still on the window.

Harriet's cross little face appears in front of me, her dark brown hair and thick fringe swishing around her face like a mop. "But you SAID . . ."

"Never mind what I said. A few minutes won't hurt."

The cop looks to be midtwenties, thirty at a push. His police hat is in his hand but he wedges it under one arm to tug at the front of his too-tight trousers. A short, rotund policewoman of a similar age gets out of the passenger side, her hat firmly on her head. They come around the car and start up the path side by side. They are definitely coming to our place. *Nettie*, I think suddenly. *It's about Nettie.*

It's possible. Ollie's sister has certainly had her share of health issues lately. Or maybe it's Patrick? Or is it something else entirely?

The fact is, part of me knows it's not Nettie or Patrick, or Dad. It's funny sometimes what you just *know*.

"Burgers are up."

The fly screen door scrapes open and Ollie appears at the back door holding a plate of meat. The girls flock to him and he snaps his "crocodile tongs" while they jump up and down, squealing loudly enough to nearly drown out the knock at the door.

Nearly.

"Was that the door?" Ollie raises an eyebrow, curious rather than concerned. In fact, he looks animated. *An unexpected guest on a week-night! Who could it be?*

Ollie is the social one of the two of us, the one that volunteers on the Parents and Friends' committee at the kids' school because "it's a good way to meet people," who hangs over the back fence to say hi to the neighbors if he hears them talking in the garden, who approaches people who look vaguely familiar and tries to figure out if they know each other. A people person. To Ollie, an unexpected knock on the door during the week signals excitement rather than doom.

But, of course, he hasn't seen the cop car.

Edie tears down the corridor. "I get it, I get it."

"Hold on a minute, Edie-bug," Ollie says, looking for somewhere to put down the tray of burgers. He isn't fast enough though because by the time he finds some counter space, Edie has already tossed open the door.

"Poleeth!" she says, awed.

This, of course, is the part where I should run after her, intercept the police at the door and apologize, but my feet are concreted to the floor. Luckily, Ollie is already jogging up behind Edie, ruffling her hair playfully.

"G'day," he says to the cops. He glances over his shoulder back into the house, his mind caught up in the action of a few seconds ago, perhaps wondering if he remembered to turn off the gas canister or checking that he'd placed the burger plate securely on the counter. It's the classic, unassuming behavior of someone about to get bad news. I actually feel like I am watching us all on a TV show—the handsome clueless dad, the cute toddler. The regular suburban family who are about to have their lives turned inside out . . . ruined forever.

"What can I do for you?" Ollie says finally, turning his attention back to the cops.

"I'm Sr. Constable Arthur," I hear a woman say, though I can't see her from my vantage point, "and this is Constable Perkins. Are you Oliver Goodwin?"

"I am." Ollie smiles down at Edie, even throws her a wink. It's enough to convince me that I'm being overly dramatic. Even if there's bad news, it may not be that bad. It may not even be *our* bad news. Perhaps one of the neighbors was burgled? Police always *canvased the area* after something like that, didn't they?

Suddenly I look forward to that moment in a few minutes' time when I know that everything's fine. I think about how Ollie and I will laugh about how paranoid I was. *You won't believe what I thought,* I'll say to him, and he'll roll his eyes and smile. *Always worrying,* he'll say. *How do you ever get anything done with all that worrying?*

But when I edge forward a few paces, I see that my worrying isn't unnecessary. I see it in the somberness of the policeman's expression, in the downward turn of the corners of his mouth.

The policewoman glances at Edie, then back at Ollie. "Is there somewhere we can talk . . . privately?"

The first traces of uncertainty appear on Ollie's face. His shoulders stiffen and he stands a little bit taller. Perhaps unconsciously, he pushes Edie back from the door, behind him, shielding her from something.

"Edie-bug, would you like me to put on *The Wiggles*?" I say, stepping forward finally.

Edie shakes her head resolutely, her gaze not shifting from the police. Her soft round face is alight with interest; her chunky, wobbly legs are planted with improbable firmness.

"Come on, honey," I try again, sweeping a hand over her pale gold hair. "How about an ice cream?"

This is more of a dilemma for Edie. She glances at me, watching for a long moment, assessing whether I can be trusted. Finally I shout for Archie to get out the Paddle Pops and she scampers off down the hallway.

"Come in," Ollie says to the police, and they do, sending me a quick, polite smile. A *sorry* smile. A smile that pierces my heart, unpicks me a little. *It's not the neighbors,* that smile says. This bad news is yours.

There aren't a lot of private communal areas in our house so Ollie guides the police to the dining room and pulls out a couple of chairs. I follow, pushing my newly folded laundry into a basket. The piles collapse into each other like tumbling buildings. The police sit on the chairs, Ollie balances on the arm of the sofa, and I remain sharply upright, stiff. Bracing.

"Firstly I need to confirm that you are relatives of Diana Goodwin—"

"Yes," Ollie says, "she's my mother."

"Then I'm very sorry to inform you," the policewoman starts, and I close my eyes because I already know what she is going to say.

My mother-in-law is dead.

2

Lucy

Ten years ago . . .

Someone once told me that you have two families in your life—the one you are born into and the one you choose. But that's not entirely true, is it? Yes, you may get to choose your partner, but you don't, for instance, choose your children. You don't choose your brothers- or sisters-in-law, you don't choose your partner's spinster aunt with the drinking problem or cousin with the revolving door of girlfriends who don't speak English. More importantly, you don't choose your mother-in-law. The cackling mercenaries of fate determine it all.

"Hello?" Ollie calls. "Anybody home?"

I stand in the yawning foyer of the Goodwins' home and pan around at the marble extending out in every direction. A winding staircase sweeps from the basement up to the first floor beneath a magnificent crystal chandelier. I feel like I've stepped into the pages of a *Hello!* magazine spread, the ones with the ridiculous photos of celebrities sprawling on ornate furniture, and on grassy knolls in riding boots with golden retrievers at their feet. I've always pictured that this is what the inside of Buckingham Palace must look like, or if not Buckingham, at least one of the smaller palaces—St. James's or Clarence House.

I try to catch Ollie's eye, to . . . what? Admonish him? Cheer? Quite frankly I'm not sure but it's moot since he's already charging into the house, announcing our arrival. To say I'm unprepared for this is the most glorious of understatements. When Ollie had suggested I come to his parents' house for dinner, I'd been picturing lasagna and salad in a quaint, blond-brick bungalow, the kind of home I'd grown up in. I'd pictured an adoring mother clasping a photo album of sepia-colored baby photos and a brusquely proud but socially awkward father, clasping a can of beer and a cautious smile. Instead, artwork and sculptures were uplit and gleaming, and the parents, socially awkward or otherwise, are nowhere to be seen.

"Ollie!" I catch Ollie's elbow and am about to whisper furiously when a plump ruddy-faced man rushes through a large arched doorway at the back of the house, clutching a glass of red wine.

"Dad!" Ollie cries. "There you are!"

"Well, well. Look who the cat dragged in."

Tom Goodwin is the very opposite of his tall, dark-haired son. Short, overweight and unstylish, his red-checked shirt is tucked into chinos that are belted below his substantial paunch. He throws his arms around his son, and Ollie thumps his old man on the back.

"You must be Lucy," Tom says, after releasing Ollie. He takes my hand and pumps it heartily, letting out a low whistle. "My word. Well done, son."

"It's nice to meet you, Mr. Goodwin." I smile.

"Tom! Call me Tom." He smiles at me like he's won the Easter raffle, then he appears to remember himself. "Diana! Diana, where are you? They're here!"

After a moment or two Ollie's mother emerges from the back of the house. She's wearing a white shirt and navy slacks and brushing nonexistent crumbs from the front of her shirt. I suddenly wonder about my outfit choice, a full-skirted 1950s red and white polka-dot dress that had belonged to my mother. I thought it would be charming but now it just seems outlandish and stupid, especially given Ollie's mum's plain and demure attire.

"I'm sorry," she says, from several paces away. "I didn't hear the bell."

"This is Lucy," Tom says.

Diana extends her hand. As I reach for it, I notice that she is almost a full head taller than her husband, despite her flat shoes, and she is thin as a street post, apart from a slight middle-aged thickening at the waist. She has silver hair cut into an elegant, chin-length bob, a straight Roman nose, and unlike Tom, bears a strong resemblance to her son.

I also notice that her handshake is cold.

"It's nice to meet you, Mrs. Goodwin," I say, dropping her hand to offer the bunch of flowers I'm carrying. I'd insisted on stopping at the florist on the way, even though Ollie had said, "Flowers aren't really her thing."

"Flowers are every woman's thing," I'd replied with a roll of my eyes. But as I take in her lack of jewelry, her unpainted nails and sensible shoes, I start to get the feeling that I'm wrong.

"Hello, Mum," Ollie says, pulling his mother in a bear hug, which she accepts, if not quite embraces. I know, from many conversations with Ollie, that he adores his mother. He practically bursts with pride as he talks about the charity she runs single-handedly for refugees in Australia, many of them pregnant or with small children. *Of course* she would think flowers were trivial, I realize suddenly. I'm an idiot. Perhaps I should have brought baby clothes, or maternity supplies?

"All right, Ollie," she says after a moment or two, when he doesn't let her go. She pulls herself upright. "I haven't even had a chance to say hello properly to Lucy!"

"Why don't we head to the lounge for some drinks and we can all get to know each other better," Tom says, and we all turn toward the back of the house. That's when I notice a face peeking around the corner.

"Nettie!" Ollie cries.

If there is a lack of resemblance between Ollie and Tom, there is no doubt Antoinette is Tom's daughter. She has his ruddy cheeks and stockiness, while at the same time being endearingly pretty. Stylish too, in a grey woolen dress and black suede boots. According to Ollie, his younger sister is married, childless and some sort of executive at a marketing company who is often asked to speak at conferences about women and the glass ceiling. At thirty-two years old, only two years older than me, I'd found this impressive and a little intimidating, but it is all swept under the rug when she greets me with an enormous bear hug. The Goodwins, it appears, are huggers.

All of them, perhaps, except Diana.

"I've heard so much about you," Nettie says. She links her arm with mine and I am engulfed in a cloud of expensive-smelling perfume. "Come and meet my husband, Patrick."

Nettie drags me through an arched doorway, past what looks like an elevator—*an elevator!* As we walk we pass framed artwork and floral arrangements, and photos of family holidays on the ski slopes and at the beach. There is one photo of Tom, Diana, Nettie and Ollie on camels in the desert with a pyramid in the background, all of them holding hands and raising their hands skyward.

Growing up, I used to go to the beach town of Portarlington for holidays, less than an hour's drive from my house.

We stop in a room that is roughly the size of my apartment, filled with sofas and armchairs, huge, expensive-looking rugs and heavy wooden side tables. A gigantic man rises from an armchair.

"Patrick," he says. His handshake is clammy but he looks apologetic so I pretend not to notice.

"Lucy. Nice to meet you."

I'm not sure what I expected for Nettie—perhaps someone small, sharp, eager to please, like her. At six feet three inches, I thought Ollie was tall, but Patrick is positively mountain-like—six seven at least. Apart from his height, he reminds me a little of Tom, in his plaid shirt and chinos, his round face and eager smile. He has a knitted sweater around his shoulders, preppy-style.

With all greetings out of the way, Ollie, Tom and Patrick sink into the large couch and Diana and Nettie wander off toward a drinks table. I hesitate a moment, then fall into step beside the women.

"You sit down, Lucy," Diana directs me.

"Oh, I'm happy to help—"

But Diana raises her hand like a stop sign. "Please," she says. "Just sit."

Diana is obviously trying to be polite, but I can't help but feel a little rejected. She isn't to know, of course, that I'd fantasized about bumping elbows with her in the kitchen, perhaps even facing a little salad crisis together that I could overcome by whipping up a make-shift dressing (a salad crisis was about all my culinary capabilities could stretch to). She isn't to know that I'd imagined nestling up to her as she took me through photo albums, family trees and long-winded stories that Ollie would groan about. She doesn't know I'd planned to spend the entire evening by her side, and by the time we went home, she'd be as enamored with me as I'd be with her.

Instead, I sat.

"So, you and Ollie work together?" Tom asks me, as I plant myself next to Ollie on the sofa.

"We do," I say. "Have done for three years."

"Three years?" Tom feigns shock. "Took your time, didn't you, mate?"

"It was a slow burn," Ollie says.

Ollie had been the classic, solid guy from work. The one always available to listen to my most terrible dating stories and offer a sympathetic shoulder. Ollie, unlike the powerful, take-charge assholes that I tended to date, was cheerful, unassuming and a consistently good guy. Most importantly, he adored me. It had taken me a while to realize it, but being adored was much nicer than being messed around by charismatic bastards.

"He isn't your boss, is he?" Tom twinkles. It's horrendously sexist, but it's hard to be annoyed with Tom.

"Tom!" Diana chides, but it's clear she finds it hard to be annoyed with him too. She's back now with drinks, and she purses her lips in the manner of a mother trying to discipline her very cute, disobedient toddler. She hands me a glass of red wine and sits on the other side of Ollie.

"We're peers," I tell Tom. "I recruit for the technical positions, Ollie does support staff. We work closely together."

It began, oddly enough, in a dream. A bizarre, meandering dream that started at my great-aunt Gwen's ninetieth birthday and ended at the house where my best friend from primary school lived, but she wasn't a little girl anymore, she was an old lady. But somewhere in the middle, Ollie was there. And he was different somehow. Sexier. The next day, at work, I sent him an email saying he'd been in my dream the night before. The expected "What was I doing?" banter followed, with an undercurrent. Ollie's office was right next door to mine, but we'd always sent each other emails from the next office—witty commentary about our shared boss's Donald Trump hair, suspicious behavior at the office Christmas party, requests for sushi orders for lunch. But that day, it was different. By the end of the day my heart was skipping a beat when his name appeared in my in-box.

For a while I'd kept my head about it. It was a rendezvous, a tryst . . . not a relationship and certainly not *the* relationship. But when I noticed him giving money to the drunk at the train station every morning (even after the drunk abused him and accused him of stealing his booze); when he'd spotted a lost little boy at the shopping center and immediately lifted him up over his head and asked if he could see his mum anywhere; when he began to occupy more and more of my thoughts, a realization came: this is it. He's the one.

I tell Ollie's family the story (minus the dream), my arms

spinning around me as I talk quickly and without a pause, as I tend to do when I get nervous. Tom is positively enraptured at the storytelling, patting his son on the back at intervals as I talk.

"So tell me about . . . all of you," I say, when I've run out of steam.

"Nettie is a marketing executive at MartinHoldsworth," Tom says, proud as punch. "Runs a whole department."

"And what about you, Patrick?" I ask.

"I run a bookkeeping business," Patrick says. "It's small now, but we'll expand with time."

"So tell me about your parents, Lucy," Diana jumps in. "What do they do?"

"My dad was a professor of modern European History. Retired now. And my mother died of breast cancer." It's been seventeen years, so talking about it is uncomfortable rather than upsetting. Mostly the discomfort is for other people, who, upon hearing this news, have to figure out something to say.

"I'm sorry to hear that," Tom says, his booming voice bringing a palpable steadiness to the room.

"I lost my own mother a few years back," Patrick says. "You never get over it."

"You never do," I agree, feeling a sudden kinship with Patrick. "But to answer your question, Diana, my mum was a stay-at-home mother. And before that, a primary schoolteacher."

I always feel proud to tell people she was a teacher. Since her death, countless people have told me what a wonderful teacher she was, how she would have done anything for her students. It seems a waste that she never went back to it, even after I started school myself.

"Why bother having a child, if you're not going to stick around and enjoy her?" she used to say, which is kind of funny since she wasn't able to stick around and enjoy me anyway, dying when I was thirteen.

"Her name was . . ." I start at the same time as Diana stands. We all stop talking and follow her with our eyes. For the first time, I understand the term *matriarch*, and the power of being one.

"Right then," she says. "I think dinner will be ready, if everyone would like to move to the table."

And with that, the conversation about my mother seems to be over.

We have roast lamb for dinner. Diana prepares and serves it herself. Given the size of their house I almost expected caterers to show up, but this part of the evening, at least, is comfortable and familiar.

"I was so impressed to hear about your charity," I say, once Diana is finally sitting rather than serving. "Ollie is so proud of you, he talks about it to anyone who'll listen."

Diana smiles vaguely in my direction, reaching for the cauliflower cheese. "Does he?"

"You'd better believe it. I'd love to hear more about it."

Diana spoons some cauliflower onto her plate, focusing intently on the transaction as if she were performing surgery. "Oh? What would you like to hear?"

"Well . . ." I feel under the spotlight suddenly. "I guess . . . what gave you the idea to start it? How did it get off the ground?"

Diana shrugs. "I just saw the need. It's not rocket science, collecting baby goods."

"She's humble." Tom pushes more lamb onto his fork, still

chewing what's in his mouth. He shoves the forkful into his mouth and keeps talking. "It's her Catholic upbringing."

"How did you two meet?" I ask, realizing that Ollie has never told me this.

"They met at the movies," Nettie says. "Dad saw Mum across the foyer and sparks flew."

Tom and Diana exchange a glance. There is affection in their gaze but something else too, something I can't quite place.

"What can I say? I knew right away that she was the one. Diana wasn't like anyone else that I knew. She was . . . smarter. More interesting. Out of my league, I thought."

"Mum came from a well-to-do family," Nettie explains. "Middle class, Catholic. Dad was a country boy, no connections, no money. Nothing but the shirt on his back."

I take a moment to undo the unconscious conclusion I'd come to the moment I walked into the house—that Diana had married Tom for his money. It's a sexist thought, but not a ridiculous conclusion to come to, seeing the disparity in their looks. The fact that she'd married him for love raises Diana a few notches in my opinion.

"And how about you, Diana," I ask. "Did you just know?"

"Course she did!" Tom says, framing his face in his hands. "How could you not, seeing this face?"

Everyone laughs.

"Actually I've been trying to tell him I'm not interested for nearly forty years but he just keeps speaking over the top of me," Diana says wryly. She and Tom exchange a smile.

After her earlier formality, it's nice to see this side of her. I allow myself to hope that once we've spent some more time together, she'll let me into this inner sanctum of hers. Maybe one day I'll even start helping her with her charity? Diana might not be the easiest nut to crack, but I'll get there. Before long, we're sure to be the best of friends.

I was thirteen when my mother, Joy, died. Mum was aptly named—always having fun, never taking herself too seriously. She wore kerchiefs and dangly earrings, and she sang loudly in the car when the radio played a song she liked. At my birthday parties, she came in fancy dress, even though none of the other adults did, and she had a pair of tap shoes that she liked to wear from time to time, even though she'd never learned how to tap.

That was the kind of person my mother was.

The only time I saw Mum dress in black—without so much as a headband or wiglet or adornment—was when she attended a conference or dinner with Dad. Dad is the polar opposite of Mum—conservative, serious, gentle. The only time Mum reined in her personality, in fact, was for Dad. When Dad decided to switch tenures midway through his academic career—something tricky and likely to undermine his career and our livelihood—she supported him without question. "Dad's job is to look after us, our job is to look after him."

Dad never recovered after she died. Apparently statistics indicate that most men remarry within three years of a previous relationship ending, but twenty years on, Dad is still happily single. *Your mother was my life partner*, he always says, *and a life partner is for life.*

Dad hired a housekeeper after Mum died, to cook and clean and shop for us. Maria was probably fifty, but with her black hair flecked with grey and rolled into a coil she may as well have been a hundred. She wore skirts and pantyhose and low-heeled court shoes, and floral aprons she sewed herself. Her own children were grown and the grandchildren hadn't shown up yet. She came from twelve noon until six P.M. every day. I don't know what Maria's official role was insofar as I was concerned, but she was always there when I got home from school and it seemed like it was the best part of her day. It was the best part of my day too. She'd empty my bag and rinse out my lunchboxes and chop up fruit and cheese on a plate for my afternoon tea—things Mum wouldn't have done in a blind fit. With hindsight, some may have felt smothered by Maria.

I simply felt mothered.

Once, when I had the flu, Maria came for the whole day. She pottered around, checking on me periodically, bringing me water or tea or a cool cloth for my forehead. A couple of times, when I was dozing and heard her enter the room, I'd let out a little moan, just to hear Maria fussing. She'd kiss my forehead and bring me water. She even fed me soup with a spoon.

It was, hand on heart, one of the best days of my life.

Maria left when I turned eighteen. She'd had her first grandchild by then, as well as an aging dog with glaucoma, and besides, I was nearly grown so there wasn't much for her to do anymore. After that, Dad got a regular cleaner, and started doing his grocery shopping on his way home from work. Maria kept in touch with birthday gifts and Christmas cards, but eventually her life got filled up with her own family. And that's when I realized. I needed *my own* family. A husband, some children, an old blind dog. Most importantly, I needed a Maria. Someone to share recipes, to give wisdom, and to drown me in waves of maternal love. Someone who wouldn't leave and go back to her own family because I *was* her family.

I didn't have a mother anymore. But one day, perhaps, I'd have a mother-in-law.

After dinner, Tom tells us to go hang out in the "den," which is a room with soaring cathedral ceilings and floor-to-ceiling bookshelves and masses of leather. It reminds me of a gentlemen's club. It has an enormous TV that rises up out of a buffet, as well as an actual bar, loaded with spirits. Ollie has been called into the kitchen to help with coffee and dessert (which I assume means they want to debrief about me) so I am kicking it in the gentlemen's club with Nettie and Patrick.

"So," Patrick says, from the bar. He is making us some sort of cocktail, which I don't need because I've already had two glasses of wine, but he seems so happy messing about with all the spirits that I don't have the heart to tell him. "What do you think of Diana?"

"Patrick," Nettie warns.

"What?" A smile curls at the corners of his mouth. "It isn't a trick question."

I scramble pathetically for something to say but honestly, there isn't much. Diana spent most of dinner intermittently asking if anyone wanted any more vegetables. She deflected any questions I asked her, and apart from her little chuckle about her first meeting with Tom, she remained frustratingly distant all evening. Honestly, if it hadn't been for Tom and Nettie and Patrick, it wouldn't have felt like a social function at all. All I know is that Diana is nothing like I was hoping.

"Well . . . I think she . . . is . . ." I roll several words around in my mouth—*nice, interesting, kind*—but none feel right and I don't want to be insincere. I am, after all, not just here to impress the parents. If things work out between Ollie and me, I'll be spending alternate Christmases with Nettie and Patrick for the rest of my life . . . so it is important to be real. Problem is, it is too early to be *really* real. Meeting the family, I realize, requires you to be a politician. You need to know where to throw your support at what time to yield maximum results. I decide to do as my mother always told me and find something true to say.

"I think she is a wonderful cook."

Patrick laughs a little too heartily. Nettie looks daggers at him.

"Oh come on, Nets." Patrick gives her a poke in the ribs. "Listen, she could be worse. At least we have Tom, right?"

It's cold comfort. I'd had such a distilled picture of what I wanted in a potential mother-in-law—no father-in-law, not even Tom, could take its place. Patrick, on the other hand, seems to have accepted his frosty mother-in-law without too much concern, despite the fact that she clearly isn't his cup of tea either.

"Well," I say after a few minutes, when Ollie has still not showed his face and I get the feeling Nettie wants a moment alone with Patrick. "I might go see how dessert is coming along."

I walk through double doors into the great room that feeds into a wide kitchen, centered on a huge granite island. Ollie and Diana are at the island with their backs to me, and appear to be arranging items onto a cheese board.

"It doesn't matter what I think," Diana is saying.

"It matters to me," Ollie says.

"Well it shouldn't." Diana enunciates her words like a librarian or piano teacher, crisply and properly, not in the least uncertain. I pause in the doorway.

"Are you saying you *don't* like her?"

Diana pauses for far too long. "I'm saying it doesn't *matter* what I think."

I pull back, out of sight, tucking myself around the corner. I feel as though I've been sucker punched. Of all the worries I'd had—that she wasn't the mother-in-law I'd wanted, that she didn't live up to my expectations—I hadn't, narcissistically as it turns out, considered that she wouldn't like me.

"Seriously, Mum? You're not going to tell me what you think of Lucy?"

"Oh, Ollie!" I picture her shaking her hand like she's swatting a fly. "I think she's *fine*."

Fine. I take a moment to digest that. I'm *fine.*

I search for an upside to *fine*, but I can't seem to find one. Being called *fine* is like being told your outfit doesn't make you look fat. Being called *fine* is like being the day-old sandwich that doesn't give you food poisoning. Being called *fine* is like being the daughter-in-law that you didn't want, but who could have, on balance, been worse.

"There you are, Lucy!"

I whirl around. Tom is at the mouth of the hallway, beaming. "Come and help me choose some dessert wine. I never know which one to go for."

"Oh, I don't really know much about w—"

But Tom is already dragging me down to a cellar with an astonishing array of wines. I fake my way through a dessert wine tasting session, grateful for the dark to hide the tears that I blink back.

To me, *fine* is as good as dead.

3

Lucy

The present . . .

The police are in my kitchen. The guy cop, Simon, has found mugs
and tea bags and milk without having to ask where they are, and
now he's making me a cup of tea. The female cop, Stella, is beside
him, loading up the dishwasher with plastic plates and tipping the
remnants of burger buns and ketchup into the rubbish.

Ollie is in the hallway, on the phone with Nettie. I can hear him
explaining that he's not sure . . . that he's told her everything he
knows . . . that *he said he doesn't know!* . . . that she should just come
over and talk to the police herself.

He is talking about Diana, I remind myself. Diana is *dead*. The
fact that we never got along seems to vanish in the face of this, or
at least soften a little, and I find myself gripped by a profound sad-

ness. It's as though Diana's death has elevated her to a higher, almost noble status—making our past issues seem trivial, even petty. After all, no one gets along with their mother-in-law, do they? No one! My friend Emily's mother-in-law refuses to believe that Poppy is lactose intolerant (*what a load of nonsense, they didn't have all these "intolerances" in our day,* she says.) Jane's mother-in-law can't fathom how she can use disposable nappies, especially after she'd gone to the trouble of purchasing Henry a box of cloth ones. Sasha's mother-in-law talks incessantly about the inheritance she is apparently going to receive, making sure to remind her how lucky she should feel. Danielle's mother-in-law is a gratuitous advice giver, Kena's is an interferer. Sara is the only one who adores her mother-in-law, and that's because Marg looks after Sara's children two days a week, while also doing the family's laundry, ironing and preparing homemade meals for the freezer. (Marg is what we call a mother-in-law unicorn.)

The kids are finally in bed. Unfortunately, the moment after the police told us about Diana, they decided to show up and demand our attention, so Simon and Stella kindly offered to hang around until they'd been fed and put to bed. (Simon had even gone as far as to *serve* up the burgers and chat to the kids while they ate!) It had been hell, having to wait for the details, but we couldn't see any way around it. When it came to bedtime, Ollie took Edie (the easiest of the three to put to bed, requiring nothing more than a chorus of "Twinkle Twinkle," her lambie and a pacifier) and I let him because, after all, his mother has just died. I took the older two, who, it seemed, had finally twigged that the police must have come to our house for a reason. At a loss, I told them they had come to ask us about a stolen bike.

"Whose bike?" Archie demanded as I piled the covers on him, trying to push him down with them. "Not mine?"

"No, not yours." He popped up again.

"Harriet's?" I pushed him back down. "She probably dumped it somewhere and is pretending it was stolen. She's been wanting a new one. If she gets a new one, I want a new one."

"No one is getting a new bike."

He regarded me skeptically but remained in a supine position. I'm about to kiss his forehead when, *bounce*, he's upright again.

"Do they think *I* stole the bike?"

"No, Archie."

He settled after I managed to convince him that Harriet was not, under any circumstances, getting a new bike.

Harriet's concerns were a little different. As I tucked her under the covers, she shifted and squirmed at my side. "Why would the police come to *our* house about a bike that isn't even ours?"

"Well . . . they thought we might know where it is."

"Why would they think that?" There was something all-knowing in her unblinking blue eyes. Harriet often caught me off guard with this all-knowing look. "Maybe," she said, before I could answer, "they are just *saying* they are here about a bike, but really they are gathering information about something else?"

Harriet had watched *Spy Kids* at a sleepover last weekend and I suspected *that* was responsible for all this *gathering information* talk. But who knew? Harriet had always been a perceptive little thing. Too wise for her four years.

"There's only one way to find out," I told her. "I'll go speak to them and I'll let you know tomorrow. You get some sleep."

She nodded slowly and slipped under the covers, looking anything but sleepy. She actually looked a little *rattled*. Which was odd, considering she didn't even know that her grandmother had died.

I look up as Ollie emerges from the hallway, his phone in his hand. He thumps down on a kitchen chair and I slide down from my bar stool and sit beside him at the table. "How was Nettie?" I ask.

Ollie rests his elbows on the table, rests his forehead in his left hand. "She's on her way over."

"Nettie is?"

"And Patrick."

I inhale, ignoring the tiny flutter of panic this kicks off in me. For goodness sake! *Of course* Patrick and Nettie were coming over. Nettie's *mother* has just died. It's a good thing, us being forced together like this. Hadn't I been hoping for weeks that Nettie would reach out to us?

Simon brings my cup of tea to the kitchen table, and he and Stella pull out chairs and sit. We all square up, preparing ourselves. Any informality we'd adopted while the kids were awake is gone and we're ready for business.

"So . . . ?" Ollie prompts.

"I'll get straight down to it," Simon says. "We don't have all the information yet; the cause of death is still being investigated. What we do know is that a neighbor alerted police just after five P.M. this afternoon, reporting that she'd seen your mother's unmoving body through a window. By the time the police got inside it appears she'd been dead for several hours."

"Yes, but what *caused it*?" Ollie can't keep the frustration out of his voice. I reach out and place a hand over his.

"We won't know for sure until the results of the autopsy," Simon says, "but some materials were found, as well as a letter, which appear to indicate that your mother may have taken her own life."

In the silence that follows I find myself aware of everything, the faint sheen of rain or sweat across the police officer's temples, the fly caught between the curtain and the window, the blood pulsing wildly around in my head.

"I realize this must be a shock," Stella says.

"Yes," I say.

I turn my attention to Ollie, who is oddly still. I put an arm around him, rubbing his back in swift rhythmic circles, like I do to the kids when they fall over and hurt themselves. Still, he doesn't move.

"Are you sure?" he asks finally. "That she . . ."

"The note was quite clear about what she'd decided to do. And the . . . materials must have been purchased in advance, which indicates this wasn't a spur-of-the-moment act."

Ollie stands suddenly and begins walking with purpose in one direction, then back the other way. Then, abruptly, he plants his feet.

"What materials did you find?"

"Unfortunately, we're not permitted to tell you that at present. Until the coroner rules it a suicide we have to treat it as a potential homicide—"

"*A potential . . . ?*" Ollie's mouth hovers open, but he can't seem to finish the sentence.

"It's just something we can't rule out until we're told to. I understand this is difficult to hear." Simon's demeanor is competent and professional, yet I find it difficult to take him seriously. He is just so young. How much could he *possibly* understand with that youthful, unlined face?

"Can you think of any reason your mother might have wanted to take her own life?" Stella asks. Her focus is on Ollie, but her gaze flickers to me every so often, as if surreptitiously. "Maybe she was depressed? Did she suffer from mental or physical illness?"

"She had breast cancer," Ollie says. "But she wouldn't take her own life. I don't believe it."

Ollie drops his head into his hands. But a moment later, when light beams in the front window he looks up again. Patrick's car is pulling into the driveway.

"They're here," I say needlessly.

"Go ahead," Stella tells us.

Ollie and I walk to the door. Patrick unpacks himself from the driver's side, standing a full head and shoulders above the vehicle. He walks around the car to open the door for Nettie, but she is slow to emerge. When she finally appears, it's a shock. Her face is gaunt; her eyes are sunken. It's only been a few weeks since I've seen her, but in that time, she must have lost a stone.

"Nettie," I say, as she makes her way up the steps. "I'm . . . so sorry."

"Thank you."

She keeps her eyes down so it catches her off guard when Ollie throws his arms around her. Perhaps because of the surprise, she allows it. Patrick waits a few paces behind, greeting me with a single nod.

I turn and head back into the house.

Inside, Simon and Stella are gathering up mugs and talking

quietly. I slip into the bathroom. Bath toys are scattered all over the floor and the kids' toothbrushes are lined up on the vanity, still loaded with toothpaste because we forgot to brush their teeth. I rinse them off and put them back into the plastic cup where they live. Then I open the cupboard under the sink and reach for an old yellow towel, one so threadbare I've only been keeping it for those occasions where one requires an old towel—mopping floors or shining shoes or cleaning up vomit. Ollie, of course, doesn't understand the concept of old towels and somehow always manages to select this one to put on display when we have guests over. But all of this is insignificant, of course, because Diana is dead.

"Lucy?" Ollie calls out from the next room. "Lucy? Where are you?"

"Just a minute," I say and I press the yellow towel to my face so no one will hear me cry.

4

Diana

The past . . .

"Oh that's right," Jan says. "You met the new *girlfriend* last night, didn't you? How did it go?"

Kathy, Liz, Jan and I are on the deck of the Baths, with the water a pane of blue-green glass behind us. We've ordered a seafood sharing platter, a bowl of shoestring fries and a bottle of Bollinger and the whole affair is both extremely pleasant and frightfully pretentious. A seagull hovers over Jan's right shoulder watching the fries with interest.

I lift my hand to block the sun from my eyes and notice the girls all looking at me intently.

"Yes, do tell, Diana," Kathy says.

The girls lean forward and I feel the self-conscious prickle of being the center of attention. At the same time I feel indignant. One of the reasons I enjoy the company of this particular group of friends—the wives of Tom's friends—is that they are usually far too interested in their own business to care about mine, and if there's one thing I *loathe*, it's people knowing my business.

"Yes, I met Lucy," I say vaguely. "It was fine."

I sip my drink. It's the first Wednesday of the month, our usual meet-up at the Brighton Baths. Once upon a time our meet-ups had, ostensibly, been a book club, and I'd been quite keen on that idea. The first book I'd suggested was a biography of Clementine Churchill, and I'd come to the Baths all prepared with a list of discussion points, only to find no one had read the darn thing. At the end of the meeting, no one suggested another book and since then, Jan had started calling it *drinks club*.

"Fine?" Jan whistles. "Oh dear."

"Why 'oh dear'?" I ask. "What's wrong with fine?"

"Damning with faint praise," Liz mutters.

"Nothing good ever started from *fine*," Kathy agrees.

I don't understand. As far as I am concerned, *fine* is an appropriate seal of approval for the son's new girlfriend. What else am I to say? *Love* is obviously too strong a word, and even *like* would be overstating it after a mere evening together—*Heaven forbid* I be one of those overbearing women that fawned all over the new girlfriend, begging to be best friends and shop together and go to the spa. As far as I am concerned, if Lucy loved my son and he loved her, she was fine by me. Absolutely *fine*.

"Come on, we're talking about Diana," Kathy says, lifting the champagne bottle from the ice bucket and finding it empty. She signals to the waiter to bring another. "Fine is actually very high praise."

Everyone chuckles, which I find perplexing. What was so wrong with *fine*? This was the problem with new friends. New, admittedly, was a stretch, as I'd been friends with Jan, Kathy and Liz for thirty years, but there was nothing like the friends you'd known all your life, the ones you never had to explain things to. Cynthia would have understood what I meant by *fine*. To this day, I still miss Cynth a lot.

"Did you give her a hard time?" Kathy asks. "Ask her about her intentions for your darling son?"

Why, pray tell, did everyone care so much what I thought anyway? Surely it was Ollie's opinion of her that mattered? In the grand scheme of things, after all, what I thought of her was largely unimportant. Some parents—including my own, Maureen and Walter—made their opinions count a little too much if you asked me. I grew up Catholic, with a mother who kept a close eye on what everyone in our neighborhood was up to, but especially her child. I'd promised myself long ago I wouldn't be like that. And, indeed, I won't.

"Were you pleasantly surprised?" Jan asks. "Horrified?"

"Neither," I reply because Lucy is exactly what I expected—pretty, neurotic, desperate to impress. Ollie's type to a tee. Born clever and attractive and a little bit quirky, she'd have spent her life being adored—by her parents first, and later, by the boys. She'd have been teacher's pet, a school prefect, a sporting champion. Things came easily to girls like her. And while I'd have liked to be happy for her, I'd seen too many girls for whom things didn't come so easily, for this not to irritate me.

"Not good enough for your son, is that it?" Jan asks knowingly.

"No one ever is," Liz agrees, bizarrely, as she doesn't have a son.

"I don't know," Kathy says, "I'd *pay* someone to take my Freddie off my hands. I'm terrified he's going to want to move in with me one of these days so he can quit his job and sit on his backside and watch reality television programs all day, calling himself a 'carer.' I'd give *anything* for a daughter-in-law. Someone to pluck the hairs from my chin and put on my lippy for me when I'm old and grey. Sons are useless at that sort of thing."

I munch on a couple of fries, and hope they'll argue it out among themselves. The bottom line is, it always takes a little adjustment when a new spouse joins the family. They have different values, different histories, different opinions. It might all work out wonderfully, but, of course, it might not. Patrick has been around a few years now and while I'd been less than thrilled about him, we've adjusted. I don't doubt it will be the same for Lucy if she sticks around. Still, it's natural to brace a little. A change is coming—of course we're going to be on our toes for a while.

"Do you think she's a gold digger?" Jan lays a hand on my forearm, making the comment a little more sinister and exciting.

"No."

The girls can't hide their disappointment. "Not another Patrick then?"

I don't respond. I have my own feelings on Patrick's little bookkeeping business, which he runs with the enthusiasm of someone who is expecting a sizable inheritance to come and take over his problems. It's none of my business, and it's certainly none of Jan's. Besides, no matter his work ethic, Patrick is family and Nettie loves him. As such I owe him a little loyalty.

"Well, the only thing that matters is that she makes Ollie happy," Kathy says after a long pause, and everyone hums in agreement. Everyone except me.

If you ask me, everyone is a little too interested in their children's happiness. Ask anyone what they wish for their kids and they'll all say they want them to be happy. Happy! Not empathetic contributing members of society. Not humble, wise and tolerant. Not strong in the face of adversity or grateful in the face of misfortune. I, on the other hand, have always wanted hardship for my kids. Real, honest hardship. Challenges big enough to make them empathetic and wise. Take the pregnant refugee girls I deal with every day. They've been through unimaginable hardships, and here they are working hard, contributing and grateful.

What more could you want for your kids?

The engagement came faster than I expected—within the year. Ollie announced it at dinner one night, wearing the same proud smile he'd worn at two years old when he'd carried in a dead bird from the garden. Tom, of course, had just about combusted at the news, at one point bursting into actual, flowing tears. For heaven's sake! That was five months ago. Before the real work of the wedding planning had begun.

"Ready, Mum and Dad?"

I'm sitting beside Lucy's father, Peter, in Louis XV upholstered armchairs, angled toward a blush, velvet curtain. At intervals, Lucy comes out from behind the curtain and stands on a stage while Rhonda, the assistant, fusses around her. It is, quite frankly, agonizing, for many reasons, not least of which is the fact that Rhonda continues to refer to us as "Mum and Dad" despite that fact that I have twice pointed out that I am not Lucy's mother, and I am certainly not *hers*.

"Ready," we chorus.

I think of what my mother would have said if I'd invited her to a place like this. ("What a load of nonsense! *I'll* make your wedding dress, and Ida and Norma from church will help. Ida did the most beautiful little rosettes for her niece Mary's wedding dress, you should have seen them! Of course she had to let it out because the poor dear had thickened up around the middle by the big day. Got everyone talking, you know . . .")

I'll admit I was surprised when Lucy invited me to have an audience today. (Apparently the matron of honor's daughter had broken her arm falling from the monkey bars this morning and was currently at the children's hospital awaiting surgery, and Lucy wanted a female opinion.) It was quite the unorthodox little group actually, with Lucy's father in attendance as well, but Lucy had been firm about that. "He's been my mother as well as my father since I was thirteen years old, I think he's more than earned his place here."

Fair enough too, I thought, though I daren't give my opinion either way. Mothers were to weigh in on such matters. Mothers-in-law were to wear beige and shut up.

Funnily enough, Lucy had been quite shy when she asked me to come. "I'm sure you're really busy, but just in case you were free I'd love it if you could make it."

At fate would have it, I wasn't busy, and I'd never been much good at making up false excuses. Nettie had been invited too, apparently, but she'd had a conflicting doctor's appointment much to her chagrin.

"Here she comes!" Rhonda cries, flinging open the velvet curtain and frog marching Lucy onto the stage in a dress that looks exactly like the last one—strapless and full skirted, like Barbie pressed into a child's birthday cake. She forces Lucy to do a ridiculous twirl.

"Do you like it?" Lucy asks shyly.

Peter tears up, predictably. He rises to his feet, the archetypal ex-professor, from his tweed jacket to his soft white beard and leather lace-up shoes. He produces a handkerchief from his pocket and presses it to his eyes.

"I think we can take that as an approval," Rhonda says, thrilled. "And what do you think, Mum?"

Everyone looks at me.

All I can think is the whole thing is monstrously indulgent. The dress, the blush curtains, the Louis XV chairs. But what am I supposed to say?

"Doesn't she look beautiful?" Rhonda prompts.

Lucy is a pretty girl, certainly, but I've come to realize that one of the most interesting things about her is her unusual style—the clashing prints; the pops of color; the sequins all over everything. Today, when she'd arrived at the bridal shop she'd been wearing an enormous, wide-brimmed straw hat and clogs. *Clogs!* It was a little over the top if you asked me, but you couldn't deny the girl made a statement. In this dress, however, she looks utterly forgettable. A classic, generic bride.

"Well, I think it's—"

"What do you think, Lucy?" Peter says, emerging from behind his handkerchief. "Do you love it?"

A cautious smile appears on Lucy's face. "I do."

At this, Rhonda takes off for the back room, returning with a veil that she affixes to Lucy's head, and a plastic bouquet of roses for her to hold. It is such a sales strategy I find myself glaring at her. Not that there's anything wrong with making a sale, of course, one needs to earn a living. But this feels untoward somehow, coercive.

Peter clears his throat. "Okay, Rhonda. What's the damage?"

Rhonda goes to her computer and taps away for an unreasonable amount of time. Apparently, at bridal stores, providing a price is incredibly complicated. I turn and pretend to look at satin-covered wedding shoes. Peter is paying for the dress as well as the wedding, and has turned down every offer from us to pay half. Tom, predictably horrified, had practically *begged* him to reconsider until I convinced him Peter might find it insulting. Besides, Lucy and Ollie are planning a very low-key wedding, to my relief, so I'm confident that Peter should be able to stretch to it. That is, until I hear Rhonda whisper an amount that could purchase a brand-new family car.

The color drains from Peter's face.

"Oh, God," Lucy says. "Really?"

Rhonda nods earnestly. "Those are real Swarovski crystals. And it's a ball gown, so there's a lot of material."

"I'll try something else," Lucy says immediately. "Something off the rack or a sample—"

I pick up a wedding magazine and focus on it intently. *This* is why mothers-in-law aren't invited to this sort of thing. Peter will feel incredibly awkward with me here to witness and will feel backed into a corner. If Tom were here, he'd be on his feet, holding out the black Amex, forcing Rhonda to take it. My style would be to suggest to Lucy that there must be a perfectly nice dress that isn't the same price as a down payment on a house.

I think of Amina, whom I visited in her home earlier today. She arrived from Sudan three months ago, pregnant with twins, with three more children under the age of five. This morning I brought her a well-used double pram and she broke down in tears and asked Allah to bless me and my family. She was going to use it to push her youngest two kids to the supermarket, she said, because usually her two- and three-year-olds had to walk and their little legs got terribly tired. Some days, she told me, it took them an hour to make the one kilometer walk.

"This is the one you really want?" Peter says.

"Dad . . . are you sure? It's a lot of money."

"I've only got one daughter," he says. "And you're only a bride once."

"Will you be wanting the veil as well?" Rhonda says, a vulture circling. "I just ask because this is the last one we have in stock. I can give you ten percent off," she says, and begins tapping on her computer again. After a moment or two, she announces a price that makes my eyes water.

"No, I don't need the veil," Lucy says.

"But it really does cap off the look, doesn't it, Mum?" Rhonda says, dragging me into her ugly plot. "And it's a small price to pay, when it comes to giving your daughter the perfect wedding, am I right?"

Rhonda has taken on a new level of evil in my mind. Guilting a poor father into buying a veil he can ill afford. Encouraging me to join her side and gang up on the man. Insinuating that if he doesn't buy the ludicrously overpriced piece of lace, it means he doesn't love his daughter or want to give her the perfect wedding. If it were up to me, the woman would be taken out onto the street and horse-whipped.

"Frankly, I don't think anyone outside the royal family would consider that amount a small price to pay," I tell her. "It's daylight robbery and you should be ashamed of yourself. I don't know how you sleep at night."

Peter and Lucy turn to stare at me, and Rhonda adopts the sullen, red-faced expression of a teenager who feels like the world is against her and nothing—none of it—is her fault.

"And one other thing," I say, since I have everyone's attention. "As I've pointed out several times, I'm *not* Lucy's mother." I fold my hands in my lap. "I'm her mother-*in-law*."

5

Lucy

The present . . .

"Would anyone like tea?" I ask.

No one responds but I head to the kitchen anyway to put the kettle on. My thoughts skitter about. Diana is dead. Intellectually I understand this, but somehow it doesn't feel true. This peculiar, anesthetized feeling is familiar, it reminds me of the days following my own mother's death when I walked around in a daze, oblivious to the day of the week and the time of the day. It wasn't until days later that the pain hit—fast and hard, as if it had been loaded into a slingshot and fired at me. It was during my mother's funeral that I'd finally broken under the weight of it, sobbing so hysterically my poor father had no idea what to do.

I slide the mugs off a high shelf and line them up on the counter.

The sky beyond the window is black. Patrick, Nettie and Ollie are in the living room, spread across furniture, staring out in different directions. I get the feeling that Patrick and Nettie would like to leave but they feel they shouldn't, as though it might be considered dismissive to Diana. These are, after all, times for family to be together.

Simon and Stella left over an hour ago, leaving behind two shiny business cards and a sober environment. Since then Nettie appears to have rethought her initial embrace with Ollie and has perched herself as far away from him as possible while still being in the same room. Patrick sits right beside her, patting her leg, sincere but unemotional. Tears stream from Nettie, filling and falling without much apparent effort on her part.

Ollie is surprisingly dry-eyed, and seems to be an impossible combination of bewildered and irritated, alternately shaking his head *no*, then nodding it *yes*, whatever that is supposed to mean. Peculiarly, it's exactly how I feel. *No, Diana can't be dead,* followed by *Yes, she is and it isn't the worst thing in the world.* After all, I've never made a secret of my dislike for Diana. Our relationship had been volatile. It has even, at one point, been *violent.* I wonder if the police will discover this while they are investigating Diana's death.

As I get down my "visitor tea" (I'm getting the feeling that Nettie might do well with chamomile), I can't help but think of the day Tom died. We'd all been called away from home and work mid-morning to come and say our good-byes, but by midnight that evening, he was still hanging on. It wasn't the first time we'd gotten the call. We'd given our teary farewells twice before, only to have Tom battle on, but this time, the doctors told us, was *it*. Apparently.

After twenty-four hours, as Tom continued to hang in there,

Ollie had asked the nurse if there was something she could give Tom to "end his suffering."

When the nurse explained that there wasn't anything—and that it could take as much as a few days before Tom died—Ollie had reached for a cushion and announced that he'd like "a few minutes alone with Dad."

Everyone had become slightly feverish with exhausted hilarity— even Diana, amazingly, had smiled as she explained to the nurse that, obviously, her son was joking. But there are no jokes to be had today. Everything is utterly somber.

I take the tea into the living room and hold out a mug to Nettie, but she doesn't seem to notice. After a second or two, Patrick takes it and sets it on the coffee table.

"I guess it's too early to talk about the funeral," I say. It *is* too soon, but I can't bear the silence anymore and what else are we supposed to talk about? Nettie stares at the blank television screen. Ollie looks at his shoes.

Only Patrick looks at me, shrugs slightly. "Depends when we get the body, I suppose," he says.

Nettie visibly stiffens.

I sit on the arm of the sofa, next to Ollie. "When will that be?"

"There'll be an autopsy, I guess," Patrick says. "That'll take time."

"But . . . why are they doing an autopsy?" Nettie asks. She glances around the room, half dazed, like she's just woken up.

"The police said they are treating it as a homicide," Ollie explains.

Nettie's eyes widen. Everyone seems to have forgotten that we're not supposed to be making eye contact and we all look intently at each other.

"They said they *have* to treat it as a homicide," Patrick says, "they don't actually think it was one. It sounded pretty clear-cut to me. The letter, the . . . materials."

"What kind of materials are they talking about, do you think?" Ollie says. His face is the image of bafflement. "A rope? A gun?"

"Ollie!" I say.

Nettie has gone so pale she looks like she might faint. Somewhere in the next room, Ollie's phone begins to ring. Eamon, Ollie's business partner, would be the only one to call this late. I'm relieved when Ollie doesn't move to answer it.

"If they think it could be a homicide," Nettie says, her eyes searching, "will they be speaking to people? Investigating?"

Patrick looks at his lap. "I guess they'll have to."

"But who would they investigate?" Ollie says. "Who'd want to kill Mum?"

It's a slow process, but one by one, Patrick, Ollie and Nettie all turn to look at me. I drop my gaze and stare into my tea.

6

Lucy

The past . . .

"I don't have something borrowed," I say to Claire, my matron of honor. She sits in the armchair in my Dad's bedroom with her three-year-old daughter, Millie, in her lap. Millie is going to be a flower girl at the wedding, a role that has delighted her until about two minutes ago when she realized she'd have to have her hair brushed. Now, Claire grips Millie between her knees as she drags the brush through her coils but Millie is twisting and wriggling like someone being tickled with a thousand feathers.

"Leave her," I say, watching them in the reflection of the mirror. "Her hair is fine the way it is."

"How do you not have something borrowed?" Claire exclaims, releasing Millie from her thigh grip and putting down the brush.

"It's your *wedding day*. Speaking of which, are you having any Runaway Bride feels? Will I need to winch this window open and saddle up a horse so you can make a run for it, Julia Roberts style?"

"No chance of that," I say.

"Are you sure? I could have a mare waiting in case you want to make a quick getaway. From your mother-in-law, perhaps?"

I check my teeth for lipstick. Fire engine red is a risqué color for one's wedding day, but I think I can get away with it. "Maybe keep the car running just in case."

My friends and I have unpacked my relationship with Diana at length, from her calling me *fine,* to insisting she wasn't my mother while bridal dress shopping, to intimating that the wedding dress I selected was frivolous and over the top. Admittedly, she had a point about the dress. I knew I'd gotten carried away with the bridal dress shopping, but it was a rare bride that couldn't say the same. And at least I was big enough to admit it! After Diana's outburst at the bridal store, I'd convinced Dad—much to the sales lady's horror—that I needed time to think about the dress. It had taken a few days, but I'd realized Diana was right, it was ludicrously overpriced—daylight robbery even, just as she'd said. And a few days later, while looking at my parents' wedding album, I'd noticed how beautiful Mum's dress was. I wasn't sure why I hadn't thought of it. I'd always loved wearing Mum's clothes. Barely was there a day when I wasn't wearing a coat or a scarf or a piece of jewelry from her collection. There was just something about having something of hers wrapped around me that made me feel close to her. On days that I really missed her, I wore multiple items of Mum's.

I take a few steps back from the mirror and look at my reflection. Mum's dress is my *something old.* A 1970s ivory silk dress with a high neckline, long sleeves and an empire waistline and covered buttons traveling from the left shoulder to just under the chin. When I asked Dad about it, he had produced it from the attic, lovingly wrapped in acid-free tissue thirty years earlier. There were a few yellow stains, but they were on the waistline and were able to be hidden by the wide, mint green sash I'd added. My pillbox bridal hat with birdcage veil, which I *did* purchase from the bridal store is my *something new*. My sapphire earrings that Ollie gave me for my birthday are my *something blue*.

"Right then," Claire says. "Something borrowed." She points to the diamond studs in her ears. "How about my earrings?"

"But the sapphires in *my* earrings are my something blue."

"My shoes?"

Claire's feet are a size and a half larger than mine. Also, her shoes are pink, the same color as her dress.

"My lipstick? My hair brooch?" Claire tries, but she's just stabbing in the dark now. I've already had my makeup done by a makeup artist. My hair is out with a loose wave, soon to be topped with my hat and veil. Millie, who is jumping on Dad's bed now, will wear a flower crown, as will Claire.

There is a gentle tap at the door. "Come in, Dad," I call.

Despite telling Dad repeatedly that it is not bad luck for *him* to see me before the wedding, he has covered his eyes every time we've crossed paths this morning. I wait for his bearded face to appear around the corner, eyes closed, but the door remains closed.

"*Dad?* You can come in."

"Lucy? It's Diana Goodwin."

Claire and I lock eyes. Silent horror travels between us. Diana is at the door. What on earth is *she* doing here?

"Hello, Diana," I say tremulously. I wonder why there isn't a rule forbidding the mother-in-law from seeing the bride on the day of the wedding. "Would you . . . would you like to come in?"

There is a short pause, and then the door handle twists. Diana's face appears in the opening. "I'm sorry to show up like this. I just have something to give you."

"Oh?"

I open the door further and Diana casts a brisk smile at Claire and a slightly less brisk smile at Millie, who pauses mid-bounce on Dad's bed. She stares at Diana. I get the feeling she is as terrified as I am.

"I'll give you a minute," Claire says, gathering up Millie and scurrying out the door. Diana waits for them to leave and then enters the room fully.

"You look lovely," I say.

It isn't lip service, I've actually never seen Diana look so lovely. She's wearing a navy linen shell top with a soft blue A-line floor-length skirt. She is wearing makeup—pink lips and smoky eyes—and she smells like a bouquet of fresh-cut flowers. I suddenly get a glimpse of Diana as a young woman, a beautiful young woman, and I understand why Tom always looks so pleased with himself around her.

"Thank you," Diana says. "So do you. I called your father this morning to see if there was anything I could do and he told me you didn't have something borrowed." Diana reaches into her clutch, pulling out a navy leather jewelry box, trimmed with gold. "I wore this on my wedding day." She opens the box and produces a silver necklace with a small flat, twisted pendant. "It's a Celtic knot. It represents strength. If it doesn't go with your dress you could perhaps hide it underneath the bodice."

"I love it," I say immediately. "And I'm not hiding it anywhere. I'll wear it around my neck where everyone can see it."

Diana looks as pleased as Diana can look. She comes around behind me and I lift my hair for her to fasten it. When she's done, she gestures to my hat and veil. "Do you need help with this?"

"That . . . would be wonderful."

Diana is tall, nearly a full head taller than me, and as she fastens the hat at my temple I can see her eyes. They are narrow with concentration as she fusses around, fixing the birdcage veil around my face and then smoothing the dress out behind me. Of course, I think of my mother. If she were here, she would have been the one fastening my necklace, smoothing my dress. A lump forms in my throat.

"Thank you," I say turning and wrapping my arms around Diana. She stiffens slightly, neither returning my hug nor pulling away, but I hang on all the same. She is thin and knobby and it feels like I'm embracing a sack full of coat hangers.

After a moment or two, I untangle myself.

"Right," Diana says, clearing her throat. "I'd better get back to Ollie."

And that appears to be that. I try not to focus on the fact that the hug wasn't really returned. After all, she showed up! She brought me a beautiful, meaningful piece of jewelry that she herself had worn on her *wedding day*. We'd made progress. And I was going to celebrate it.

Diana makes it to the door before she stops suddenly, pivots back. "Oh er, Lucy?"

"Yes?"

"That necklace is your something borrowed."

"I know," I say. I glance at it in the mirror again, marveling at how perfect it is. It is actually hard to believe I almost *didn't* wear it.

"Good," she says, "because *borrowed* means you have to give it back."

A long silence.

"I understand that," I say slowly, and Diana gives a little nod and lets herself out of the room.

"The girls will want champagne," Eamon tells the waitress in the black pants and crisp white shirt. "If there's one thing I know about girls, it's that they always want champagne."

Eamon's wife, Julia, nods enthusiastically. She calls over the waitress and points to a bottle of Dom Pérignon.

"Lovely choice," the waitress says.

The blood drains from Ollie's face. Even before we arrived, he was nervous about how much this meal is going to cost (meals with Eamon were never cheap) but when we arrived at Arabella's and saw the white table cloths and the menu with no prices . . . I could see he was panicking. Now, Dom Pérignon. It's a choice made even more frustrating by the fact that I'm eight weeks pregnant . . . thus neither able to drink it, nor disclose that I'm not drinking it, which means leaving a very expensive glass of champagne undrunk at the end of the night.

"So how's the house hunting going?" Julia asks us, once the waitress has disappeared. Her face creases with worry, as if she is asking about a rare disease with which one of us has been recently diagnosed. "You know, we used a great buyer's advocate when we bought our place in South Yarra. Why don't we give you his details?"

The fact that Ollie and I rent a home is an endlessly perplexing fact to all of Ollie's friends. At some point it seems to have been universally accepted that we simply couldn't find the right place, the assumption being that Ollie's parents would foot the bill for the place of our choosing. Unfortunately, this isn't the case. Instead, in the year since we married, Ollie and I have been saving hard for a down payment. Currently, with both of us working, we earn a good income but soon, fingers crossed, I'll be at home with the baby. And sadly, no buyer's advocate will be able to help us if we don't have any money.

If it were up to me, I'd simply point out the fact that Ollie's parents aren't footing the bill, but Ollie can be oddly coy about these things. And so I say nothing, and play along.

"Why not?" Ollie says. "Can't hurt, can it?"

Julia nods, delighted she can be of assistance, and Eamon fumbles with his phone, firing off the contact to Ollie. I really don't understand the games Ollie's friends sometimes play, spinning every failure or downturn as "a wonderful opportunity to go in a new direction." I'd love to see Eamon's and Julie's faces if we were to say, "Actually we're struggling to even pay rent right now, and I can guarantee your buyer's advocate would not be advocating properties in the areas we're looking at! Ha, ha, ha."

"Anyway," Eamon says, sliding his phone back into his jacket pocket. "S'meals!"

Eamon has been trying in vain to explain his new business to Ollie from the moment we arrived. Lord knows why! Every time I see him, Eamon appears to be cooking up a new business idea, claiming it was going to be the next big thing, talking about how people needed to get on board early. For a while he franchised mobile spray tan businesses, then he manufactured children's fingerprinting kits. He'd had varied success, according to Ollie, and you couldn't fault his tenacity. I just wished he'd stop discussing it all in painstaking detail over dinner, when anyone could see Ollie was entirely focused on figuring out how we could get out of the restaurant for less than five hundred bucks.

"They're a smoothie for a meal. Chock full of superfoods. The fresh food is delivered to your door in ziplock bags, you just have to stick it all in your NutriBullet and voilà!"

I blink. "So . . . fruits and vegetables? In bags? That's what it is?"

"Not fruits and vegetables." There's a note of triumph in Eamon's voice. "Nutritionally balanced *meals*. You can drink it at your desk and call it lunch."

"Like meal replacement shakes?"

"But with actual fresh food, instead of chemicals. *Superfoods*."

Eamon has said "superfoods" at least seventeen times since we arrived and I find myself desperate to ask what a superfood is because I suspect he doesn't know. But again, for Ollie's sake, because they have been friends since kindergarten and their parents know each other, I force myself to abstain.

"Interesting. Well, good luck!" I say.

He'll need it.

But Eamon isn't listening to me, he's too focused on Ollie. "How are things with you then, old boy? How are things in the recruitment world?"

"Things are good. Did a great placement last week, actually. The guy, Ron, was sixty, and he'd been out of work for six months. He really needed to work for another five years before he could retire, but everyone was telling him he had no hope, because his entire specialty was in a system that was now obsolete. I promised him I'd find him something and then boom, last week, I found a client who was upgrading their ERP from a system that Ron virtually wrote during the 80s. Now he's the head of data conversion. Neither Ron nor the client could believe their luck."

Ollie beams. I love seeing him like this. He *lives* for putting the right candidate in the right job, particularly the ones that are hard to place. He listens to candidates during the interview process and by the time they leave, they are friends. Unfortunately it is an asset that is rarely rewarded in an industry that values goals and targets, and for this reason most of Ollie's colleagues have risen ahead of him into management while he stays exactly where he is, agonizing over placements for candidates like Ron.

"Cool, cool," Eamon says. "You've been there a while though, right? Don't suppose you've thought about extending your wings a bit? You've got some pretty valuable contacts now. The world's your oyster. You can't keep working for the man forever."

This little speech reeks of someone who wants something. I feel myself brace.

"All right, spit it out," Ollie says, clearly interpreting Eamon's speech the same way I had. "You want me to join your business, is that it? Or start a new business with you? Or invest in a business?"

Eamon tries to look insulted. "Can't a guy be interested in his old mate's career? But . . . since you mention it, I might be looking for a business partner." He grins.

"In your smoothie business?"

"Meal replacements," Eamon corrects. "With *superfoods!*"

"How could I possibly help you with that?" Ollie asks.

You could give him money, I think to myself. *Or, rather, your father could.* At least that is what Eamon is thinking.

"Don't undersell yourself, mate," Eamon says. "You'd be a massive asset to any business. You're a people person. Every business needs that."

Ollie doesn't respond right away, and for a horrible moment, I think he might be considering joining Eamon in his smoothie business. I look at him. He appears to be thinking deeply. But this proposition doesn't require even a moment's thought. Does it? Unless . . . have I missed something? Is Ollie not happy in his job? What about what he just said about placing sixty-year-old Ron? Surely a man happy in his job wouldn't consider a career move on a whim just because his friend suggested it at dinner?

"Have you all had a chance to look at the menu?" the waitress says, appearing at the table. But none of us has had a chance to look at the menu.

"Why don't I tell you about the specials?" the waitress suggests, when none of us speak. "We have a lovely thrice-cooked pork belly tonight and the fish is blue grenadier with a Parmesan crust."

"Give us a few minutes," Eamon says to the waitress, his eyes not leaving Ollie. He's practically salivating, ready to go in for the kill. Ollie's eyes are skyward, his lips pinched as though he's actually taking this seriously.

"Ollie," I say, desperate to interject before he says something he can't take back.

"I'm just not sure," he says. "Pork or fish?"

Eamon explodes. "Pork or fish? I thought we were talking about S'meals!"

"What?" Ollie frowns. "Oh, your smoothie business. No, listen, I wish you all the best, mate, but *come on*. Mixing business with pleasure. Bad idea, right? Everyone knows that."

I feel Ollie's hand squeeze my leg under the table and I exhale. My husband may have his pride, but he's not stupid. Maybe, when it comes to money, Ollie is savvier than I thought.

7

Lucy

The present . . .

The next day, I focus on the kids. Despite the police showing up last night the kids seem to be narcissistically unaware that anything is up, even though Edie has been allowed to chow through seven squeeZ-fruit pouches (normally her limit is two per day), and Archie and Harriet haven't been taken to karate or gymnastics or forced off their devices at midday on a Saturday. But now we have to tell them. We might not be able to tell them how she died, but at least we can tell them Diana is dead. We can say that we don't know why yet, that the doctors are looking into it. That will satisfy them. Honestly they'd probably be satisfied with "she was very old."

I look at Ollie. After yesterday's protesting that it couldn't be real, he seems to have moved into the next level of grief, whatever that is. All morning he's been utterly silent, apart from the odd spasm of bizarre emotion. Like a few minutes ago when Harriet—in the middle of a spontaneous arabesque—slipped on a cushion and went, quite literally, head over heels. She landed flat on her back, face up on the floor, and promptly began to wail. Ollie stared at her for a second or two, then, inexplicably, began to laugh. By the time I made it over to Harriet, he was positively wild with hilarity.

Grief.

I catch Ollie's eye on the couch and mouth, "Let's tell them now."

I half expect him to keep staring into space, but he nods, picks up the remote control and turns off the screen.

"Hey!" Archie cries. Harriet and Edie glare at us. I sit on the arm of the sofa and the kids look back at the television, more comfortable with the blank screen than with actual human faces.

"Kids, we have something to tell you."

"What?" Archie moans, throwing down the Xbox controller.

"We've had some sad news."

Both Archie and Harriet spin around. *Sad news.* We have their attention now. They've watched enough kids movies (Is it just me, or do the parents die in every damn kids movie?) to know about sad news.

After Tom died the kids were devastated. Archie began wetting the bed again, and Harriet had started getting panicked if Ollie was even a little bit late home from work. ("Is he *dead*?" she'd ask, her little saucer-eyes gawping up at me.) Edie, of course, had been none the wiser back then, but this time it's different. She adores Dido (the inane name Diana insisted on being called). They all love Dido. Loved Dido.

I take a deep breath. "Dido died yesterday."

Harriet is the first to react, with a gasp. Her hands rise, forming a tent around her mouth, and she breathes in and out loudly. There's something false about it, like she's reenacting something she's seen on television.

Archie is still yet to react so I focus my attention on him. "Did you hear me, buddy?"

Archie nods. His expression is somberish, but more collected than if, say, I'd told him he couldn't have ice cream for dessert. "Dido died," he repeats, hanging his head.

Harriet drops her hands from her face and bursts out laughing. "*Dido died.* That rhymes." She falls back onto the empty couch, chortling so hard she has to hold her belly.

"It doesn't rhyme, idiot," Archie says.

"It does."

"Doesn't."

"*Does!*"

"Kids," I say. "Do you understand what I'm saying? Remember when Papa died? He went up to Heaven and we couldn't see him anymore. Well . . . now Dido has died."

Harriet laughs again. "*Sorry!* It just sounds funny."

Archie lets out a chuckle. Then Edie, of course, joins in though she has no idea what's going on.

"Aren't you sad that Dido's dead?" Ollie asks, a slight inflection to his voice. I turn to him, suddenly worried that he might start to cry. Not that that would be a bad thing, but the timing wouldn't be ideal. The kids also register the inflection, and one by one, stop laughing.

"Yeah," Archie says, but he doesn't sound sad. He sounds like he knows that's what he is expected to say. Archie is dutiful like that. Edie is looking at her feet, marveling at the spot where her big toe peeks through her sock. Harriet is rolling her eyes and inspecting her fingernails, which are covered in chipped lolly-pink sparkly nail polish.

"I'm not sad," she mutters.

I frown at her. "Why aren't you sad, Harriet?"

She shrugs. "Dido was mean to you. I don't like people who aren't nice to my mum."

Ollie and I look at each other.

"It'll be much nicer now that she's not here, won't it, Mummy?" Harriet continues. She bounds out of her seat and flings her limbs around, trying for, perhaps, a leaping pirouette. But she misses her footing and this time she lands flat on her face. She howls. Edie squeals. And Archie, in a delayed reaction, suddenly bursts into tears.

8

Diana

The past . . .

I pull up to the traffic lights and glare at the enormous stuffed teddy bear on my passenger seat. Tom had bought the ridiculous toy, obviously, and as if that wasn't bad enough, he insisted that I be the one to take it along *to the hospital* to give to Lucy.

"What on earth for?" I'd said to him on the phone. "It's not like Archie will be playing with it in the next few days!"

"It's our first grandchild," he'd replied. "Besides, Lucy will love it."

He was probably right about that. His perfect understanding of our daughter-in-law's psyche was almost as spectacular as my lack of understanding of it. Lucy had given birth to Archie in the early hours of this morning, after a short, uncomplicated labor. Tom had wanted to go to the hospital the instant we heard the news, but I'd managed to convince him to go into work for a couple of hours to give them some time alone with the baby. Now though, even *I'm* itching to get there. Tom is going straight from work and I'm meeting him there.

The traffic lights turn to green at the same time as my phone rings. I stab at a few buttons on the steering wheel, until finally it connects. (Usually I drive my little Ford Festiva around when I'm doing errands, but it has gone in for a service so I'm in the Range Rover and you honestly need a Ph.D. in car mechanics to make the darn thing work.) "Hello?"

The car fills with the sound of heaving breathing. "Mrs. Diana?"

I recognize the voice immediately. "Ghezala?"

Twenty-two and pregnant, Ghezala has been in Australia for five months since escaping Afghanistan. In recent weeks I'd visited her several times, to drop off a pram, a bassinette and some newborn baby clothes, and each time, Ghezala had put on a pot of Kahwa tea and we'd settle in for a good old chinwag. Ghezala's English isn't great and the conversations are often lists of what she's had for breakfast, what the weather is going to do this week, what she's watched on the television . . . yet I always enjoy the simplicity of it.

"Mrs. Diana?" More puffing and panting. "The baby."

I pull to the side of the road, calculating dates in my head. It's a few weeks early, not dangerously early, but early. And Ghezala has no family or friends in Australia. Her partner, Hakem, is at least in the country, but his capabilities as a birth partner remain to be seen.

"You need to go to the hospital, Ghezala. Remember the voucher I gave you for a taxi? Call the taxi and use the voucher to pay the driver. Ghezala? Do you remember the voucher?"

I hear another contraction take hold, so I wait. The fact that she can't talk through it worries me and I wonder if I should call an ambulance.

"Ghezala," I repeat when the panting stops. "Do you have the taxi voucher?"

"I . . . I don't know." She sounds spent. Without thinking about what I was doing, I've already done a U-turn and am headed toward her house, but it's a good twenty minutes' drive from here. "Where is Hakem, Ghezala?"

"Outside."

I bite back an urge to scream, "What is he doing outside?" and instead ask: "And how bad is the pain? Out of ten."

"It's . . . a four."

But I get the feeling Ghezala's four is most women's eleven. Her next breath catches on another contraction.

"Ghezala, I'm going to call an ambulance."

"No," she says. "Can . . . you come, Mrs. Diana?"

"I'm on my way to your house right now. Ghezala—"

But the phone goes dead. And when I call again, it rings out.

It takes twenty-five minutes to get to her house and when I get there, Hakem is in the front yard, smoking a cigarette. He must spend half his life in the tiny, overgrown courtyard of theirs, smoking cigarettes. I leap out of the car and run toward the house. "Hakem? Where's Ghezala?"

He gestures toward the house with his head. "Inside."

"*Inside?* Why aren't you in there with her?"

He looks at me like I've suggested he book a holiday to the Bahamas. I get the feeling he's being intentionally obtuse.

"Have you called an ambulance?"

He turns away, takes a drag of his cigarette. "You might think you are our savior, but you know nothing. You are different from us. Different from Ghezala."

"Hakem. Have. You. Called. An. Ambulance?" I ask through my teeth.

He takes a step toward me. The whites of his eyes are yellow and filled with little red cracks. "No. I. HAVEN'T."

Hakem is thickset, and a good thirty years younger than me but I match him in height, inch for inch. I square up against him. "Do not try and intimidate me, young man. I promise you, you will come off worse."

It's not true, of course. I would come off worse, *far* worse, but if there's one thing I've learned in life it's that minds win wars, not muscles. And as I've made up my mind to get Ghezala's baby delivered healthy and well, I'll be damned if I don't do exactly that.

I'm still right in Hakem's face when he holds up his hands in defeat.

"Call an ambulance," I say, as the screen door slaps closed between us. "Now!"

I find Ghezala on the tiled kitchen floor, her back against pillows. I skid and almost fall in a wet patch, gasping when I see that the baby's head is already out. There's no time for an ambulance, I realize as Ghezala shudders and I drop to my knees. She gives a great moan and I only just have time to grab a tea towel before Ghezala pushes her baby boy right into my hands, pink and bloody and squirming. I wrap him in a towel and rub him vigorously until he lets out a piercing, glorious cry.

It takes me back to another time. *The single bed with moonlight streaming in the curtainless window. The pop followed by a feeling deep within of something bursting. My breath is a cloud in the room.*

Hakem is wrong, I am not different from Ghezala. We are exactly the same.

9

Lucy

The past . . .

"Where on earth has she got to?"

Tom shifts newborn Archie in his lap, and glances at his watch. Diana should have been at the hospital an hour ago, and she has a surprise, he tells me (only holding out about thirty seconds or so before letting it slip that the surprise was a giant teddy bear). Now he is positively jittery with impatience to give it to his grandson, who is all of six hours old. God love him.

Ever since I announced my pregnancy, Tom has been the *image* of a devoted grandfather—dropping to his knees every time I visited to "talk" to my belly, or reaching out to feel the baby kick. Diana had chastised him: "Give the girl some space!" but I didn't mind. Actually I preferred Tom's tactile approach to Diana's style, which was barely mentioning the baby at all. Of course, I'd steeled myself for the fact that my pregnancy wasn't likely to be the bonding point I hoped it would be for Diana and me, but I was nonetheless disappointed to find that it hadn't injected even the *slightest* warmth into our relationship.

When the alarm on my phone goes off, signaling three hours since Archie's last feed, I adjust the pillow on my lap and gesture to Tom to bring him over. Tom does as he's told, carrying Archie as if he is made of glass, then backs away again, his eyes theatrically averted, as I fiddle with my nursing bra.

"Where on earth could she *be*?" Tom says, glancing at his phone again.

"Traffic?" Ollie suggests. He's stretched out beside me on the hospital bed, watching football on the television in the corner, but his eyes dart back to Archie every minute or so, as if checking that he hasn't gone anywhere.

"I have texted her twice," Tom says. "I hope she hasn't gotten into an accident."

I lift Archie to my breast and try to latch him on, but the little guy is still deeply asleep. I blow gently on his face like the nurse showed me, but to no avail. He's out cold. "Why don't you call her?" I say. "For your peace of mind, if nothing else."

The fact is, I'm getting impatient to see Diana too. I'm having crampy afterpains from the birth, I feel oddly teary, and there is a lot of testosterone in the room. Before Tom arrived, I had a visit from Dad, and while I love having all these menfolk around, I'm craving a maternal figure, someone to lean on.

Also, in the back of my mind, I'm painfully aware that this is our very last chance, Diana and I. If she doesn't warm to me after I've birthed her first grandchild . . . what hope do we have?

"Yes," Tom says. "Yes, all right. I'll call her."

Tom is just reaching for his phone when suddenly, there she is, in the doorway. We all do a double take at Diana standing there. She looks flustered . . . no, she looks like *a wreck*. The knees of her linen trousers are damp and dirty, and her linen shirt is rumpled. I've actually never seen Diana look so disheveled.

"Di!" Tom says, standing. "Are you all right?"

"I'm fine. Sorry I'm late, I had a . . . oh, never mind, I'm here now. Oh." She stops a few paces from the bed and inhales sharply. "There he is."

Archie is showing no signs of waking or feeding, so I turn him around to face his grandmother. I smile. "Here he is."

Diana remains rooted to the spot for several moments. I might be imagining it, but I think her eyes are a little misty. It makes me a little teary too.

"Would you like to hold him?" I ask.

Diana is silent for several seconds before nodding. Then she washes her hands in the sink—nice and thoroughly—and comes to my bedside. I hold Archie out to her and she takes him gently from me, cradling his tiny head in both hands.

"Well, hello there, young man," she says quietly. "It's very nice to meet you."

Tom rises from his chair and stands beside Diana, looking down at Archie. Everything is quiet, apart from the blissful sound of Archie breathing. For a few moments, I feel at ease, totally filled up.

"Where is the teddy bear?" Tom asks Diana.

"Oh." Diana looks up, suddenly flustered again. "Actually my . . . client, as it happened, gave birth today. That's why I was held up. And . . ."

There is a long, charged silence. Tom's jaw drops.

"She didn't have any toys for the baby, and I guess . . . I just . . ."

I don't know why, it's not as though I have any particularly affinity for teddy bears, and I certainly don't think Archie needs one at one day old, but for some reason Diana giving his teddy bear away . . . it feels deeply personal. A betrayal.

"We'll buy Archie another one," Diana says finally.

"Yes," Tom says, recovering. "*Of course* we will. We'll buy it this afternoon. We can bring it back tonight!"

"Guys, guys!" Ollie says, holding up his hands. "Calm down. Archie doesn't need a giant teddy bear, and he certainly doesn't need it today." He grins, enjoying being the reasonable one, the peacemaker. "I'd say it's much better off with your refugee lady and her kid. We have nowhere to put a giant teddy bear anyway, do we, Luce?"

They all turn to look at me. I drop my gaze.

"I'd better take Archie," I say, taking my sleeping boy from Diana's arms. "He's due for a feed."

10

Diana

The past . . .

I stand on Ollie and Lucy's doorstep and knock briskly. The brisk-
ness is an attempt to counteract the doubts I'm already having.
Archie is two weeks old. Would Lucy want me showing up like this
unannounced? Would she hate it? Who knew? Tom has dropped in
several times, of course, never once questioning whether or not he'd
be welcome. It's self-fulfilling, that kind of confidence. My lack of
confidence also seems to be self-fulfilling.

In truth, I think I've stayed away because of that damn bear.
When I gave it to Ghezala it seemed, absolutely, the right thing to
do. That teddy would likely be the best toy that child would ever
receive. Perhaps even the only toy. And as I handed it over to

Ghezala and watched her tear up, suddenly it didn't seem so silly after all.

I should have known Tom would tell Lucy and Ollie about the teddy bear. When I showed up to the hospital, late and empty-handed, I'll admit I felt guilty. I should have done better than that for my first grandchild. I should have done better than that for Lucy.

So today I am going to do better.

I knock on the door again, even though part of me wants to get back in the car and drive home. But if I did that, what would I do with the chicken? I look down at it doubtfully, raw and heavy in its blue plastic bag. Lucy is probably asleep or having some quiet time while the baby naps. *If* the baby is napping. According to Ollie, Archie has barely slept a wink since he was born. The maternal health nurse was saying he had colic. The last thing Lucy will want through all of that is her mother-in-law showing up unexpectedly.

I should take my chicken and get out of here.

"Diana?"

I look up. Lucy is standing in the doorway, dressed in a grey tracksuit and a pair of fluffy pink slippers. Despite her quick smile, it is clear that she's not thrilled to see me. Archie is perched on her shoulder, wailing.

"This is a surprise," Lucy says, sweeping a few threads of hair off her face.

"Yes. I, er . . . just brought you a chicken."

I'm aware it's an odd gift; I'm not stupid. But when Ollie was a baby, someone delivered me a chicken to my home and it was one of the most thoughtful gifts I've ever received. It was before the days of Uber Eats and home delivery and the idea of having to get dressed and take the baby to the supermarket was simply too much to handle.

I thought today, I might tell Lucy the story and . . . I don't know . . . it could become a Goodwin family tradition or something, bringing a chicken to women who'd just had a new baby. Now it just sounds dreadfully twee.

"Oh," she says. "Well, why don't you come in?"

I follow her into the house registering the milky deposit on Lucy's shoulder, and another one farther down her back. Archie's little hands stretch up and I have a full view of his perfect, angry little face as he howls. Sweet boy.

The sitting room is glorious in its filth. A bag of popcorn has spilled on the floor, a bowl of cereal is congealing on the coffee table. Packets of baby wipes, diaper bags and dirty dishes are strewn all about. In one corner of the room, I notice a used diaper is rolled into a ball, unbagged. It takes all of my self-control to stop myself from gasping.

"I cleaned last night," Lucy says defensively, "but it just . . . Archie has been so unhappy . . . he has colic . . . and I just haven't had a minute to . . ."

"I'll do it," I say, because honestly I can't stand to be in this filth a moment longer. Not to mention the fact that cleaning, unlike small talk, is something I know how to do. Besides, Archie is clearly hungry, and his cry is like nails on a chalkboard. "You sit down and feed the baby."

"Oh, well, if you're sure—"

"I'm sure."

I set the chicken on the kitchen counter and get to work. I roll up the diaper, bag it, and carry it to the outside bin, then I gather up the dirty mugs and plates and take them to the kitchen. I have no idea how they can live like this. The last time I visited—Ollie's birthday, I think—the place had been tricked up like a show home, with flowers and cushions and soft music. Poor Lucy had spent the entire evening sweaty-faced in the kitchen, cooking the most ridiculous Vietnamese banquet. I'd suggested that she might just order in, but Lucy insisted. It was some new recipe she wanted to try, she said.

For goodness' sake.

I empty and reload the dishwasher, and I'm about to set it going when I notice something in the oven—half a dozen old chicken nuggets. They're hard as rocks. *Classic Lucy*, I think to myself. Feast or famine.

Lucy appears behind me as I drag the tray of nuggets out of the oven. "*Oh!* They must be Ollie's . . . oh my goodness . . . he's always putting things in the oven and then forgetting about them. Oh no, let me."

She snatches the tray out of my hands. Archie screams on her shoulder. I want to tell her to deal with him and let me sort out the kitchen, but I've tried that and it clearly didn't work. So what do I do? The problem is it's so easy for a mother-in-law to get it wrong. It seems there is an endless list of unwritten rules. Be involved but not overbearing. Be supportive but don't overstep. Help with the grandkids, but don't take over. Offer wisdom but never advice. Obviously, I haven't mastered this list. The sheer weight of the requirements makes it intimidating even to try. The most frustrating part is that it's nearly impossible for a father-in-law to mess it up. He has to be welcoming. That's it.

People have higher expectations of a dog.

Archie is still wailing, pulling his little legs up toward his belly as Lucy struggles with the tray. Up close, I can see Lucy's exhaustion. She has acne on her chin, and it has to be said, she's a little on the whiffy side. On her T-shirt I see an old stain . . . spaghetti sauce by the look of it.

"Lucy, please let me do it," I say. There's a hint of begging in my voice which I'm not proud of. "You sit down and feed that baby. Go on!"

I must have said it right because Lucy nods and disappears to the sitting room. I let out a long breath. It's so rare that I get something right with Lucy, and it's not for want of trying. I tried when I lent her my most beloved possession, my Celtic necklace, on her wedding day. My own mother-in-law, Lillian, had lent it to me on *my* wedding day. The symbol represented strength, and Lillian had bought it to stay strong while Tom's dad was away at war. She left it to me in her will, with a note that said: *For strength*. It occurs to me now, that perhaps I should have told Lucy the story when I gave it to her. Silly me.

"Has he been fussy all day?" I ask Lucy, when I've finished tidying the kitchen. I bring her a cup of tea which I set on the coffee table. Archie lies flat on her lap, red-faced and wailing, despite having been fed.

"All day every day," she says. "And all night every night."

"Have you tried gripe water?" I sit beside her. "When Ollie was a baby, it used to sort him out when he was gassy."

"I've tried it. I've tried *everything*."

"May I?"

Lucy gives a helpless shrug. "Why not?"

I pick Archie up and place him vertically against her chest, so his head is nestled under Lucy's chin. Then I pat the midsection of his back firmly. Almost instantly he belches—a loud, cavernous sound, utterly incongruent with the size of him. It's incredibly satisfying, I will admit. For a moment, Archie looks like he might cry, but then he closes his eyes and promptly falls asleep.

"There," I say happily.

Lucy is staring at me as though I've grown another eyeball. "How did you do that?"

"Burp him?" I stare at her. "Oh, Lucy. *Tell* me you've been burping this child."

Lucy's eyes fill with tears. I kick myself.

"Well," I say quickly. "You must burp him after each feed. Sometimes even *during* the feed. Otherwise wind gets trapped and hurts his tummy."

"Okay," she says, nodding. It's as though no one has ever given her any mothering advice before. "Okay, I will."

"Good. Now pop him in his crib and take yourself off to bed. I'll just turn on the dishwasher and then let myself out."

Lucy looks surprised. "But . . . aren't you going to . . . stay for a while?"

I know the right answer to this. No one wants her mother-in-law to stay for a while. The baby is asleep and the house is tidy. Now is the time to leave. I'm not sure of much, but I'm *absolutely* sure about this.

"No, no. Things to do. Must get on."

I gather up my things, and set the dishwasher going. I'm out the door before I realize I never explained the significance of the chicken.

11

Lucy

The present . . .

In the three days since Diana died, I haven't cooked a meal, done a
load of laundry or been to the supermarket. I haven't disciplined a
child, helped anyone with homework or hidden any vegetables in
spaghetti sauce. I haven't done anything normal at all. It's as though
we're caught in an unmoving, timeless void while the rest of the
world keeps moving around us, oblivious.

The big kids have returned to school today, but Ollie still hasn't
been back to work. It's a surprise, even in light of his mother's death.
In the past two years my previously unambitious husband had turned
into a workaholic, heading to work on weekends, evenings, public
holidays. Now, he's sitting on the couch next to Edie, staring into
the ether as if he's in some sort of trance. At intervals I go and tell

him how sorry I am, that I wish there was something I could do. Each time I have to wonder: do I wish that?

I head to the kitchen, deciding it's time to reinstate some order and routine. This seems the very *least* I can do. A pile of unopened mail sits at the end of the counter so I start there, tearing each envelope open with my thumbnail and folding the papers flat, one by one.

The first document is a bank statement. I tend not to look at bank statements as a rule—since I'm the one managing the parenting load, I am happy to let Ollie manage the financial load (it's not sexist as much as fair responsibility distribution). But when my eye catches the seven-digit closing figure—debit, rather than credit—I can't help but draw in a breath. My eyes jump back to the top where the name *Cockram Goodwin* is printed. The Cockram part comes from Eamon, his business partner. How on earth could they be this far in the hole? More importantly, why hasn't Ollie mentioned it to me?

I open my mouth to ask him but before I speak there's a knock at the door. I glance at Ollie but he barely registers, too lost in his seven-mile stare.

"I'll go," I say needlessly.

When I open the door, two people are standing there, not uniformed, but clearly police. My instincts tell me this, and also the badge that is proffered by the female.

"I'm Detective Sr. Constable Jones," the woman says. "This is Detective Constable Ahmed."

"Hello," I say.

It is not Simon and Stella, the young, fresh-faced cops who informed us of Diana's death. Detective Jones is fortyish, slim, medium height. She has an attractive, if slightly masculine face, chin-length brown hair flecked with golden highlights. Her clothes are plain and practical, white shirt, navy trousers, fitted enough to suggest she takes pride in her figure.

"And you are?" she asks.

"Oh . . . I'm uh . . . Lucy Goodwin."

"The daughter-in-law." Jones nods. "I'm sorry to hear about your loss."

Ahmed bows his head. His crown is thinning and a ring of pale brown skin can be seen through his sweep of black hair.

"May we come in?" she asks.

I move back out of the doorway and Jones and Ahmed step into the front hall.

"Nice place," Jones says.

"Thank you," I say, though it isn't especially nice. Then again, police detectives probably saw a lot of houses that were a lot *less nice.* "What can I do for you, detectives?"

A wedding photo catches Jones's eye and she pauses briefly to look at it. "This is a nice picture. Is that your mother-in-law?"

She points to Diana, standing to Ollie's left in the picture. "Yes. That's Diana."

"I imagine it's a hard time for you all. Were you very close to your mother-in-law?"

Jones continues looking at the picture, and those surrounding it on the wall, seemingly uninvested in the answer.

"It's complicated."

"Isn't it always?" Jones smiles. "My ex's mother was a real piece of work. I could barely be in the same room with the miserable old cow. It killed my marriage in the end. So how about you? How was it complicated for you?"

"Oh, you know. Just . . . complicated."

Jones and Ahmed pick their way down the hall, pausing to look at the photos that dot the walls.

"Did you spend much time together as a family?" Jones continues. "Birthdays, Christmases, that kind of thing?"

I think of the last Christmas we spent together. The ugly words, the gnarled faces, the screaming over the turkey. It wasn't exactly a Hallmark commercial.

"I'm sorry, did you say which unit you were from?" I ask. For a moment I feel like a character out of *Law & Order: SVU*, which is, of course, my only point of reference for police showing up on the doorstep.

"We're from homicide," Jones says evenly.

"Lucy?" Ollie calls from the next room. "Who is it?"

I take a deep breath and walk into the living room. Jones and Ahmed are at my heels. The back door is wide open and Edie appears to have disappeared—a ball must have landed in our yard. Edie adores nothing more than throwing a ball back over the fence.

Ollie stands up, confused.

"It's the police," I say.

Ahmed approaches Ollie and extends a hand. "You must be Oliver Goodwin?"

"Ollie," Ollie says, shaking Ahmed's hand.

I see Ollie through the police's eyes. He looks like hell. He's wearing navy track pants and a maroon rugby sweater, his hair is a shambles, his skin has an odd, grey tone to it. It reminds me of the way he used to look when our kids were newborns and not sleeping, when he would appear in the doorway and beg to go back to sleep "just for half an hour" despite the fact that *I* was the one who'd been up most of the night.

"I'm Detective Senior Constable Jones and this Detective Constable Ahmed," Jones says. "We have a few questions, if you don't mind."

"Questions about what?" Ollie asks.

There's a pause, then Jones gives a slight chuckle. "Uh . . . about your mother's death?"

Ollie's eyes shoot to me and I shrug. Finally, after a second or two, he gestures for the cops to sit down. They do, on the couch.

"So what can we do for you?" I ask, sitting beside Ollie, on the arm of the armchair. "Do you have any more information about Diana's death?"

"We don't have the coroner's report yet," Jones says, "but we'll have it soon. In the meantime, we're gathering information. You mentioned to Constables Arthur and Perkins that your mother had cancer, is that correct?"

"It is," I say, when Ollie fails to reply. "Diana had breast cancer."

Jones flicks open a black notebook embossed with a gold police logo and holds her pen poised. "And can you tell me who her doctor was?"

"Her GP was Dr. Paisley," I say. "At the Bayside Medical Clinic."

"And her oncologist?"

Everyone looks at me. Everyone, including Ollie. "Actually . . . I'm not sure. She never mentioned her oncologist's name to me."

Jones closes her book. I get the feeling this isn't news to her. "I see."

Ollie blinks. "What do you see?"

"We haven't found any evidence of your mother's cancer. There is no record of her visiting an oncologist. No mammograms or ultrasounds, no chemotherapy. As far as we can see, she didn't have cancer at all."

Jones seems irritated by this, as though their incompetence is somehow *our* fault. "Well, obviously you haven't looked in the right place," I say. "You can't have checked with every doctor—"

"There's no referral from Dr. Paisley," Jones tells us calmly. Her elbows rest on her knees, her hands are clasped together. "There are no scans or blood test results, or anything that might indicate cancer."

I feel my face screw up. This is just ridiculous. People didn't say they had cancer if they didn't. Or perhaps *some* people did, people with hypochondria or Munchausen's, those who wanted to garner sympathy or money or friendship. But Diana hated sympathy and she certainly didn't need money. As for friendship, she hated people fussing around her or offering her so much as a tissue. Diana would *never* say she had cancer if she didn't. I'm as sure of this as I am of my very existence.

And yet.

"A problem with the system," Ollie says. "That must be it. Why would she say she had cancer if she didn't?"

"That's what we're trying to figure out."

Ollie shakes his head. "But she committed *suicide*. That's what *you guys* said."

"We don't know that for sure."

Now Ollie seems to snap to attention. "But . . . you said there was a letter?"

"There *was* a letter."

"Can we read it?"

"Eventually. But it's currently part of our investigation."

"What does that mean?"

"We're checking it for fingerprints. Doing a handwriting analysis."

"You think it was *forged*?"

"We're trying not to make too many judgments until we know more."

"This is ridiculous," Ollie says, standing up. He begins to pace. "Just ridiculous."

"Listen, there is evidence to suggest she committed suicide. The materials. The letter we found in her desk drawer."

I blink. "Her desk drawer?"

"Muuuuuum, I'm huuuuuungry."

Everyone glances in the direction of the voice. Edie is standing at the back door. Jones and Ahmed rise to their feet.

"Who are these people?" Edie asks, walking up to Jones, not stopping until she's practically between her thighs.

"My name is Detective Jones," Jones says. "This is my partner, Detective Ahmed. We're police."

Edie frowns. "But you don't have police clothes on."

"Some police don't wear uniforms. But I have a badge. Here. Look."

Jones, I notice, has changed temperaments as if on an axis. Suddenly she is, perhaps not quite maternal, but certainly friendly and warm. It's clear to me somehow that she doesn't have children of her own, but she appears the type who might very well be someone's favorite aunt.

"I think we'll leave it at that for today," Jones says, taking her badge back from Edie and putting it in her jacket pocket. "But if you think of anything significant, or remember Diana's oncologist's name, please do give me a call." Her tone indicates that she doesn't expect that call to come.

"It just doesn't make sense," Ollie says, as they walk toward the front door. "Mum wouldn't lie about having cancer."

But my mind is caught up with something else, something irritating and itchy, like having someone's name on the tip of your tongue. No matter how many times I turn it over, I can't make any sense of it.

If you committed suicide, why did you leave the letter in the study drawer, Diana? Why wouldn't you leave it where you knew someone would find it?

12

Lucy

The past . . .

A week or two before Archie's first birthday, Ollie and I arrive at Tom and Diana's house. We are immediately shuffled into the front living room, the "good room" all the Goodwins call it, which is strange because all the rooms seem pretty good to me. Still, it's a novelty as we usually gather around bar stools in the kitchen, or hang out in the den.

"Can I get you another mineral water, Lucy?" Diana asks.

"No, I'm fine, thank you."

Diana and Tom's sofa is so plump with stuffing that I have to clutch the armrest for stability. It doesn't help that my knee is doing its nervous bounce thing. Diana does nothing to put me at ease. She is her classic self today—her gaze beady and guarded. She sits right on the edge of the couch, her legs crossed at the knee. Nettie and Patrick were here when we arrived, but after giving us a quick, apologetic wave, they made themselves scarce. I wish I could make myself scarce.

Diana and I attempt to make small talk—about work (mine, never hers), about my dad's health (the precancerous mole he recently had removed), about the 70s zebra-striped jumpsuit and jacket combo I'm wearing (which Diana mistook for pajamas), but I sense Diana's heart isn't in it and neither is mine. We both want to get on with what we came here for, and it's clear from the fact that Ollie and I suggested this meeting that we want something.

"Cheese?" Diana says, holding up an antipasto platter.

"No," I say, and we drift back into silence.

Unfortunately, Ollie is still locked in conversation with Tom, long after Diana and I have exhausted all avenues of conversation. Tom, it appears, is talking about the inheritance again. He adores talking about *the inheritance* and drops it into conversation as often as he possibly can. It reminds me of a child desperate to tell their friend what they'd gotten them as a birthday present before they can tear off the paper. The *inheritance*, he says, will look after us in our old age. Admittedly, it's nice to know we'll be looked after and it does give me some comfort in those times we eat instant noodles for dinner because we can't afford anything else . . . but at the same time, it feels like poor taste to talk about what we'll get when someone dies *before they are dead.*

"Anyway, we wanted to ask you something," Ollie says, after what seems like an eternity. Diana and I sit a little straighter. Tom is the only one who seems surprised that there is a purpose to our visit. For someone so successful, he really can be quite thick.

"We've found a house," Ollie announces.

"And not a moment too soon!" Tom says eagerly. He, like the majority of Ollie's friends, has been unsettled about the fact that we're renting and likes the security of bricks and mortar for investment.

"It's a two-bedroom worker's cottage in South Melbourne," Ollie continues. "It's pretty run-down, but we could renovate it. We've got a good deposit, just short of twenty percent." He hesitates here, steals a quick glance at his mother. "Problem is, without a twenty-percent deposit we'd need to pay mortgage insurance, which is just throwing money down the drain. We hate to ask but—"

"South Melbourne, eh?" Tom says. "A good spot. Close to the city. Near the market, near Albert Park Lake. It's not easy for you young folk, is it? Everything is so expensive. I read the other day that a lot of kids are not buying their first home until they are in their forties, can you believe that? What do you think, Di?"

Tom is the only one I've ever heard call Diana "Di." Once, I heard him call her Lady Di. The strangest part was, Diana had actually *smiled*. Tom brought out an entirely different side to her. A softer side. Unfortunately, now, Diana doesn't look soft. Her lips are pressed tightly together as though she's trying to break something with her teeth.

"Life has never been easy," she says finally, folding her hands primly in her lap. "Every generation has its challenges and I dare say, most have had to suffer through worse than unaffordable housing. You and Lucy both have good heads on your shoulders. If you want this house badly enough, I don't doubt you'll make it work. Otherwise you'll find something else . . . something you *can* afford."

Silence follows. Deafening silence. I stare at the swirls of the rug on the floor, unable to meet her gaze. After a moment or two, I steal a look at Ollie and Tom, who both look disappointed, though not surprised.

"Diana," Tom starts, but Diana is already holding up a hand.

"You asked what I thought, that's what I think. Now that's all I'm going to say on the matter." Diana uproots herself from the over-stuffed couch. "Will you kids be staying for dinner?"

Ollie and I stare at her, blinking.

"I'll take that as no," she says, and disappears out of the room.

"I'll walk you out," Tom says.

"No, no," I say hurriedly. "Don't get up, please. We can see ourselves out."

I expect Tom to insist but he just nods. "Rightio then. You kids take care."

I am sick with mortification. What were we *thinking* asking Diana for money? Suddenly it seems so obvious. With what Ollie has told me about his upbringing—how Diana insisted he and Nettie be raised with part-time jobs and secondhand cars and an understanding that not everyone is as privileged as them—*of course* Diana wasn't going to be in favor of giving them a handout. Sure, they'd gone to private schools and had some pretty amazing holidays (at Tom's insistence), but they'd also spent weekends picking up donations for her charity, and serving at the local soup kitchen. The worst part is, as humiliated as I am, Diana had made some very good points when she'd turned us down. Other generations *had* had it harder. Ollie and I *did* have the ability to get a house within our means. Which means I can't even *hate* her for what she'd said.

As we reach the foyer, Nettie and Patrick materialize, as if from nowhere.

"How'd it go?" Nettie whispers. Her face is apologetic, as if she already knows exactly how we went. "Did she give you the spiel about how every generation has its challenges?"

Ollie nods. "But if we want it badly enough—"

"—you'll make it work?"

Nettie and Ollie all chuckle quietly.

"Commiserations," Patrick says. He's obviously been sampling some of Tom's top-shelf drinks while we were being given the lay of the land because he smells of whisky.

"Thank goodness for Dad, eh?" Nettie says. "If it wasn't for him, we'd all be left penniless on the street."

"What are you talking about?" I ask.

"Oh, don't look so worried, Lucy!" Nettie says, putting an arm around my shoulders. "Dad's not going to let you miss on your house. He's probably already written Ollie a check, am I right, Ol?"

Ollie pats his jeans pocket and grins.

"*What?*" I say.

"We all knew Mum wouldn't go for it. She never does." He glances at Nettie who nods. "We also knew Dad would."

"So *that*," I point toward the good room, "was . . . what exactly? A performance you put on for your mother's benefit?"

Ollie, Nettie and Patrick all look mildly perplexed. It is like everyone is in on a joke I don't understand.

Ollie gives a small, hapless grin. "I mean, I guess so. It's no big deal, Luce. It's just . . . the way the Goodwins do things."

Now it's my turn to look perplexed. I shake my head, sincerely stunned. "Well, I'm sorry to tell you that the Goodwins are going to do things differently from now on."

"Can you pull over, please?" I ask as soon as we are out of Tom and Diana's driveway.

Ollie glances at me then sighs and the car rolls to a stop.

"Please don't ever involve me in these games with your parents again."

Ollie pulls up the hand brake and shifts in his seat so his knees are angled toward me. He is attempting, I know, to be conciliatory. "I told you, Luce. This is just how it works in our family. You heard Nettie. It's just the process."

"The *process*?" I blink hard. "What does that even mean?"

"Don't you and your dad have processes around money? Like when we got married, you asked him for money then."

"I never asked him for anything. He *offered* to pay for our wedding."

"But you knew he would offer. That's a process. Kind of." Ollie smiles a little, but it slides away when I don't return it. "Listen, I'm sorry. You're right, I shouldn't have involved you."

"You shouldn't have involved *yourself*." I look at the dashboard. "Your mother was right. We're adults, we're smart. We need to take responsibility for our own lives now. I don't want to ask them for money again. Not for a house. Not for a car. Not for a liter of milk. Okay?"

"Okay just hang on a min—"

"I'm serious, Ollie. We'll pay the mortgage insurance and bug the house ourselves. This is a deal breaker for me."

"A deal breaker?"

"Yes."

Ollie takes a deep breath, lets his head fall back against the head rest. Silence hangs between us and I can feel Ollie wrestling with it. It's hard; I get that. It's instinctive to reach out to your parents for help when you need it, everyone does it. It's as familiar and comfortable as getting dressed in the morning. But at some point in adulthood, you have to teach yourself a new way to be. It's infuriating that Diana had to be the one to teach me that.

Finally Ollie nods. "Okay, fine. I'll never ask them for money again."

"Even if we're poor and starving and can't find a crumb between us?"

"Even then." He gives me a resigned smile. "There is no one I'd rather starve with than you."

We laugh and I find myself impressed with the speed in which Ollie came around. I wonder if it's because, in the back of his mind, he knows that we will never have to starve. He knows that at some point a huge amount of money will be coming our way, more money than we could possibly know how to spend.

And to access it, all we need to do is wait for someone to die.

13

Diana

The past . . .

The kids have barely left the house before Tom starts pouting. I knew this would happen, with the same certainty that *he* knew I was going to turn down Ollie's request for money. When you've being married for as long as we have, while you may hope for different results, you stop expecting them. And, if you want a happy marriage, you have to look to the other things, the things you do see eye to eye on. Lucky for me, when it comes to Tom, there are many of these.

Tom sits heavily in his wingback chair.

I hold up a hand, palm forward. "I know what you're going to say, Tom, so please save it."

"Did I say anything?" He lets out a long, world-weary sigh.

"I don't like being the bad guy, Tom. You know that."

He shifts in his seat, his expression resigned rather than annoyed. "I *do* know that."

As far as arguments between Tom and I go, this is as heated as they get. Once upon a time, Tom had more fire to him, but now there's only a handful of things that really make him fly off the handle. Traffic. People leaving lights on around the house. Racism. You know, the important things. Today, despite our differing views, Tom and I respect where the other is coming from. Tom grew up in the outskirts of Melbourne where the suburbs meet the country, a low socioeconomic area even before he was orphaned and had to move further out to live with his grandparents. He was schooled in a rough area, and left at fourteen to do his apprenticeship with a local plumber. Once qualified, he found himself a job on a residential development project, befriended the owners, and suggested they try their hand at retirement communities—a suggestion so profitable he wound up a business partner in one of the largest residential development companies in Australia.

"I would have thought that you of *all people* would understand that you don't have to be given a handout to succeed, Tom."

"But things are different now," he says. "Everyone is going to university, working for free to get experience, using their private school networks. It's harder than in my day."

But of course this is just part of the waffle that private school parents tell each other to justify the exorbitant fees they pay. After Tom badgered me for years, I finally relented and allowed Ollie and Nettie to attend schools with term fees high enough to feed an entire Afghan village for a year. Years later, I'm still doubtful as to whether the schools were any better than the local ones. What I *am* sure about is that giving children handouts—no, not children, *adults!*—after they have already been privately educated and given every advantage in life, simply to keep pushing them further ahead of those who are trying to make their way without assistance, is not the right thing to do for anyone involved.

"It's always been hard, Tom. You were hungrier for it than our kids are, that's all."

Unlike Tom, I grew up in a fairly middle-class family. We didn't have the kind of wealth Tom and I live with now, but we were comfortably off. The fact is, I wouldn't have been hungry for it either if my circumstances hadn't taken a drastic dive in my youth.

"I think Ollie could do with being a little hungry. A little hunger is good for young people. It was the making of you."

Tom slides over and I sit beside him in the wingback chair, which is generous enough for two middle-aged bottoms. "Actually . . ." Tom smiles. "It was the making of you."

1970

Cynthia and I called it the summer of the Falcon, mostly because the rest of our friends were in Europe and we wanted to make it sound more exciting than it really was. The Falcon XR GT was a car, and it belonged to Cynthia's boyfriend, Michael. I knew, of course, what happened in the back of the Falcon, what Michael and Cynth had done in the Falcon many times. I wasn't desperately in love with David, though I liked him well enough. He was tall, and he was studying engineering at university, which seemed to be enough, back then. Height and smarts. What else could a woman want?

As it turned out, when I discovered I was pregnant, David's

smarts came in useful. "There's a place in Broadmeadows," he said. "A home for unwed mothers. You go there, you have the baby, and then you come back. You can just tell everyone you went to Europe."

I was glad he hadn't suggested the other type of place you went as an unwed mother. An abortion clinic. I may not have been the most maternal of girls, but I'd always been a believer in taking responsibility for your actions. It wasn't the poor baby's fault that I'd gotten into the back of the Falcon with David; I didn't see why it should have to pay the ultimate price for it. My mother agreed that David's plan was wise and my father tended to agree with my mother when she thought something was wise. The idea that I would have to give my baby away before leaving the home was a thought so far off in the distance that I didn't even bother to think about it. After all, when you're drowning and someone offers you a life raft, you don't check it for punctures before climbing aboard.

"Are you feeling all right?" David asked me the night before I left for Orchard House. He waved a hand vaguely in front of my midsection, indicating he was asking about pregnancy-related symptoms.

"I'm fine."

It was a warm evening and I was sitting on the brick steps of my parents' bungalow with a bag of grapes in my lap. (I'd had morning sickness for nearly six months, and grapes were the only thing that staved it off.) I'd put off my secretarial course, and told my friends I was spending a semester in Sicily. No one apart from my parents and David knew the truth. Not even Cynthia. Turned out that Catholic shame fell harder than I'd thought.

I'd only seen David a couple of times since I'd been accepted into

Orchard House. While I'd been lying low, David, apparently, had been working around the clock to help my father pay for the home. My father had been impressed with David's commitment to help. I'd once heard him tell mother that he'd been glad "I was consorting with an honorable sort of boy, at least." I remember looking through the crack in my bedroom door one evening and seeing my father shaking David's hand while my mother thanked him profusely. In contrast, my father had barely looked at me in months.

"Maybe I'll see you again when you get out," he said.

"Maybe," I agreed. But we both knew it was a lie.

My mother drove me to Orchard House.

"It won't be forever," she said at the door, giving me a brusque kiss and hurrying back to the car. I was startled that this was the extent of her good-bye but I forced myself not to call her back. I was humiliated enough as it was.

After a moment or two, a pinched-looking woman in a navy pinafore came to the door. She opened the security door and surveyed me silently. "You must be Diana," she said. "Well . . . you'd better come inside."

Orchard House had the look and feel of a hospital. It was three floors high, with wide halls, linoleum floors and vinyl furniture. Matron took me up the stairs to the second floor, which had a communal area in the center and burgundy doors around the edges, presumably leading to dormitories. Pregnant women in small clusters looked up when I entered, then quickly down again.

"You're among the oldest at Orchard House," Matron told me, leading me around the edge of the room. "The youngest is a girl named Pamela, who you'll be sharing with. Pamela is just fourteen." Matron tutted with disapproval. "We only exchange first names at Orchard House, and we don't talk about the schools we went to, the people we know, or anything that can distinguish us to the outside world. It's to protect your identities," she said, but I suspected it was more to protect our parents' identities. Matron stopped just shy of a door which I assumed led to my room. "You should know that Pamela is a little troubled. I thought an older, well-spoken girl like yourself might be able to help her, teach her how to behave properly." She gestured inside, where a girl sat on one of the twin bed. She wore a sour expression, and her hair in two greasy plaits.

"Pamela?" Matron said. "This is your new roommate, Diana."

"Hello," I said as Pamela looked resolutely at the floor.

"Don't look so glum," Matron said to her. "You girls are lucky. Your families have helped you. If you keep your head down until you have your baby, you can return to your old lives and forget this ever happened. Not everyone is as fortunate."

Matron left us then, telling me to "make myself at home." As I sat on the narrow twin bed, opposite the strange, reticent girl, I felt the tears stack up in my eyes. But I brushed them away. After all, I was lucky.

After dinner that night I went to the communal area, which was filled with pregnant girls on brown vinyl couches, watching the television or staring at novels. At one table a girl sat painting another girl's nails a pretty, pale pink that reminded me of Cynthia's nails.

"May I sit here?" I asked a blond girl on the couch, who was in her pajamas and slippers, her hair pinned up in rollers. She was chatting to the girls on her right and she slid along without looking up.

The couch was startlingly uncomfortable, but as I wasn't sure I could physically stand again, I didn't bother trying to move. All around the room, girls were pinned to their seats by their enormous watermelon-shaped bellies. I counted seventeen girls, seventeen watermelons. Pamela was the only one who didn't sit. She stood by the bookshelves to the right of the television, ostensibly choosing a book, but mostly fidgeting. She was one of those types that couldn't sit still, I'd noticed. She was jittery, anxious. It was distracting.

The blond girl—Laurel, I found out—talked quietly to the two girls on her right. As I eavesdropped, I found out that this was her second time at Orchard House. She'd been here two years earlier, when she was just sixteen. Funnily enough, rather than people finding this startling and horrifying—as I did—she was treated as a celebrity of sorts, and regarded as the fountain of all knowledge about Orchard House. As I listened, conversation drifted from the terrible food, to Matron's crush on Arthur, the gardener, to Laurel's suspicion that one of the girls was pregnant with her own brother's baby. The banter, inane as it was, reminded me of conversations with my own friends, and made me feel lonely and comforted in equal parts.

At ten minutes to ten, Matron appeared. "Ten minutes until lights out, girls!" Matron had a shrill voice that pierced the air and knocked any sense of normality out of the room. "Come on, now. Don't dillydally."

She disappeared, and the girls dutifully shuffled their hips to the edge of the couch, ready to hoist themselves to standing. I found out, via the girls' grumbling, that the lights did indeed go out at ten P.M., and if you weren't in your room, you had to find your way back there in pitch darkness.

"Ten minutes until lights out," Matron said again. "Don't dillydally."

We all glanced at the door again.

"If you dillydally I won't be able to dillydally with Arthur after lights out."

Matron was nowhere to be seen. A slow giggle broke out across the room as everyone glanced around. I noticed Pamela's back was to us.

"Pamela?" Laurel cried, delighted. "Was that you?"

Pamela bent over, fiddling with the spine of a book, pretending not to hear. If she was doing the impersonation, no one could deny that it was spot-on.

"Oh, Arthur, *stop* that!" came Matron's voice again. "Oh, go on then. Don't stop."

The giggles became a fever-pitched chortle.

"Just take me into your shed and I'll . . . I'll . . ."

"What are you girls still doing in here?"

The voice was louder now, more shrill. Our heads swung toward the doorway where Matron—actual Matron—stood, hands on hips.

"Didn't I tell you not to dillydally?"

"Right away, Matron," Pamela said and she was the first one to exit the room.

Our bellies grew. We weren't told much about what was coming. We guessed when our babies were due by the size of our bellies. In public, we talked about our pregnancies insofar as they affected our bodies: "My bladder is the size of a walnut," or "I can hardly walk up this flight of stairs," but we didn't talk about the "babies," as such. No one told us not to, we just didn't . . . a natural form of self-protection perhaps. I avoided making friendships, which was surprisingly easy when you were forbidden to talk about who you were and where you came from. In any case, I'd never been much good at small talk.

During the day, Pamela didn't talk to me at all. I tried to teach her things, as Matron had asked. How to speak nicely. How to sew. But each time I tried, she just stared at me or rolled her eyes or muttered under her breath. Once, as I was showing her how to hold cutlery properly, she picked up a fork and threw it across the room. The problem, I realized, was that Pamela was damaged. I wasn't sure how to teach her *not* to be damaged.

Pamela's impersonations became a nightly ritual. She could "do" almost anyone—Dr. Humbert, the obstetrician with the bushy moustache who came by once a week to take our blood pressure; Arthur, the gardener and Matron's love interest; any of the girls. She was a master at finding people's quirks, the tiniest detail that brought the impersonation to life. Every evening, she stood by the bookshelves and we waited. It was my solace, these few minutes of giggles each day. It didn't occur to me until later that it might be a comfort for her too. A few minutes of being someone else.

One night, when I'd been at Orchard House nearly a month, she impersonated me.

"Oh, yes, I'm Diana, I know how to use cutlery and talk posh."

Everyone giggled. Even me. Perhaps it was her tone that made it funny rather than mean-spirited. Or maybe it was because it was the first time she'd acknowledged me at all. A part of me was glad to realize that someone in here knew I existed.

One night, as we gathered in the communal area, someone noticed Mary wasn't there.

"She went into labor last night," Laurel, her roommate, told us, her voice hushed.

Everyone gathered in close. We knew that people went to have their babies, but we were starved of logistics. It was rare to get any actual details.

"It was pretty tough. She waited as long as she could before she called Matron. She didn't want to go to the hospital."

That had been a surprise. Mary had been one of the braver girls. She'd been saying for weeks she couldn't wait to get her baby out, that when it was all over, she was going to buy a pair of hip-hugging flares and a bottle of whisky.

"Why didn't she want to go?" someone asked, the question on everyone's lips.

Sixteen pairs of eyes gawped at Laurel.

"Because you go into the hospital with a baby," she said, "and you leave without one."

Later, when Matron came to announce lights out, we were all animated.

"Did Mary have her baby, Matron?" Laurel asked.

Matron looked guarded. No one used the word "baby" with Matron. Even Dr. Humbert had managed to avoid using it, at least in front of us.

"She did," Matron said eventually.

We all waited. I noticed Pamela, by the bookshelves, standing so still I doubted she was breathing.

"What did she have? A boy or a girl?"

"The baby was healthy," Matron said, and that was the last time I heard her say the word "baby" at Orchard House.

After news of Mary's birth, the impersonations stopped. It was as though for a time we'd forgotten what we were doing there, but then, just like that, we remembered. During the day, Pamela barely spoke at all. But at night, when we lay in bed, she sometimes said a few words. Something vulnerable happened to you at night at Orchard House. You took off your clothes, you took off your armor.

"I think I'm having a girl," she whispered one night, as we lay in our twin beds. "What about you?"

In the darkness I could just about make out the outline of her body, under a mound of blankets. It was cold in the room and her breath was a cloud in the air.

"It doesn't matter," I said. "It won't be my baby."

"But what would you call it?" she insisted. "If you were keeping it?"

I shook my head. "I wouldn't have the faintest idea, Pamela."

"I'd call my girl Jane. Jane Pamela. It's pretty, don't you think?"

Outside, a car drove past and a streak of light crossed her bed, illuminating her face. It was light, hopeful. Utterly unlike Pamela. A lump filled my throat.

"Diana?" Pamela said after a moment.

"Mmm?"

"My friends call me Pammy."

I inhaled sharply, swallowed hard. All at once I felt pinned by the weight of what was coming.

"Diana? Did you hear me?"

"Yes," I said, coughing to clear my throat. "I heard you, Pammy."

As our due dates drew closer, Pammy shared a few little details about her life. She told me the father of her baby was a man named Christopher, a doctor. Christopher had a wife, Pammy said, but she didn't love him, only his money. Christopher paid for Pammy to come to Orchard House because he didn't want her to have to lift a finger while she was with child, that's how much he loved her—at least that's what Pammy said. I had my doubts about Pammy's version of events, but I was happy to listen. It was better than when she started talking about the baby.

"I wonder if Jane will look like me or Christopher."

"I bet Jane will be smart, like Christopher."

"Oh look, Jane is kicking me. She's a feisty one!"

Sometimes, when Pammy talked about Jane, I wanted to scream. Pammy wouldn't be allowed to name her baby. She wouldn't even be allowed to hold her. That was hard to think about. As the days moved on, my urge to hold my baby was nearly overwhelming. At night, when I felt it kick and move, I wrapped my arms around my belly. I assumed it would be my only chance to hold it.

I do have a name," I told Pammy, one night. "For a boy, that is. Oliver."

"Oliver," Pammy said approvingly. "What a lovely, posh name. Lovely and posh, like you."

Despite my hurt, despite *myself* . . . in the darkness, I laughed out loud.

. . .

One evening, I realized I hadn't seen Pammy all day.

"Matron?" I said when she came to tell us it was ten minutes until lights out. "I haven't seen Pammy today. Has she gone to have her baby?"

Matron pursed her lips. "Pamela has been moved."

"Moved where? It's too early for her to have her baby."

"That's none of your concern." Matron clapped her hands together twice. "All right girls, time for bed, don't dillydally."

"*Matron*," I said, louder now. "Where has Pammy been moved?"

Matron's turned to look at me, pinning me in her beady gaze. "Are you going to start causing trouble, Diana? That's disappointing. I thought you were one of the more sensible girls."

I felt Laurel tug my hand. I abandoned the conversation with Matron and followed her into the corridor.

"Has Pammy been saying anything about wanting to keep her baby?" Laurel said.

"No . . . not really." I thought about that. "Well she did give her a name."

"*Her?*"

I shrugged. "She thinks it is a girl."

Laurel nodded sadly.

"What is it?" I asked.

"The same thing happened to Josephine, the first time I was at Orchard House. One day she told everyone she'd decided to keep her baby. The next day Josephine was gone."

"She kept her baby?" I couldn't keep the awe out of my voice.

"We assumed so," Laurel said. "But I saw Josephine on the outside, a year or so later. After she told Matron she wanted to keep her baby, Matron kept her downstairs in a different room and wouldn't let her see anyone. They put her to work, night and day—cleaning, doing dishes, cooking. They said that if she wasn't giving her baby up she'd have to pay for all of her living and hospital expenses herself, and she needed to start working for them right away. They worked her so hard she went into labor a month early. And when she had her baby, she hadn't paid off her debt, so they held the baby for ransom. Eventually she had no choice but to hand the baby over. My guess is that's where Pammy is."

"Enough of that chatter," Matron said from the other end of the corridor. "Off to bed with you all."

I hoped that Laurel was wrong, that Pammy had got out and was somewhere with Christopher and her baby. I hoped for it, longed for it . . . but I never really believed it.

Mother came to visit when my belly was so round and tight that I couldn't put on my shoes and had been wearing slide-on slippers for weeks. Mother was wearing her hat and gloves, like she was going to church.

"I want to keep my baby," I told her, as she sat on the vinyl back chair. "But I need your help."

"Diana," Mother said. "You're being utterly ridiculous."

"I'm not. It's 1970. Single women have babies nowadays."

Mother smiled. "Oh? Which women are you referring to?"

I didn't know any, of course. But they existed. The news said things were changing, that women were gaining more rights.

Apparently single women were able to access welfare to help them support themselves and their babies.

"Meredith is divorced," I said, because Meredith was the closest thing I knew to a single mother. Unfortunately it wasn't the best example. My dad's cousin Meredith had left her husband a couple of years ago after finding out he was unfaithful, but divorce had ruined Meredith socially, not to mention financially. Meredith had been tossed out of her family home and last Diana heard, was living in a rented house in Melbourne's West, in an industrial area. She'd gotten herself a job, apparently, in a factory cafeteria.

"Do you want to end up like Meredith?" Mother asked.

"I can just leave here, you know," I said, defensively. "There's no lock on the door." In fact, I had no idea if that was true. In any case, I certainly wouldn't be telling Matron about my plans.

"I suppose that's true," Mother said thoughtfully. "But what would you do then? Bring the baby back to your father's house? I don't think so."

"I'd get my own place."

"With what money? Who would rent a house to a pregnant single woman with no qualifications to work?"

"I'd stay with friends."

"Which friends?"

I said nothing, trying to make my expression defiant. But I didn't have any friends that could help me. The only friends I had that weren't overseas or at university lived with their parents, most of whom were friends of *my* parents. I had nowhere to go. My plan was a giant bluff and my mother was calling it.

She placed a cold hand on top of mine. "Come on now, Diana,

you're nearly there. Have your baby, come home and make better choices next time." She kissed my forehead and the matter, as far as she was concerned, was laid to rest.

That night, I ran.

14

Lucy

The present . . .

The funeral director's name is Pearl. She's a kindly woman in her midfifties with a puff of overdyed chestnut hair and the patience of a kindergarten teacher. Thank goodness for her because, as it turns out, there's a lot to do after someone dies. When Tom died, Diana organized everything and I never appreciated how heroic that was until now. How does one, through his or her grief, meet with funeral directors and select caskets, figure out readings and choose flowers, all the while supporting others and managing the minutia of their lives at the same time? I guess I'm going to find out.

We've been at the funeral home for several hours selecting things, but my mind is elsewhere. Apparently Jones and Ahmed paid a visit to Nettie and Patrick yesterday too and told them about the cancer . . . or lack of it. Nettie and Patrick agree it all must be some sort of misunderstanding, but I can't seem to shake the feeling that something isn't right. Why hadn't Dr. Paisley referred Diana to an oncologist? Why weren't there any records of mammograms or ultrasounds? Why would she lie about it?

None of it makes sense.

"What about the wake?" Pearl asks us. "Will it be at your mother's house?"

Nettie shudders. "No. Let's do it somewhere else."

"I agree," Ollie says. "Knowing Mum died there . . . it's different now."

"How about a local bar or restaurant?" Pearl suggests and we all mutter our agreement.

"Now, for the service. Some people who have nondenominational services like to have a few church hymns. Do you think Diana would—"

"No," Ollie and Nettie say in unison.

"Mum wasn't really into hymns," Ollie explains.

"No hymns," Pearl says, making a note in her paperwork. "That's fine."

While I hadn't thought about it much in the past, Diana's harsh rejection of her Catholic upbringing is curious to me now. I find myself wanting to ask her about it . . . and I'm hit by a jarring sadness that I can't.

"All right," Pearl said. "Moving on."

For the most part, Nettie and I do the choosing. Ollie and Patrick sit there like a couple of teenagers, nodding and grunting and looking at their phones. Around lunchtime, Pearl suggests Nettie and I pop down to the corner store for sandwiches.

"I'm not hungry," Nettie says.

"It's important that you eat," Pearl says. She's entirely firm and also entirely serene. "And grab something for the men while you're at it."

Outside, we shuffle along the street. A train track runs along the side of the road and the noise of a passing train takes the edge off the silence for thirty seconds. Then it's gone, and there's nothing but the sound of our breathing. Nettie lifts a hand to scratch her nose and her shirt sleeve rides up revealing a thick purple ring around her left wrist.

"What happened to your wrist?" I ask.

Her gaze flickers to me, then back to the road. "What's it to you?"

"Nettie. Come on."

"Let's just get the sandwiches, shall we?" she says quietly.

We walk a few more paces.

"I *hate* this," I explode, suddenly unable to keep it in any longer. "Diana would hate it too. You know she would."

Nettie stops.

"Now of *all times* we should be coming together as a family."

"Family?" Nettie squares up against me. "You and Ollie and the kids are a family. Patrick and I, we . . . we're just two people. Two people who don't even—"

"I know—"

"You *don't* know. You couldn't possibly know."

I sigh. "Nettie, I want so much for us to put this behind us. I want to help you through this."

I'm not hopeful, but I think I have a chance. Here, without Patrick, without Ollie, I feel like I might be able to get through to her.

And I want to get through to her. There has already been too much loss for this family. First Tom. Then Diana. I can't lose Nettie too.

"I don't care what you want."

She turns away and continues walking down the street. It's not until later that I realize she never told me what happened to her wrist.

15

Diana

The past . . .

I've heard it said that every parent spends 80 percent of their energy on one child, and spreads the remaining 20 percent among any other children. Ollie has always been my 80 percent child. I spent most of his childhood wondering if he was eating enough, learning enough, doing enough. He wasn't the most popular kid in school, but he wasn't a social leper by any means either. His general contentment, which should have comforted me, somehow only served to baffle me. Did he want to invite his little friend over to play, or did he wish I'd stop inviting that friend over? He never seemed to care either way.

Nettie, on the other hand, was born so capable and articulate, I never bothered worrying about her. Being her mother was like having a tiny little peer that accompanied me everywhere. If some-one picked on her at school she'd simply have a quiet word with them, saying if they didn't stop being mean they'd have no friends left, and wouldn't that be silly? When I served them vegetables for din-ner and Ollie, five years her senior, refused to eat them, she'd ask him: "Don't you want to be big and strong like a superhero, Ollie?"

Once, when Ollie was eleven and Nettie was six, they'd been swimming in the pool for most of the afternoon when I had to go inside. Ollie and Nettie were both strong swimmers, so it wasn't a big deal to pop back to the house for a short while.

"Keep an eye on your sister," I must have said, or something to that effect.

I went to the kitchen and started on dinner, peeling potatoes. It was a warm day, and the sun beamed in through the window. As I picked up the last potato, a funny feeling came over me. Mother's instinct, perhaps. *I should check the kids.*

When I got outside, I saw a tangle of bodies just under the sur-face of the water.

I didn't pause even to take off my shoes before leaping into the water.

I grabbed Nettie first, but Ollie had ahold of her and wasn't letting go. I pulled and twisted her but he was like an anchor, weighing her down. Finally, I gave Ollie a kick in the stomach, and she came free. I pushed her to the side of the pool and a mo-ment later, did the same for Ollie. He clung to the side of the pool, blood and water dripping down his face, landing in the hollowed-out part of his collarbones.

"What . . . on earth . . . happened?" I said, panting.

"Ollie did a flip and hit his head," Nettie gasped. "I saw blood and he wasn't moving. I tried to save his life and then he tried to drown me!"

I looked at Ollie, sucking in wild breaths at the side of the pool. "Did you panic, Ollie? Is that why you were holding onto Nettie?"

Ollie didn't reply. He seemed just as confused as Nettie was.

That's when I realized. Some people jumped in and tried to save someone who was in trouble; others did anything they could to save themselves. Ollie hadn't meant to drown Nettie, he was simply following his instincts, just as she was following hers.

My children had just shown me who they were.

When I arrive home, Nettie is sitting on a bar stool in my kitchen, leafing through the newspaper. Her suit jacket is on the counter and her hair is swept into a very corporate-looking chignon.

"Hello, darling," I say, jostling with my bags from the supermarket.

Her eyes flicker up from the newspaper. Nettie stops by like this from time to time on her way home from work, sometimes under the guise of dropping something off, sometimes just *because*. I don't really understand it, but I've come to quite enjoy the routine of it. "Hey, Mum," she says.

"I saw your friend Lisa in the supermarket just now." I haul the bags onto the counter. "She mentioned a bunch of you were going to Hong Kong for a girls' trip."

"I'm not going," Nettie says.

"Oh. Why not?"

She sighs. "Money. Time."

I nod. But it seems to me that a girls' trip might be exactly what Nettie needs.

"Have you seen Lucy and Archie?" I ask her.

"Not since the hospital."

"I've just been to visit them."

"Oh." Nettie turns the page of the newspaper, studiously uninterested. "How are they?"

"I think Lucy's had better days. But that's what it's like with a new baby." The clock on the oven catches my attention. It's not even five o'clock. "Nettie, shouldn't you be at work?"

"I left early."

I look at her. "Are you allowed to do that?"

"I'm allowed to do anything I like."

I look at her. She's in a strange mood. Her posture is sullen, almost teenage.

"Is something the matter, Nettie?"

She shakes her head, of course. My daughter, for all her softness and light, is fiercely private, at least with me. She's actually one of only a handful of people who can make me uncertain of myself. I enjoy this about her, the juxtaposition of it. There was a time though when Nettie did use to open up to me. When she was younger, I practically had to tell her to *stop* telling me things. *Some things*, I'd say, *are for sharing with your girlfriends, Antoinette.* But somewhere along the line she'd stopped sharing so much. Started talking to Patrick, I assume.

"Are you sure?" I ask.

She'll never divulge that she'd dearly love a baby. That she wished it was *her* holding a newborn instead of Lucy. I know it's true just the same. The poor girl is so desperate for a baby it's practically written on her skin. Her polycystic ovaries make it tricky to conceive, but there must be things she can do to help. She's probably already doing *things*. But she won't tell me and I won't ask, instead we'll just be together for a little while, not saying anything at all.

"Would you like to stay for dinner?" I ask.

"No," she says. "I need to get home to Patrick."

"Patrick is welcome to join us too," I say dutifully.

In the early days, Nettie and Patrick would come to dinner often. They'd retire to the den after dinner and Patrick would mix drinks and smoke cigars with Tom. Patrick always seemed so comfortable that for a while, I'd worried we'd never have a night to ourselves. But a year or two in, he'd stopped coming, save for Christmas and family occasions.

"No," she says. "I'll go home."

"You know, if something is bothering you, you can talk to me about it," I say. "I might not be the best conversationalist . . . but I'm not a bad listener."

Nettie looks at me, and for a long moment, I think she might cry. Nettie is not a crier, she hasn't been since she was a very little girl. But a few seconds pass and Nettie regains her composure, sits straight. "Thanks, Mum," she says. "But everything is fine."

16

Lucy

The past . . .

"Are you feeling okay?" Ollie asks.

I nod gloomily.

"Not carsick?"

"No."

I *do* get carsick, but that's not what's bothering me. We're in the car, on our way to the Goodwins' beach house. I understand, of course, that it is a privilege to be miserable about this. There are people with worse problems. Certainly, Ollie isn't unhappy about it. He loves Sorrento. All year he romanticizes it, waxing lyrical about how nice it is to have the whole family together under the same roof for a week. He is utterly oblivious to any undercurrents of tension. If I mention anything to him, he always looks baffled. ("Mum, stressed? *No.* That's just how she is! She *enjoys* the stress.")

Perhaps it's just Ollie who enjoys the stress. He's been whistling all morning, and his entire body is growing more spongy and relaxed as we inch along the foreshore in bumper-to-bumper traffic, catching the odd glimpse of sapphire blue through the beach scrub.

Whenever I tell anyone my in-laws have a beach house in Sorrento, they make appreciative noises. *Sorrento, ooh la la.* I understand why. Tom and Diana's clifftop beach house is arguably one of the most spectacular houses on the Mornington peninsula, a 1900s sandstone braced into the cliff with manicured gardens and a white-washed timber path built down to the beach. There is a pool, a tennis court and a three-tiered limestone patio with uninterrupted sea views.

I hate it.

"How on earth can you hate *that*?" Claire demanded recently. "I would kill to have a beach house that I could visit whenever I liked. I mean, I'd literally kill for it."

I would kill not to have such a place. For one thing, the Good-wins' place is entirely un–child friendly. Artwork, pottery and sculptures adorn every wall and surface. I can barely set Archie on the floor without Diana gasping. It's so foreign to me. My own mother couldn't have cared less about artwork or sculptures. If she'd had the chance to be a grandmother, all the artwork on her walls would have been painted by her grandchildren, and she only would have gasped when I told the kids it was bedtime. ("Don't be ridiculous kids! You're staying up late with Nana tonight.")

Growing up, we'd spent our summers in Portarlington, a quaint beach town on the less glamourous side of the bay. On the main street opposite the beach was a fish and chips shop, a pub, and a shop that sold beach chairs and tents. For the entire month of January, old bald men sat in deck chairs along the sand, exposing their enormous bellies, and middle-aged women in sun hats stood in the shallows in frilly turquoise one-piece swimsuits, offering children watermelon from Tupperware containers. Prior to visiting Tom and Diana's place, I'd always thought of a beach house as a place that had sand on the floor, beach towels on the rail of the deck and a jumble of little plastic shoes inside the front door. But Sorrento is something else entirely.

"The Greenans are coming for dinner tonight," Diana had said on the phone to Ollie this morning. "You remember Amelia and Jeffrey, don't you?"

I remember Amelia and Jeffrey. Amelia was nice enough, but Jeffrey, a colleague of Tom's, was awful. All of the *ists*: sexist, racist, classist. The first time we'd met (within minutes of meeting) he'd asked me what school I went to, and when I'd said Bayside High School, he'd scrutinized me a moment and then said with a little awe, "Wow. You'd never know."

When we arrive, Nettie and Patrick are still unloading their bags from the car. Patrick resembles a packhorse, lumbering under a dozen smallish bags while Nettie only carries her purse. Nettie looks a little green.

"Welcome!" Tom says, standing in the grand front doorway, his arms outstretched. "Diana, they're all here!" He beams at us. Having all the family down at the beach house—this is his happy place. "Where's my grandson?" he says to me. I put Archie down and he toddles over to Tom. "Well, hello there, my boy. Haven't you grown?"

I kiss Tom and then walk past him into the house. I set my purse on the oak dining table, custom built to seat sixteen guests. ("Why sixteen?" I'd asked Tom when he'd pointed that detail out, but he just seemed baffled by the question and moved on to the next item on the tour. I suspected he himself wasn't entirely sure.) Though it's not exactly to my taste, there's no denying the house has its wow factor. The soaring ceilings, the vast open spaces, the floor-to-ceiling windows with views of the sea and the cliffs. Walking in the door feels like stepping into the pages of an interior design magazine (and in fact, according to Tom they had been "begged" to feature the Sorrento house in several publications, but Diana had declined, calling it "vulgar"). Diana catches my eye now, fussing around in the adjoining gleaming-white and marble kitchen.

"Diana," I say.

She smiles. "Hello, Lucy."

"Hi, Mum," Ollie says, entering the house behind me. He puts down the bags and plants a kiss on her cheek. Besides Tom, Ollie is one of the few people who is always pleased to see Diana. If the feeling is mutual, it's hard to say. She always seems shy, almost embarrassed by the attention.

"Hello, darling," she mutters.

Tom strides into the house, holding Archie up like a trophy. "Di! Come and see our gorgeous grandson."

A flurry of activity follows—Patrick appears, asking for some acetaminophen for Nettie, who has a headache; Archie spots a bowl of nuts on the coffee table and upends them, spilling them all over the floor; and Tom tries to figure out which remote control (there are six) opens the garage door. Meanwhile, Ollie picks up the bags again and walks toward our usual room.

"Ollie, wait!" Diana cries.

Ollie freezes midstride.

"I've set up the rooms downstairs for you and Lucy and Archie," she says, with less certainty.

Miraculously, all the action stops and there is silence. Even Archie looks up from the spilled nuts, sensing something is up.

"I . . . thought you might prefer having your own space," she says.

It's a good suggestion, a practical suggestion. The downstairs area is huge, and we'd have our own bedroom for Archie. If he cried during the night, it wouldn't disturb anyone; I could walk the hallways with him all night if I needed to.

So why does it feel so much like a slap?

That evening, we are bathing Archie when the Greenans arrive. Actually, *Nettie* is bathing him and I am sitting on the vanity with a glass of rosé. Out in the hallway, Ollie and Patrick are sitting on the floor with their backs to the wall, drinking cocktails that Patrick has made. I find, to my surprise, that I'm not having an awful time.

Nettie has been a godsend. When she heard we'd been relegated to the downstairs rooms (admittedly "relegated" is a little harsh, our room is grander and more spacious than most hotel suites), she'd promptly told Diana they would be moving their bags downstairs too. ("We'll make a party of it," she'd said, winking at Archie.) Patrick and Nettie were wonderful with Archie. All afternoon they'd taken turns to play with him, taking him on walks around the garden or swimming in the pool while Ollie and I ate lunch and unpacked. In fact, I've hardly held him all day.

"What time does he go to bed?" Nettie asks.

"Seven," I say.

"So what happens now?"

"Once he's in his pajamas he'll play for a bit. Then I read him a story, give him a bottle and put him to bed."

"Will he wake during the night for a feed?"

Nettie wants to know every detail. It's funny and also unnecessary because she is natural with babies in a way that few people are. In the past I'd gotten the impression she and Patrick were waiting a while before having kids, perhaps until Nettie's career was more established, but now I wonder if that's the case. I think of Nettie's green complexion earlier and wonder if it was more than just travel sickness. Maybe she's pregnant?

"The Greenans are here," Diana's voice announces from the top of the stairs, as Nettie is washing Archie's hair. "Can you kids come up?"

"We're bathing Archie," Nettie replies, grinning at Archie. He grins back.

There's a pause. "All of you?" Diana asks pointedly.

I open my mouth, ready to say that I'll finish up, that everyone else should head on upstairs. After all, I'd rather be down here than up there. But Nettie, to my surprise, gets in first. "Yes. All of us."

The silence stretches on and on. I find myself desperate to fill it, but Nettie looks at me and shakes her head. In the tiny gesture, I realize I'd underestimated Nettie. She's a better ally than I'd originally thought.

"I'll go," Ollie says, climbing to his feet. Patrick also rises, though I expect it's his desire to drink Tom's top-shelf wine rather than a desire to appease Diana. Nettie remains where she is on the floor, rinsing Archie's hair and babbling to him in a low, soothing voice.

. . .

By the time Nettie and I make it upstairs, everyone is sitting at the outdoor table and the pleasant hum of music and chatter can be heard from halfway down the stairs. I watch the scene through the huge glass doors, taking it all in—water as far as the eye can see; twinkling fairy lights strung up on the trees, the peach glow of sunset spilling its light all over everything and everyone. The table has been decorated in white and burlap with silver lanterns, candles and flowers . . . it's breathtaking.

"Here they are," Tom says, spotting us.

Everyone turns. Jeffrey Greenan's teeth are already stained red from wine. He makes a great show of getting up when we appear, despite our insistence that he remain seated.

"Ladies!" he says, swaggering over. His white shirt is unbuttoned just a little too far and grey-black hair curls up his chest almost as far as the jugular. "My, my, Lucy, motherhood suits you. And Nettie, aren't you growing up?"

He winks and Nettie's smile tenses.

He is, already, more awful than I remembered.

I walk over to the outdoor outlet and plug in the baby monitor. I flip the switch and the green light illuminates, indicating that it's working.

"What is that noise?" Diana exclaims, and my stomach pulls tight. "That . . . crackling?"

Admittedly, the monitor has seen better days—it's a second-hand one I found at the charity shop. It works fine, but when it's switched on, it hums a slightly static tune. I'd become so used to it I'd stopped noticing. "Oh, Archie was a little fussy so I brought the monitor up."

Diana looks perplexed. "Does it always make that *sound*?"

Everyone quiets down and listens while I stand there like a fool. Somewhere in the back of my mind I think, *if you didn't send us downstairs to the dungeon, we wouldn't need the damn monitor.*

"Oh, but aren't they great, these little devices they have nowadays?" Amelia, Jeffrey's wife, says, touching Diana's arm. Amelia is petite and freckled in a white linen dress and gold slide-on sandals. She is, at once, pretty and plain, with small blue eyes and a grey-blonde bob and a propensity to touch that somehow makes her endearing, the very opposite of her husband. I find myself fantasizing about having Amelia for a mother-in-law. Even with Jeffrey for a father-in-law, it might be worth it.

Might be.

"Wouldn't we have wished for monitors when we had little ones, Diana?" Amelia continues.

Clearly Diana wishes nothing of the sort. She is a no-nonsense kind of mother and grandmother, the kind that thinks breastfeeding and back-to-sleep and seat belts are all nonsense because *her kids didn't have them and it never did them any harm.* At least I think she is that kind of mother, but I don't know because she rarely bestows me with any actual advice or opinions. This should be a good thing, but instead it just leaves me with a general feeling of getting it wrong without any idea of how to do better.

"Just make sure the volume is turned down," Diana says finally, under duress, and begins to hand out the plates.

"Come and sit next to me," Jeffrey says to me. Nettie has already taken the other remaining chair so I don't have a lot of choice. "Tell me how are you enjoying motherhood so far?"

"I'm enjoying it a lot more now that those first few months are over."

"Yes." He nods as though he knows exactly how those first few months are, then he looks knowingly at Ollie. "All tits and shits, those first few months, right, Ollie?"

Ollie's face remains carefully neutral and Jeffrey breaks into a laugh more suited to a five-year-old. "Not that they'd have it any other way, ladies, am I right? It's primal. A mother just wants to be with her baby. It's how it should be."

On the monitor, Archie lets out a short whimper. Diana stands, goes to the kitchen. The rest of us serve ourselves chicken and a variety of interesting salads—ancient grain, couscous, kale and almond. I deduce that Amelia must have brought them as Diana doesn't do interesting salad.

"What about you, Nettie?" Jeffrey asks, his mouth full of couscous. "When are you and Patrick going to take the leap? You don't want all your eggs drying up, do you? Having a career is all well and good, but a job isn't ever going to love you back, you know!"

Amelia, on the other side of Jeffrey, puts a hand on her husband's arm. "That's enough, Jeffrey."

But Jeffrey is unperturbed. "What? Everyone wonders why there is a fertility crisis these days. You must be . . . what . . . thirty-five, Nettie? You'd be a grandmother if you were in Africa. You girls just leave your run too late, that's what it is. You need to get in that saddle, so to speak. Am I right?"

He looks at Tom, then at Ollie for support. They both studiously avoid his gaze.

I visualize shoving a chicken breast directly into Jeffrey's mouth.

Nettie keeps her gaze forward, on the table. Jeffrey opens his mouth again, and I am about to say something—anything—when Patrick stands.

"Enough."

His voice is cool, calm. I haven't seen this side of Patrick before, the protective side. Standing over us like this, he looks quite ominous. In an odd way, I feel quite . . . impressed.

Jeffrey, blessedly, looks a little uncertain. "All right, no need to get upset. I was just saying—"

"*Enough.*"

Nettie touches Patrick's arm, while Tom nimbly takes over the conversation, steering it toward football. He and Jeffrey are both mad Hawthorn supporters, so it's likely a good choice. Patrick keeps his gaze on Jeffrey for a few moments longer before lowering himself into his seat.

"Well," Amelia says some time later, when the tension seems to have slipped away. "Archie's been a good boy, hasn't he? Is he sleeping through, Lucy?"

"Not exactly. He tends to be unsettled in the first half of the night, but he usually gets a good stretch in after midnight. It's actually a miracle we haven't heard from him tonight." I glance at the monitor. "Uh oh."

I walk over to the monitor. The power is off. I look at Diana.

"Did you turn this off?"

I don't sound accusing, because I don't believe it. What kind of grandmother would turn off the baby monitor? But the way she sets her jaw, I start to wonder if she did.

"I turned it *down*," she says.

"Down to *off*?" I twist the dial, increasing the volume until Archie's hysterical sobs pierce the air. I can tell from the pitch, he's been crying for a while.

"Mum!" Ollie says. "Tell me you didn't—"

But I don't hear the rest because I'm already running down to get my baby.

It takes me twenty minutes to calm Archie down. When he finally stops crying, he will only sleep in my arms. I pat and soothe him while whispering furiously to Ollie in the dark. "We're leaving tomorrow. First thing."

Ollie stares at me. I know what he's thinking. For him, this isn't a big deal. Tomorrow it might be a bit awkward, but then things will go back to normal. After all, Archie is fine. No need to cut short a holiday.

Sure enough, he says: "Luce, let's not make a bigger deal of this than it is."

"This *is* a big deal. Diana has no respect for me as a mother, so I can't stay here. How dare she turn off my baby monitor? How *dare* she?"

Ollie shrugs helplessly. "Maybe she thought it was the right thing to do, to give you a little break?"

"She had no right. No right at all."

"But—"

"If you want to stay, Ollie, knock yourself out. But I'm leaving tomorrow and so is Archie."

We go back and forth for a few minutes more before Ollie agrees, out of exhaustion more than anything else. Almost immediately afterward, he slides down in the bed, his breathing becoming steady and rhythmic. I stay awake a few minutes longer, patting and rocking Archie into a deep sleep. I've just placed him into the port-a-cot when I hear a whimper, a gentle muffled sob. But it's not coming from Archie. It's coming from somewhere nearby—just across the hall.

Nettie's room.

17

Lucy

The present . . .

Something is niggling at me.

I lie on the sofa with my feet in Ollie's lap. The kids are in bed and I am nursing a glass of pinot noir. Ollie is nursing his own glass—usually it's my favorite part of the day. But today, something is niggling at me. And I have a feeling I know what it is.

Guilt.

Ollie's mobile starts to vibrate and we both spring to life as though we're are expecting it.

"Who is it?" I ask.

"Don't recognize the number . . ." he says.

"Why don't I get it?" I say. "It could be the funeral home or . . . I don't know . . . something important. Maybe the police?"

He shakes his head. "I'll get it," he says, pressing the phone to his ear. "Oliver Goodwin speaking."

He frowns, cocks his head. Then he meets my eye. *It's Jones,* he mouths after a second or two.

"Put it on speakerphone," I mouth back, and he does. Jones's cool, efficient tone fills the room.

"We've received your mother's autopsy report. We'd like to talk to you about it down at the station."

"The station?" Ollie blinks. "Can't you tell me over the phone?"

"It's easier if you come here. Your sister and her husband are coming down too."

Ollie looks at me. I shrug, baffled. "I mean . . . if that's what we need to do. I'll be right there—"

"Actually, we'd appreciate it if both you and Lucy came down. We'd like to talk to both of you."

"Both of us? Together?"

"Yes."

"It's eight-thirty at night. Our children are in bed."

"Then I suggest you find a babysitter," Jones says. "Because this is important. And we'd like to see you both tonight."

18

Diana

The past . . .

"Have you heard the news?" Tom says, his face a shiny beacon of cheer.

I glance around in surprise. The entire family is gathered in the "good" room—Tom, Nettie, Patrick, Ollie, Lucy, even Archie. Though I've seen everyone individually, we haven't all been together as a family for nearly a year, not since the baby monitor fiasco at Sorrento when Lucy and Ollie and Archie scurried back to Melbourne after one day (a dreadful overreaction, in my opinion, even if I did overstep). In any case, I'm pleased to see everyone together again.

"What is it?" I say, stealing a glance at Nettie. I can't help it. Lucy is eight months pregnant with baby number two; it *has* to be Nettie's turn. But she just shrugs as if to say: *Don't look at me.*

"Ollie is going into business for himself!" Tom can barely contain his joy. "A boutique recruitment agency!"

"Oh!"

My voice registers my surprise. Ollie has never showed any interest in starting his own business, in fact he's always been resistant to the idea. As his mother, I'd never known him to be particularly ambitious and despite Tom's desperation to see his son "make a name for himself" I'd thought it made him happy, working for someone else, having less pressure, even if it meant less money. "Well . . . congratulations, darling."

"You should congratulate Dad," Ollie says, but he looks pink-cheeked and pleased with himself. "He's been angling for this for years. And I'm not exactly doing it myself. I've got a business partner."

"Who is your business partner?" I ask.

"Eamon."

A whisper of dread crawls up my back. "Eamon Cockram?"

"Yes."

I try for a smile but it feels more like a grimace. Eamon Cockram. I'd never liked that smarmy boy. He is that insufferable type who thinks he is charming the mothers by telling us the years have been kind (sadly the years had not been quite as kind to him—the last time I'd seen him he'd grown tubby and quite bald). I heard through the grapevine that his wife Julia had left him recently, and I couldn't say anyone blamed her.

Tom is grinning from ear to ear. "We'll have to have Frank and Lydia over for a drink, won't we, Di?"

I make a noncommittal noise. Frank and Lydia are Eamon's parents, and I will be going to the utmost lengths to avoid having this drink. Still, there is no point telling this to Tom, who is practically floating around the front room, buoyed by the close proximity of his family and his son's business venture.

Nettie, on the other hand, looks particularly melancholy. She's gained some weight and has a sheen of sweat across her face. As she reaches up to pull her sweater over her head, her shirt rides up and, even though she said she's not pregnant, I find myself looking hopefully for a bump. I don't see one. Instead to the left of her belly-button, I see a faint, oval-shaped bruise. She balls up her sweater and rests it in her lap.

"So tell me about this recruiting firm," she says to Ollie. "Will you specialize in a certain industry?"

"We'll focus on I.T. roles to begin with because that's our background."

"Well . . . that's *your* background. What about Eamon?"

If Nettie's tone is anything to go by, she shares my opinion of Eamon. I feel a swell of solidarity with my daughter.

"Eamon has done a lot of things," Ollie admits.

"Anything relevant to recruiting?"

Ollie raises an eyebrow. "With due respect, Nettie, do you think I'd be going into business with him if I didn't think he had anything to add?"

"I think Eamon could sell sand in the desert," Nettie says, and she has a point. At the same time, Ollie isn't stupid, nor is he irresponsible. He wouldn't have gone into business with Eamon if he hadn't thought it through. At least I hope he wouldn't have.

"Is it time for cigars, son?" Tom asks. "Patrick, are you interested?"

Patrick, of course, is interested. He, Ollie and Tom wander toward the den. Tom has his arms around them as he goes. I know all he wants is the best for his family, but he can be so single-minded about it.

I glance at Lucy, sitting quietly on the other end of the couch— I'd almost forgotten she was here. She is enormously pregnant. This must be unsettling for her. Starting a new business is a stressful time for anyone, let alone when you are weeks away from giving birth. I wonder, as I have wondered so many times, why she hadn't gone back to work herself. Even working part time, keeping her toe in the water, would surely give them extra security when starting a new business.

"How do you feel about the business, Lucy?" I ask.

"It's wonderful," she says. "Ollie is really excited."

She smiles, the image of the doting wife, but I see in her eyes that she is worried. And while I know I should be grateful that she is so supportive of my son, all I want to do is grab her by the shoulders and give her a good shake.

The next morning, I'm up and about early. I'll admit, it's a strange arrangement I have with the refugee girls I work with. Generally, it's a very intense relationship in the lead-up to the baby's birth that peters out when the babies reach a few months old. I keep in touch with the girls where I can—a phone call every so often or a Christmas card, but I quickly become busy with new pregnant girls, and they become busy with their own lives. Still, I'm always pleased when I have reason to hear from them again. Like when Ghezala tells me she's having another baby.

I pull into the driveway of her home—a different one, just a few streets away from the first, but just as run-down. The lawn is over-grown and the gate is hanging from one hinge. I know Ghezala has been cleaning supermarkets at night to make ends meet but, as far as I'm aware, Hakem hasn't worked since they arrived in the country, two and half years ago. When I pull up, he's sitting in a faded deck chair on the front porch, smoking a cigarette.

"Hello, Hakem," I say, slamming the door. He's aged since I saw him last. He's still a young man, barely thirty at a guess, but his black hair is swept through with grey and he's paunchy around the middle. His eyelids sit at half-mast, as though he's drunk or half asleep. I go around to the back of the car and retrieve the basket of maternity things I've brought for Ghezala. "How are you?"

He doesn't respond. I let myself in the wonky gate.

"Everything all right?"

"Fine," he mutters. He's dressed in a flannel shirt, grubby beige pants and flip-flops. "Ghezala is inside with the boy."

I stop, rest the basket on my hip. "How's the job hunt going?"

"Fine. Fine."

"What kind of jobs are you applying for?"

He stubs out his cigarette, shaking his head. "Oh. This and that."

"Need any help? I might have some contacts I could—"

He stands, yanking open the screen door. "Ghezala!"

"Have you applied for *any* jobs, Hakem? Ghezala found her cleaning job quite quickly. Surely you should be able to find something too."

He cocks his head. "And what kind of jobs would you have me apply for? Taxi driver? Supermarket shelf packer?" He laughs, revealing a mouth of eggshell-colored teeth. "In Kabul, I was an engineer. I built skyscrapers for the big Western chains. This is one of the reasons we were run out of there. Now that I'm here, no one would let me build their dog kennel."

"So you're happy to let your pregnant wife clean supermarkets but you're not willing to do the same."

He jabs a finger at my Land Rover. "You drive this car to my house and then ask me what I'm willing to do?"

"I'm driving this car so I can drive a double pram to a pregnant woman in Dandenong, Hakem."

"Tell me this," he continues, turning his finger on me now. "What would *you* be willing to do?"

"I'd be willing to do anything for my family. I might not be happy about it. It wouldn't be fair. But life isn't fair, is it?"

He shakes his head, makes a *pah* sound. After a moment, he extends his finger again, over my shoulder. "See this apartment?" he says, pointing to the shabby three-story building across the street. "The guy who lives there was a respiratory surgeon back home. He used to live in a five-bedroom house! He lives in a one-bedroom apartment now with his wife and three kids." He takes a step toward me and I can smell his breath, cigarettes and spice. It's unclear if he is doing this to intimidate me, or is simply fired up making his point. "Have you actually thought about what it would be like to go from having everything to having nothing?"

I *have* thought about it. More than that, I've lived it. But it occurs to me that I haven't thought about it, *really* thought, for quite a while.

"What's going on?" The screen door squeaks open, and I see Ghezala standing there with a little boy at her ankles. Hakem pulls back from me and I feel the welcome rush of fresh air in my face. "Hakem?"

"Aarash," Hakem says, patting the boy on his head. "Come. Let Mâmân talk with her friend."

She watches them wander out toward the street, then turns to me. I smile and hold up my basket. "I brought you some maternity clothes. And some information about a doula service in case you'd like to have this baby at home with a little medical assistance this time. Shall we talk inside?"

Ghezala nods and I hold the door open to let her walk back into the house. Before I enter myself, I glance over my shoulder at Hakem. I was wrong, I realize, when I thought he was angry. He's *more* than angry, he's bitter. It worries me. Because when left to their own devices, bitter people can do bad things.

19

Lucy

The past . . .

"You're not happy about me going into business with Eamon, are
you?"

Ollie is merely a disembodied voice as he removes a load of laundry from the washing machine in the next room and tosses it into
the dryer. For all of Diana's foibles, I will never resent her for making
the man learn how to do laundry. I lower my pregnant body onto the
couch and, after trying and failing to remove my wedges, lift my feet
and place them on the coffee table, shoes and all.

"Why do you say that?"

We've just returned from dinner at the Sandringham Pub, a
virtual heaven for parents due to its indoor playground that allows
mums and dads to consume their beers and chicken parmigiana in

relative peace while their offspring get into fights with other kids on brightly colored play equipment behind a pane of glass. Usually I enjoy the Sandy Pub for what it is, a change of scenery, a chance to drink wine and chat with Ollie without being surrounded by children, but tonight I was simply too pregnant to enjoy anything. The saving grace, at least, was that Archie fell asleep on the way home and didn't rouse as Ollie carried him to bed.

"Because," Ollie says, appearing in front of me. "You've been quiet since I brought it up."

The problem, of course, is that unlike my mother, who was happy to silently support my father in everything he did, I find it difficult to keep my opinions to myself. Or maybe Dad just never made any decisions as stupid as going into business with Eamon Cockram.

"I know you don't like Eamon." Ollie sits on the coffee table. "And I know I've joked about his business sense in the past. Obviously I'd never get onboard with one of his ridiculous enterprises. I mean S'meals? Come on." He laughs. "But I know recruitment. This isn't a bad business idea, Luce. In fact, I think Eamon and I are well suited in this venture. I have the expertise and Eamon has . . . the hustle."

It's hard to argue with that. The one thing Eamon is good at is hustling. And while no self-respecting recruiter would ever refer to themselves as such, we were, in essence, hustlers. Or at least salespeople. The candidates were the product, the client was the consumer. Ollie was dedicated to the candidate to a fault, and Eamon, on the other hand, was excessively interested in the client. Perhaps Ollie was right? Perhaps they were a match made in Heaven?

Ollie takes my feet in his lap and begins undoing the buckle of my left shoe. "Look, I should have had this discussion with you earlier. I'm sorry I didn't. But if you really don't want me to do it, I won't."

He takes the shoe from my foot and drops it onto the carpet. I believe him. I believe that if I told him I didn't want him to do this, he wouldn't do it. At the same time, I think it's no coincidence that Ollie made the announcement before asking me this question.

Perhaps he's not such a bad hustler after all?

Dad's job is to support us, our job is to support him.

"Of course you should do it," I say with a sigh. "I may not like him but it's not as if Eamon is a criminal! Besides, what's the worst that could happen?"

20

Lucy

The present . . .

"Everything okay?" I ask.

Ollie and I sit in the reception area of the police headquarters, holding white plastic cups of water. Dad is babysitting, though the poor man was out of his mind with worry when I explained we had to go to see homicide detectives. But Dad is the least of my worries, and by the look of it, the least of Ollie's. His eyes dart around and his leg has its nervous bounce. I am caught between a feeling of dread and a feeling that I'm in a TV set, like *The Truman Show,* and soon someone with a clipboard is going to call "Cut!"

"Lucy and Oliver Goodwin?"

A woman—who is neither Jones nor Ahmed—is standing by a

sliding door, looking around. Ollie and I put down our water and rise in unison.

"This way," she says.

The woman smiles, the polite kind of smile rather than the friendly kind. She is young but hard-faced, like she's seen some stuff.

We take an elevator to the third floor, then exit down a narrow corridor with doors along the left, slim enough that we fall into single file. As we pass room after room, I can't help but wonder about the people who have walked this path before us. Guilty people and innocent, I guess. I notice Patrick in one of the rooms and am momentarily surprised, but then I remember . . . Jones mentioned on the phone that both he and Nettie were coming in.

The woman leading us stops about halfway down the corridor. "Mr. Goodwin, you're in here."

Ollie frowns. "Lucy and I aren't together?"

"It's standard procedure."

"Why is that standard procedure?" Ollie's voice sounds different, more clipped than usual, brusquer. "We're not under arrest, are we? We're here to get the autopsy results for my mother's death."

The woman is unflustered. She smiles again. "It's just the way we do it."

Ollie glances at me and I shrug like it's no big deal. I know this type of woman. She's the type that doesn't deviate from standard practice. The type that makes a great debt collector, because they stay on message even in the face of terrible extenuating circumstances. ("I'm sorry your wife just died and your house has been repossessed, sir . . . you owe eight hundred and fifty-eight dollars, we take checks or EFT.") So I recognize immediately that any resistance to the separate room situation is likely to be futile.

"We can go separately," I say. "It's fine, isn't it, Ollie?"

"What's fine?"

I turn. Detective Constable Jones and Ahmed are ambling toward us down the narrow corridor. It's Jones doing the speaking, as usual. She's carrying a bright green KeepCup, and she takes a sip.

"I was just explaining that they are being set up in separate rooms," the lady says.

"Yes, sorry, I should have mentioned that," Jones says, though she doesn't sound sorry. "It's standard practice. Is there a problem?"

She shoots a glance at Ahmed. Ahmed is wearing a suit today, with tie and all. It looks good on him. Something subtle about the body language between him and Jones makes me think that Jones has noticed this too.

"No," I say, even though now Jones is looking at Ollie, whose face is saying the opposite. I wonder what's up with him. Usually Ollie is the calm, unflappable one. Usually he is the one calming *me* down.

"All right then," Jones says. "Ollie, you're with me. Lucy, you're with Ahmed."

My first instinct is to be relieved that I have Ahmed. Out of him and Jones, he is clearly the good cop, so to speak. But I worry about Ollie going off with Jones given the strange mood he is in. He's likely to get himself in trouble for something he didn't do.

Ahmed leads me to a room where a person is fiddling with a video camera. Ahmed takes off his suit jacket and hangs it on the back of his chair. "Sorry about the monkey suit," Ahmed says. "Been in court this morning."

I smile even though the idea of Ahmed giving evidence in court makes me nervous. Despite the fact that I am apparently just here for a friendly chat, it occurs to me that it's only a friendly chat until

I'm found guilty of something. Then that video footage will be wheeled out in court. Then it will be used as *evidence*.

"So . . . the autopsy report?" I start, but Ahmed interrupts, explaining that we are going to be recorded. Then we go through my particulars, my name, my address, my relationship to Diana. Ahmed's stance is casual, one elbow on the desk, his body angled to the side, one ankle on the opposite knee. As I answer each question, he nods encouragingly. His eyes, I notice, are the color of maple syrup.

"Can you tell me where you were between one and five P.M. last Thursday afternoon?" he says.

I glance at the camera. "Um . . . well, I was at home with my two-and-a-half-year-old daughter until around three-forty P.M. Then the other two kids came home."

"Can anyone verify that . . . other than your daughter?"

I think about this. "Ollie came home from work early, around two or two-thirty P.M., then he went out again to get our son, Archie. So he can verify part of the time."

"Why did he come home early?"

"He wasn't feeling well," I say, though it suddenly occurs to me that he didn't seem particularly unwell. In fact, I recalled thinking he'd been in a good mood that day.

"You said he picked up your son?" Ahmed says. "And one of your daughters was home with you. Where was your other daughter?"

"Harriet had gymnastics after school. She was dropped home by another mother, Kerry Mathis, around four P.M. I came out and waved from the doorstep."

"And Ms. Mathis will verify this?"

"I'm sure she will," I say, though I cringe at the idea of the police contacting a school mum to verify my whereabouts.

"Good." Ahmed puts down his pen and sits back in his chair. He exhales slowly. "I understand that there was an incident between you and your mother-in-law a few years back. Do you want to tell me about that?"

"Incident?" I ask. I'm just buying some time, as clearly he knows about it. I'm not going to deny it.

"An assault."

"Oh," I say. "That wasn't an assault, exactly."

"You slammed your mother-in-law into the wall, as I understand?" Ahmed watches me. "And she was unconscious for quite some time?"

"I wasn't charged with anything," I say. But of course, Ahmed already knows this. He's feeling me out, trying to gauge my reactions.

"What do you think happened to your mother-in-law, Lucy?"

"Well . . . obviously . . . I don't know. I thought that's what we were here to find out."

"It is." He's looking at me too intently. "But I'm interested in *your* opinion."

"Okay, I think she killed herself . . ." I say, with what I hope sounds like conviction. "I mean, you found a letter."

"We did find a letter. In her study drawer. Kind of a strange place to leave a suicide letter, don't you think?"

"I . . . yes, I do think so."

"Do you think it is in character for Mrs. Goodwin to do something like this?" he continues. "To take her own life?"

"It was in character for her to be headstrong," I say. "Once she had decided to do something, it was hard to change her mind."

Ahmed looks down at a manila folder on the table in front of him, then retrieves a pair of wire-rimmed glasses from his pocket and places them on his nose. "The coroner reported high levels of carbon dioxide in the deceased's blood." Ahmed glances up at me over the tops of his glasses.

"Am I supposed to know what that means?"

"She also had bloodshot eyes, bruising around the lips, gums and tongue."

That part, admittedly, sounds odd. Why would she have bruising?

Ahmed looks back at the paperwork. "The examiner also found fibers in your mother-in-law's hands. Thread . . . it looks like. Gold thread." He shuffles through some pages in the folder, plucking out one. "Your mother-in-law's house indicates she was house proud. Very tidy. Everything in its place. Matchy-matchy."

I'm thrown by the sudden change in direction. "What does her *house* have to do with anything?"

Ahmed turns the piece of paper so I can see it. It's a photo. I recoil, expecting a picture of Diana's body. But it's just a picture of Diana's place, the good room.

"Does anything look wrong to you in this picture?" Ahmed asks.

I give it an arbitrary glance. "No, nothing."

"Are you sure?"

I look a little closer. At the bookshelf, the coffee table, the deep, cream sofa with matching cream cushions . . . threaded through with gold.

"It feels like she would have a pair of these gold-threaded cushions, don't you think?" Ahmed says. His gaze feels accusing and for a moment I wonder if he is, in fact, the good cop. "But we looked and looked, and we could only find one."

I look back at the picture. He's right, there *were* two cushions, definitely. I remember seeing them recently. I was at Diana's with the kids and Harriet was picking at one, trying to pull out the thread so she could tie it to her hair and have long golden hair like Rapunzel. I had to snatch the cushion from her and put it back. Diana immediately straightened it. Ahmed was right, Diana was house proud.

"Well, I don't know. Maybe she'd spilled something on one?" I suggest. "And sent it out for cleaning?"

"We're looking into that. We're looking into a lot of things."

"Okay. But . . . wait. I thought you said you found materials in Diana's house. Suicide materials."

"We did." Ahmed surveys me closely with his shiny, syrupy eyes. "An empty bottle of Latuben was found by your mother-in-law's body. Latuben is a popular drug that people take to bring about a fast, painless death. Usually people drink two bottles of Latuben if they are trying to end their life, but even one bottle could be a fatal dose on someone Diana's size and build."

"So," I clear my throat, "there was only one bottle by her body?"

"Only one." Ahmed nods. "And in any case the drug wasn't found in her bloodstream. So we've been looking at alternate causes of death."

"Alternative causes of death?"

"Yes. So in light of everything I've told you, I'd like ask you the first question again." He watches me over the tops of his glasses. "What do you think happened to your mother-in-law?"

I open my mouth and repeat the answer I gave Ahmed the first time, that I think Diana killed herself. But this time, it doesn't come out with quite so much conviction.

. . .

Ollie emerges from his meeting room at the same time as I do, and Jones and Ahmed walk us back down the corridor. The room that Patrick was in is now empty, and if Nettie was here, she's gone too. Ahmed and Jones take us as far as the elevator, thank us for coming in and give us their business cards again. Then Jones tells us, *twice*, that she'll be in touch. Probably she is just tripping over the niceties of conversation, but then again, the police TV programs I watch lead me to believe the cops don't do anything by accident.

"It went fine," Ollie says, once the elevator door closes and we're plunging downward. But his face says otherwise. He has a blotchy look about him that he gets when he's coming down with something. The elevator doors open.

"Are you all right?" I ask.

We step out into the foyer. "Did Ahmed tell you about the autopsy?" he whispers as we walk. "The bruised lips?"

We cross the floor of the foyer, go through the automatic doors into the parking lot.

"Yes. And the missing pillow. And that's not the only thing that doesn't seem right about this."

Ollie stops. "What else doesn't seem right?"

"The cancer. Why isn't there any evidence of cancer?"

Ollie opens his mouth but I get in first.

"And the letter, why was it in a drawer? Wouldn't she leave it somewhere obvious for someone to find it?"

Ollie's expression is as puzzled as I feel. "I wish I knew," he says finally. "She was my mother but as it turns out . . . I didn't really know her at all."

21

Diana

The past . . .

The call comes at around five A.M. I turn over in bed and look at the red numbers blinking into the darkness.

"The baby's coming," Ollie says, when I pick up the phone. "Lucy's contractions are about ten minutes apart. Can you come now?"

I get out of bed and make myself a strong coffee. I don't trust myself on the roads until I've had my morning coffee; my eyes aren't what they once were. I shower quickly and get myself dressed, double-checking everything in the overnight bag I've packed. These labors can go on for a long time, so who knows how long I'll be at Ollie and Lucy's house. I've packed my pajamas, a toothbrush and a novel. I've even brought a little gift-wrapped Thomas the Tank Engine train for Archie. I plan to give the train to Archie "from the baby," because apparently that's what everyone does these days, at least that's what Jan says, and Jan seems to know these kinds of things. Once I've confirmed that I have everything, I get in the car and make the twenty-minute drive to their house, arriving at 5:55 A.M.

Ollie is on the doorstep and Lucy is half bent over the front fence, having a contraction.

"Where have you been?" Ollie exclaims.

I bristle, I'll admit it. Heaven forbid I take longer than they expect to get there. No one is asking where Tom has been. He'll wake up sometime around eight A.M., play eighteen holes of golf and then swan into the hospital when the baby is a few minutes old, bearing an extravagant gift and promises of a trust fund and he will be everyone's hero.

"Here's the taxi," Lucy says, ignoring me entirely. She is in labor, and I know the reasonable thing to do is to forgive her for this. But a "thank you," I feel, wouldn't hurt. Even a "hello."

It feels like yesterday I was in her position, doubled over in pain, waiting for my baby to come. But in my case, no one was on their way to help, no husband was there to call a taxi to the hospital. I was left on the steps of the hospital with a bag in my hand. And after that, I was on my own. I know that I should look at Lucy and see the similarities between us. We are both mothers, we have a mutual love for my son. We are also both motherless, although my mother stepped away by choice where hers was taken from her, kicking and screaming no doubt.

I know all this.

But for some reason, despite our similarities, when I look at her, all I see are our differences.

. . .

When Tom arrives at Ollie and Lucy's house later that day, I tell
him he has a granddaughter.

"A granddaughter?" Of course he is misty-eyed in an instant. "It's
like history repeating itself, isn't it? A son, then a daughter?"

"Our story is a little different, though." I say.

"A little," he agrees.

I laugh as I notice a shiny pool of liquid gathering in the corner
of his mouth. "You're drooling." I wipe it away with my thumb, the
same way I do sometimes to Archie. "Ollie wants us to bring Archie
in to meet his sister."

Tom's eyes canvas the living room. "Where *is* Archie?"

"Napping. He only just went down, so I'll give him another hour
or so." I take one of Tom's legs into my lap, and begin massaging
his calf. His eyes fall shut and he moans appreciatively. "Tom, I was
wondering . . . you're not looking for any engineers at work at the
moment, are you?"

He frowns, but his eyes remain shut. "Engineers?"

"I might know of someone, that's all."

"An engineer?"

"Yes. Very qualified. Used to build sky scrapers in Kabul." I
run my thumbs from the back of his knee, all the way down to his
Achilles heel.

"I'm getting the feeling that you're trying to influence me with a
leg rub, Diana?" Tom smiles and I feel that familiar surge of joy that
Tom Goodwin loves me. It is without question the greatest bless-
ing of my life.

"If you can vouch for them," he says. "Consider them hired."

22

Lucy

The past . . .

Lightning doesn't strike twice, that's what they say. Well in fact, there was a man, Roy Sullivan, who was struck by lightning seven times during his life. SEVEN! What must Roy have thought every time he heard someone say that lightning didn't strike twice? I get the point, of course, it's not common. But that must have just made poor old Roy feel even worse. Roy survived all seven strikes, which is more inspiring if you ask me. He was found dead in his bed at the age of seventy-one after shooting himself in the head—and I daresay all these "lightning doesn't strike twice" folk should shoulder their share of responsibility in that. Because the fact is, sometimes, lightning does strike twice. It did for Roy and it has for me.

Because I have a second child with colic.

I'm sitting in my recliner holding a nipple to my screaming infant's mouth, only this time, I have a toddler too. My recliner is in the lounge room, which is now the playroom, TV room and Harriet's bedroom. An episode of *Game of Thrones* plays on the television and I half-watch it. I've watched this episode three times now and I'm still not entirely sure what's going on. Too many characters in this damn show. Still, there's Jon Snow, which makes it worth the effort.

"Just feed!" I hiss-whisper to Harriet.

I thank my lucky stars that at least Archie is out of my hair while I do this. Diana comes on Tuesdays now and takes Archie to the park for an hour and a half and for this, I'm truly thankful. Archie adores Diana—for many reasons, not least of which is because she packs him full of babycinos and marshmallows and lets him run riot—and I am fine with this because I have a newborn with colic and if a murderous gangster offered to take my kid off my hands for a couple of hours I'd be sorely tempted.

Harriet is a piece of work, I can tell this already at three months old. She won't go to anyone else, not even to Ollie, and when I try to hand her over, she sucks in a breath and watches me with knowing eyes. *Why do you even bother, Mum? I'm about to scream so loudly the neighbors will think you are trying to kill me. They might even call the police. You'd better . . . oh there we go, Daddy's handing me back. Don't make this silly mistake again.*

Diana persists in trying to hold Harriet week after week, as if expecting her to have magically, since the week before, warmed to people. Each week, as we go through this little routine, I feel like telling her not to bother, but that would be denying Diana her grandmotherly rights, not to mention making me one of those crazy daughters-in-law, the ones that make everyone get a whooping cough shot before they can hold the baby. And so I let her hold Harriet. I've learned to play the game.

I have just managed to get Harriet latched on when I hear Archie's approaching giggle. My heart sinks. Already? I had GRAND PLANS for this afternoon but in an hour and a half, all I'd managed to do is fold a tiny pile of washing (not even put it away) and watch Jon Snow and Ramsay Bolton in "Battle of the Bastards." Now, Archie bursts through the door, clutching a fistful of lollies. I pick up the controller and pause *Game of Thrones*. Archie runs around the room in a maniacal circle, pumped up on sugar.

"Archie!" I shout as he tracks a muddy boot right across my pile of folded laundry. My breast comes out of Harriet's mouth with a painful pinch. "Shit!"

"Shiiiiiit!" Archie says.

Diana appears behind Archie, looking appalled. She surveys the room and immediately holds out her hands for Harriet who starts inhaling a nice, deep breath. I hand Harriet over and look at my ruined pile of laundry, the grand sum of my achievements in the last hour and a half. In true hormonal style, I find myself holding back tears.

"Archie, look what you've done, mate!"

I don't scream it. There's the "mate" I add to the end, for good measure. But Archie, of course, decides to burst into tears.

Diana squats down, transferring a wailing Harriet to the opposite shoulder as if that will make a difference, and tries to comfort Archie.

"That folding is all I managed to do while you were gone!" I explain. "Other than try to feed Harriet, where my efforts were just as pathetic."

Diana glances at the television where a picture of Jon Snow is frozen on the screen, then back at me pointedly. "Maybe you could try multitasking. When Ollie was a baby, I used to unload the groceries, vacuum the house and pay the bills while feeding him."

Obviously Diana is lying. She never unloaded the groceries, vacuumed the house and paid the bills while feeding Ollie. It's physically impossible. I know because I'm well-versed—not to mention *recently* well-versed—in breastfeeding. But it doesn't matter what I know because mothers-in-law are allowed to say things that aren't true. Whether they're lying or misremembering is entirely beside the point.

"Richard took his first steps at three months old."

"Mary never cried. *Never!*"

"I started feeding Judy solids while she was still in the hospital."

"I washed all of Trevor's clothes by hand in homemade laundry powder."

"Philip loved vegetables. LOVED them. He devoured everything I ever served him. Brussels sprouts were his favorite!"

Daughters-in-law *know* their mothers-in-law are lying, but it doesn't matter a jot, because how does one prove something *isn't* true? More importantly, how does one prove something isn't true *while trying to be polite to their mother-in-law?* It is as impossible as breastfeeding an infant while unloading the groceries, vacuuming the floor and paying the bills. And so, mothers-in-law get to say whatever outlandish statements they like about motherhood. Mothers-in-law *win*, every time.

"You could put Harriet down for a minute or two and do some laundry," Diana is saying. "Throw both kids in the stroller and take them to the grocery store. Put a puzzle down for Archie and pop Harriet in the bouncy chair while you cook dinner. You shouldn't need to be sitting in that chair around the clock when she's three months old."

It takes me a moment to collect myself. I should be clear, I don't have postnatal depression or anxiety or any other postnatal mood disorder to speak of. I know people who have had it. My cousin Sophie confessed to me once that she felt indifferent to her daughter Jemima. She felt hopeless about her role as a mother and would have done anything to turn back the clock and not have had her. My friend Rachel reported being trapped in a world of exhausted insomnia for months after having Remy, where she would lie in bed, her head locked in a circuitous OCD cycle of "If you don't move your right leg right now, Remy will be dead in the morning." I, on the other hand, am mentally well. I adore my children. Apart from the (I am told, totally normal) hormonal moments when I decide my baby (or husband) is the devil incarnate, I am very fond of my life. I enjoy being an at-home mum, I even like my teeny tiny worker's cottage with the unrenovated kitchen.

What I don't like is being told what to do by my mother-in-law in my own home.

"Thank you for that advice, Diana," I say finally. "That is . . . incredibly helpful. I can't wait to try your suggestions."

We lock eyes. We both know I'm being sarcastic. But calling me on it would be futile because I'll deny it. It is an unexpected and unintentional win for me and I bathe in it for a second or two.

Harriet, who is still screaming in Diana's arms, reaches for me and I take her. The crying stops instantly. Another win.

Checkmate.

It occurs to me that only a mother-in-law and daughter-in-law can have an all-out war without anyone so much as raising their voice. The funny thing is, if any of the menfolk were here, they wouldn't have a clue that anything other than a pleasant conversation was going on. If Ollie were here, he'd probably comment on "what a nice afternoon that was with Mum." In that way, menfolk are really quite simple, bless them.

Archie comes and sits on my lap next to Harriet and for a surprising second, both my children are content. I find, to my surprise, that I'm quite enjoying myself.

"All I'm saying is that I don't know if you're using your time effectively," Diana says finally.

And what business is that of yours? I want to ask, but that, we both know, would be breaking the rules. I must not assault, but defense is allowed. I think of my high school netball days. I'm goal defense. If I'm good enough at my job, the other team won't score. And so I come up with something else.

"You're right," I say with a smile. "You don't."

And even though it will never feature on the scoreboard, I'm pretty sure I just shot a goal.

23

Lucy

The past . . .

"Are you going to trade me in for a younger model one day?" I whisper to Ollie.

We're standing on the back deck by the BBQ. Ollie is barbequing and I am shuffling around, trying to look busy. It's Saturday afternoon and Eamon has brought his new girlfriend, Bella, to lunch. She is twenty-two and I have never felt older in my life.

"Can't afford to," he says. "Anyway, I married a young one to begin with."

"You've always been a forward planner."

"I play the long game," he says with a wink. "By the way, Bella's in the kitchen. You'd better get in there. She might start playing with matches." He gestures to the steps of the deck where Harriet and Archie sit, eating sausages in bread. "I'll keep an eye on the other kids."

Reluctantly I head to the kitchen to talk to Bella. It's not out of loyalty to Eamon's ex-wife—I wasn't especially fond of Julia either. It's purely the fact that I'm a married mother of two . . . and she's twenty-two.

When I get to the kitchen, Bella is standing in front of the salads, staring down at them.

"Where's Eamon?" I ask.

"He's just gone to the bottle shop for champagne. I told him I didn't want any, but he insisted." She rolls her eyes.

"Oh, well, can I get you a drink in the meantime? Or something to eat? I have cheese and crackers—"

"Water's fine," she says, gesturing to the glass beside her.

"Can I at least get you some ice?"

"No, room temperature is better."

Better for what? I wonder, but I don't ask lest she decides to tell me. I have a vague recollection of being lectured about the perils of cold drinks (something to do with damp heat collecting in the body) when visiting a Chinese doctor about a persistent neck injury a few years back, and while the acupuncture worked a treat on my neck, as someone who was partial to an ice-cold beverage, the unsolicited advice about consuming room-temperature beverages had been an unwelcome addition to my service.

"So how did you and Eamon meet each other?" I ask instead.

"He goes to my gym," Bella tells me. "He was in my body pump class."

"You're a fitness instructor?"

She nods, and I feel relieved. Ollie told me she was one of those fitness people on Instagram, the ones who post photos of smoothies and protein powder in among pictures of their abs in exotic locations. It's comforting to know she has an actual job as well.

"Well, at least I used to be anyway," she says. "I mostly fill in now, now that my business has taken off."

"Oh?" I say, looking in the drawer for salad servers. "And what is your business?"

"I'm a fitness influencer."

My hands flatten on the cutlery tray.

"I have a hundred and twenty-two thousand followers on Instagram at the moment, so yeah, things are taking off. But I mean . . . I need to keep growing it."

"And . . . how do you . . . grow it?"

I find some servers and start tossing the potato salad. I'd gone heavy on the mayonnaise, which I now suspect was a mistake. The green salad, too, is chock full of avocado and feta and oil.

"You know . . . analyzing the best-performing posts . . . looking at the hashtags you're using like #fitspo and #fitnessporn, keeping up to date with who is influencing in your field."

"Gotcha."

"Then it's pretty much about partnering with brands. I've been contacted by a really interesting up-and-coming organic juice brand and we're going to be doing some really cool stuff with them and yeah, it's good."

"Great!"

I feel like I'm babysitting a friend's teenage daughter. She is wearing a sports bra and Lycra leggings with a clear slicker over the top. To lunch! Through the slicker I notice that her breasts look suspiciously round for her slender frame. I spare a sudden thought for my own deflated breasts, destroyed by two pregnancies and two hungry babies. Ollie doesn't seem to mind my breasts, in fact he seems rather fond of them, but all the same I indulge in a moment of mourning for my pre-baby boobs, all upright and roughly the same size as the other.

A door slams and a moment later Eamon appears, a bottle of champagne in each hand. He waggles them around like an idiot. "It's party time, ladies!"

Eamon's shirt is unbuttoned too far. He's lost a bit of weight lately, the way men do when they are going through affairs or midlife crises. (Ollie, God love him, has maintained a stable weight, even gaining a little with each passing year, which is good news on the affair front.)

"Champagne glasses, Luce?" Eamon says.

A few minutes later he returns with four glasses, filled to the brim. "I said I didn't want any!" Bella exclaims, as he pushes a glass into her hand. "I'm on a cleanse."

"Nothing better for cleansing than champagne," he says cheerily.

"Who is cleansing?" Ollie asks, appearing in the kitchen with a tray of overcooked meat.

"Bella," Eamon and I say together.

Ollie glances at the meat on his tray the same way I looked at my salads.

"Don't worry," Bella says, smiling. "I brought my own food."

Ollie gawps at her. "You brought your own *food?*"

She unzips a brightly colored cool-bag that I'd previously thought was her purse. "I meal prep at the start of the week, so it's no trouble, really. All I need is a plate. Easiest guest you've ever had, right?" She laughs.

I can already hear Ollie and me impersonating her tonight after they've left. *Easiest guest you've ever had, right?* For this reason, and this reason alone, I manage to smile.

I give Bella a plate and she dishes up a sad-looking salad that appears to be brown rice and lettuce. The rest of us tuck into potato salad, sausages and burgers.

"So how's business, Eamon?" I ask. "Things going well?"

The one upside of Eamon being here is that I get to ask about the business. Since it started, Ollie has been working around the clock, but when I ask him how things are going, he says very little. He has a tendency to be a worrier, and I console myself with that when he seems less than optimistic. But today I'd been hoping for a little reassurance from Eamon as well.

"We don't need to talk shop today." Eamon puts down his glass. "It's the *weekend.*"

"I'm happy to talk shop," I say.

"You know what would be more fun? Truth or dare."

Midsip of my champagne, I choke. Truth or dare? Eamon is forty-three, I remind myself. *Forty-three.*

"Come *on.* It's a good ice-breaker. We played it the other night, didn't we, Bells?"

Bella nods, spearing a spinach leaf. She's listening, it seems, but her entire focus seems to be on her food. The poor little thing is probably starving.

"Okay, you can start, Bells," Eamon says. "Truth or dare?"

"Hmmm. I should say dare. Because I like a physical challenge.

But given the location, and the fact that we're having lunch I'll say . . . truth." She shrugs gaily.

"What was it about Eamon that you found attractive?"

It comes out of my mouth before I can help it. Normally I'd be cautious, in case it implied that there wasn't anything attractive about Eamon, but lately I am less concerned about his ego. As for Bella, I expect her to fumble, to be shy, but she just reaches across the table and takes his hand, smiling unabashedly. "Before him, I'd only been with boys. Eamon is a man."

Ollie and I exchange a glance. I try not to vomit.

"It's a tough job," Eamon says, stretching his arms out, "but someone has to do it."

"All righty then," Ollie says, clearly as appalled as I am. I take a moment to bask in the simplicity of my mostly-normal husband.

"Your turn, buddy," Eamon says to Ollie. "Truth or dare?"

"Dare," he says, which is a surprise because who, above the age of twelve, says *dare*? I tell myself he's just answering quickly to move things along. I am trying to think of something, my mind going to ideas of knocking on the neighbors' doors and running away, when Eamon puts down his glass.

"I dare you to borrow a million bucks from your dad!" he says. "His dad's minted," he explains to Bella. "He'd probably have a million bucks in pocket change."

He laughs loudly, and I'm reminded of Jeffrey Greenan, Tom's friend. Same awful laugh, same chauvinistic manner. At least Jeffrey though, had a very nice wife.

"Unfortunately . . ." Ollie wipes the corners of his mouth with a paper napkin. "There's my mum to deal with."

"His mum's tight," Eamon explains to Bella, and Ollie bristles.

Eamon's treading on rocky terrain here. Ollie understands that his mother is difficult, but she is, after all, his mother.

"Your turn, Eamon," I say quickly because the sooner this game is over the better. "Truth or dare?"

"Truth," he says.

"Let me do this one," Bella says, and she takes a painfully long time to come up with something, humming and huffing and pressing a forefinger dramatically to her lips.

"What's the worst thing that's ever happened to you?" she says finally.

Eamon is clearly surprised, and I get the feeling he was expecting something along the lines of "Have you ever had a threesome?" I have to hand it to Bella, it's not a bad question.

"Well, divorce hasn't been pretty," he says, after a slight pause. "The financial ruin of it, I mean," he says quickly to Bella. "I lost my house and a fair chunk of my savings. But I learned from it, too."

He presses a forkful of sausage into his mouth and chews slowly.

"What have you learned?" I ask.

"You know." He shrugs. "To put safeguards in place. That kind of thing."

"Safeguards against what?" I ask, with a laugh. "Divorce?"

"Safeguards against everything," Eamon says, as if it's obvious.

Even Bella is looking perplexed now. It warms her to me a little. "There's no safeguard against *everything*," she says.

Eamon swills his champagne, and winks revoltingly. "Money," he says, "is a safeguard against everything."

24

Lucy

The present . . .

The next day, we go to the lawyer's office. I try to get out of it, but Gerard, Diana's lawyer, told Ollie it would be a good idea for us all to attend, so even though Diana's funeral is tomorrow and I have several hundred funeral booklets to fold, readings to choose and catering to confirm, I go. But as we sit in the waiting room, my mind is a Newton's cradle, flicking back and forth over everything I know. Diana was found dead with an empty bottle of poison in her hand. But there was no sign of poison in her system and there is a missing cushion and evidence of smothering. Even I can see that it's starting to look like someone staged Diana's death to look like a suicide. But, if that was the case, why would they hide the letter away in a drawer instead of leaving it in plain sight?

None of it makes any sense.

When Gerard appears in the foyer of his office, Ollie, Nettie, Patrick and I are in opposite corners of the room. The arrival of Gerard, however, brings a welcome focal point and we shuffle together.

"My condolences," he says.

"Thank you," we mutter.

Gerard went to school with Tom, but they were probably more acquaintances than friends. Ollie and Nettie have met him many times, and I have met him briefly once or twice. He's always seemed harmless if a little dull. I have a vague memory of Tom telling Diana that he'd invited Gerard over for a Christmas drink once and Diana groaning. Clearly she thought Gerard was dull too.

Gerard ushers us into his office and then, noticing we are two seats short, pops out into the hallway again. Ollie, Nettie, Patrick and I remain in the room in excruciating silence, looking everywhere but at each other. Nettie, I notice, doesn't even look at *Patrick*.

"Right, then," Gerard says, returning pushing a wheely chair, "thank you for coming in. Usually we mail out letters to our clients letting them know they are the beneficiaries of an estate but I wanted you to come in to the office because this estate is a little more . . . yes, in here, Sherry," he says to the flustered middle-aged receptionist who appears, pushing a second wheely chair. She stops it in front of Ollie and scurries out again. "Thanks, Sherry. Sorry, as I was saying, your parents' estate is a little more complicated than most of our clients'."

This isn't news to us. An estate as large as Tom and Diana's is bound to be complicated. It's the reason, I assume, that Tom had Gerard act as an executor, rather than Ollie or Nettie.

"Why don't you go ahead and sit?" he says to Ollie, who is still standing despite the chair in front of him.

"I'm good here," Ollie replies.

"As you like. Anyway, as you know, Tom and Diana have a sizable estate. There are the properties, the cars, the boat. There's the share portfolio, the furniture, home décor, jewelry, and personal effects. And there is a not insignificant amount of cash."

"Tom mentioned this once or twice," Patrick says with a chuckle.

Gerard folds his hands in front of him and sits forward, as if steeling himself. "Yes, well . . . as it turns out, Tom's will named Diana as the sole beneficiary of his estate. In the event of her death, the estate was to be divided equally between Ollie and Antoinette. However . . . a few weeks ago, Diana came to see me about making some changes." Gerard rubs his brow, his face becoming pinched for a second, as though he has a migraine. His eyes remain lowered. "During that meeting, Diana requested to name her charity the sole beneficiary of the estate."

The room becomes so quiet I can hear the traffic outside, the clock ticking, even the receptionist scratching around her desk outside, filing, stapling, typing.

"Diana *did* say she was going to communicate the change to you, but it was made so recently, she obviously didn't have the chance."

I feel Ollie shift behind me and I spin to face him.

"Hang on. Diana's charity is the beneficiary of . . . ?" he starts.

"All of it." Gerard glances up, locking eyes with each of us under his thick grey eyebrows. It is a look that tells me there is no joke, no misunderstanding, no confusion. "The houses, the cars, the share portfolio, the cash."

Nettie inhales sharply. Patrick rises to his feet. Ollie's head is cocked and he is squinting a little, the way he does when Edie is trying to tell him something and he just can't understand her. We all look around the room and for the first time since arriving everyone meets each others' gaze. Several seconds pass. But no one speaks.

25

Lucy

The past . . .

I have two kids strapped into the back of the car, one of them wailing (Harriet), the other (Archie) trying to stick a grape up his nose.
We're stopped at a busy roundabout while the woman in the black
SUV in front of us hands a tennis racket through the window to
her sullen-looking teenage son then proceeds to start a conversation
with him with no regard for the growing line of cars behind her.

Harriet lets out a newly emblazoned wail.

This kind of thing is rife in Diana's neighborhood. We're headed
to Diana's now—on Tuesdays, I drive them to her house at ten A.M.
where they stay until two P.M., when I pick them up again. Harriet
is six months old now, and while I loathe the process of strapping
both kids into the car, driving the twenty minutes to Diana's house

and doing the reverse journey again a few hours later, I am not so pigheaded as to refuse free child care. Even from my impossible mother-in-law.

"Archie, can you put Harriet's pacifier in?" I say, glancing in the rearview mirror. Her pacifier is in his mouth and the grape is nowhere to be seen. "What happened to the grape?"

"I ate it," he says, removing the pacifier and pushing it right into Harriet's mouth. I try not to think about his streaming nose and the cold that he has now almost certainly passed on to Harriet. It's some consolation that she stops crying immediately.

"Are we at Dido's house yet?"

"Nearly," I say, and he settles down. As irritating as it is, he loves his grandmother. She's good with him in her own, Diana sort of way. She doesn't marvel over his artwork or beg for cuddles, but she does other things that seem to rank highly with kids . . . like looking him directly in the eye, challenging him, turning the television off and playing with him. And, of course, there's the jar of Tim Tams on her kitchen counter that is always full when he arrives and empty when he leaves.

It's a few minutes to ten when I pull into Diana and Tom's pebblestone driveway (which I hate because Archie stuffs the pebbles into his pockets and they end up all over my house). There's a battered yellow Volvo parked by the front door, one of the cleaners, probably. I park behind it and hoist Harriet's baby seat out of the car. Archie unclicks himself and launches himself out of the car, immediately grabbing a fistful of pebbles. I walk up the steps and set the baby carrier down on the landing. The front door is ajar and an unfamiliar male voice comes from somewhere nearby.

"We have an expression in Afghanistan: in an ant colony dew is a flood. It means . . . a small misfortune is not small for one in need. I applied for many jobs, each time—not even a response. So what you did, this is not nothing. This is *something*."

"Tom says you're doing a great job." It's Diana's voice now.

"Tom is very kind. And I am not as kind. I was rude to you. Forgive me."

"There's nothing to forgive," I hear Diana say. "Just go and take care of your family. I know you will do that, Hakem."

"I will."

There is movement, and I shuffle back and lift my hand to knock, like I'm just arriving. Archie is throwing rocks at Diana's Land Rover. ("Stop that," I whisper, as Diana appears in the foyer.)

"Lucy." Diana frowns. Her gaze is panoramic, sweeping the front yard, stopping briefly at Archie who has frozen in a guilty stance. She gives him a stern look and he lets the rocks drop back onto the driveway.

"We just arrived!" I say.

"I see that." She turns away from me, to face the man who has joined her in the foyer. "Thank you for coming by, Hakem."

"Thank you for seeing me. I will not forget your kindness."

We watch the man get into his Volvo and roar away. Then I grab Archie's hand and yank him off the pebblestones. Diana picks up Harriet, who has woken up and is watching us intently with blue startled eyes. Harriet doesn't cry anymore when Diana holds her.

"Who was that?" I ask, guiding Archie up the front steps.

"Hakem is an engineer who works for Tom."

"He seemed very grateful to you."

"Did he?"

"Diana. Obviously you did something for him." I'm venturing

into pushy territory, but it's not like I have a wonderful relationship with Diana that I could potentially destroy. Having nothing to lose has its upsides. "Tell me."

Diana rolls her eyes. It's as if I'm a pest that she doesn't want to encourage. "He was having trouble getting a job, that's all. He wasn't being given a chance. I just made sure he was given one."

"That's wonderful of you."

Diana sighs. "Yes, well. You probably don't think I'm especially wonderful. But I do feel strongly that everyone should be given an equal chance. Hakem was not given one. My children, on the other hand, have been given *every* chance. Now it's time for me to stay out of the way and see what they make of the opportunities they've been given."

It's the closest I've ever come to a proper conversation with Diana and for a second, I get a glimpse of who she is.

"What a good philosophy," I say.

We look each other straight in the eye for a second or two and I think something like mutual respect passes between us.

"I'm glad you think so," she says and she takes my children and bustles into the house.

26

Lucy

The past . . .

"Higher," Archie shouts. "Higher! Make it go weely high."

He's already soaring so high he looks like he might loop the loop.

"Okay," Nettie says. "Here we go!"

Nettie has taken the day off work to help me with the kids. She's done this a handful of times since Harriet was born and each time, afterward, I feel like I have a new lease on life. Right now, Harriet is strapped to Nettie's chest while she pushes Archie on the swing, but all morning she's been tossing a ball to Archie, climbing trees, and playing hide-and-seek. She's nothing if not a devoted aunt.

Unlike Diana, Nettie comes to my place because "you don't

want to be strapping all those kids in the car to come to my place."
(Hallelujah.) She nearly always arrives with treats for the kids (and
asks me if it's okay before handing them over), coffee for me, and a
ready-to-eat meal for Ollie and me to eat that evening. Sometimes
she takes the kids out to give me a break, other days, like today, we
amble around together, doing errands and visiting the park. Usually when she's around she's upbeat, happy, radiating happy energy,
but today she seems off her game. Her hair is unwashed. She's
wearing leggings and a long cardigan and sneakers which, while
perfectly appropriate for a day in the park, is a good step down in
her normal stylish attire. And while she's been talkative enough
with Archie, she's barely said a word to me all morning.

"Are you all right, Nettie? You've been quiet this morning."

Her gaze steals sideward. "Have I?"

In fairness, Nettie usually isn't a big talker, especially about herself. She plays her cards close to her chest, preferring to ask questions than give information. But I see an internal struggle in her eyes
now, and it occurs to me that maybe she *does* want to talk.

"What's going on?" I ask.

She steals another look at me, and then exhales. "Okay. The truth
is . . . I had a miscarriage a few days ago. That's why I'm off work
this week."

"Oh, Nettie, I'm so sorry."

She remains focused on pushing the swing, shrugs a little.
"It's . . . not my first, actually. Patrick and I have been trying to have
a baby for years. We've lost three others, all early, during the first
trimester."

"You've had *four* miscarriages?" My mind reels back over all the
times she might have been pregnant or miscarrying and I had no

idea. I think in horror of all the off-the-cuff comments I must have made.

"You can have this pram when I'm finished with it . . ."

"Just wait until it's your turn . . ."

"I'll repay you when you have your kids."

Narcissistically, I'd thought Nettie would tell me something like this. Foolishly, I thought I'd *know.*

"I assumed you were focusing on your career . . ."

Nettie shakes her head, laughs blackly. "I couldn't care less about my career. I want a family. I have polycystic ovary syndrome, so I knew it wouldn't be easy, but I never thought it would be this hard."

"Have you seen a fertility specialist?"

"Two. We've tried Clomid and IUI. I've injected my belly with hormones for months on end. The next step is IVF."

"Well I know dozens of people who have had babies using IVF. Half the kids in my mothers' group were IVF babies," I say eagerly.

"I know, but it's not cheap. With the mortgage and all this fertility stuff I've got nothing saved up. And Patrick's business, well, it's not exactly thriving."

"Surely your parents will help you?"

"Of course I had to go through that hideous formal process of asking them. Then Mum said no."

My jaw drops. I know Diana's rule on giving money, but I can't fathom that this would extend to Nettie's IVF.

"Dad's given me money in the past, for the IUI and some of the testing. But Mum doesn't know, and Dad hates lying to her. So . . . I guess we're on our own for the IVF."

"Sometimes I really hate her," I say before I can stop myself. Immediately I want to take it back. Diana is Nettie's mother. No matter what she does, Nettie will be loyal to her. "Nettie, I'm sorry I—"

"Sometimes I do too," Nettie says, and we drift into silence, as the swing chains squeak in the cold morning air.

27

Lucy

The past . . .

"I want to pop a cracker with Harriet," Archie says, sidling up to me in the kitchen.

He's already wearing an orange paper Christmas hat on his head and has a green plastic whistle around his neck, which tells me it wouldn't be his first cracker of the day. My dad and the entire Goodwin family are jammed around our dining room table, dipping prawns into Thousand Island sauce. The table is lined with festive napkins, paper plates and decorations made lovingly by Archie at day care.

"Pop it with me, champ," Ollie says.

"But I promised Harriet!"

"I don't think Harriet will mind, Arch," I say and we both look at her in Nettie's lap, blinking uselessly.

Our Hampton rental isn't as small as our South Melbourne worker's cottage but it isn't huge by any stretch, particularly with the Christmas tree taking up half the living room. We are short two dining chairs so Patrick and Ollie sit on bar stools at one end, looming over the rest of us. Tom looks politely befuddled by the whole thing and Nettie has said how great it all is enough times to make me wonder who she is trying to convince. In the past, Christmas has either been at Dad's or with the Goodwins at their Brighton home, and this year it was set to do the same, until I intervened. It was time to take some control back, I'd decided.

Ollie had been surprisingly enthusiastic. ("Doing our own Christmas," he'd said. "Being the grownups, setting new traditions.") It was sweet, even if he'd been less than useless when it came to preparations.

"Ollie, can you give me a hand in here, please?" I ask from the kitchen. My face is unbearably hot, and I'm guessing, beet-red. I'd underestimated the effort it took to cook a turkey for seven adults and two kids, plus vegetables and gravy and plum pudding and a seafood starter. Like a fool, I'd refused when Diana and Nettie offered to bring something, saying, as I'd always yearned to, "Just bring yourselves." (It always sounded so generous and carefree when people said that.) Unfortunately, it also meant I'd had to spend the morning in a sweat-drenched sundress, cooking up a dinner that was never designed to be eaten at a hot Australian Christmas, in a house that didn't have air-conditioning.

"Well, Merry Christmas," Tom says, raising his beer to knock against Diana's wineglass. He seems amused, though not disappointed, with his can of Victoria Bitter, and Diana, to her credit, is uncomplaining about her glass of lukewarm chardonnay, in fact, she's had more than one glass. It's one area where I'd like to give her points—especially since last Christmas we went through several bottles of Bollinger at her place—but after hearing that Diana had refused to help Nettie pay for IVF, I'm not feeling like giving Diana any points.

"Merry Christmas," Nettie says, chinking her wineglass with her dad's beer can. She'd arrived with two bottles of wine and had already polished off one. I can't say I blame her. She'd saved up and been through one round of IVF (which yielded two embryos), but neither had transferred successfully. Now, at thirty-nine, she was going to have to start saving for another round, by which point she would be nearly forty and her chances of becoming pregnant would have decreased even further. All the while her parents had more money than they could ever possibly spend. Where was the logic in that? I'd told Diana I liked her philosophy once, but there was nothing I liked about this.

Nettie had held Harriet on her lap for most of the day, refusing to put her down, even as we ate our seafood starters. Now that she was showing signs of looking a little sloshed, I wonder if I should take Harriet away. But Patrick seems to be keeping a close eye on her, and he's only on his first beer, so I decide to leave her be.

"Reporting for duty," Ollie says, joining me in the kitchen. I hand him a pair of oven mitts and he slides them on and disappears into the oven. "Maybe, by next Christmas," he calls, reaching for the turkey, "there'll be another baby around the table, huh, Nets?"

Everyone pauses, their mouths full of prawns and Thousand Island sauce.

"So what's the plan?" Ollie continues, oblivious, setting the turkey on the counter. "Are you going to be one of those types that has the baby while answering emails on her iPhone, then heads from the hospital straight back to the office?"

I send him the death stare, but it's wasted because he's happily basting.

"Actually," Nettie says, "if I was *lucky* enough to have a baby, I'd quit my job in a heartbeat. Take a few years out of the rat race and stay home with my kids, like Lucy has done. I really respect what you've done, Luce, and I think you're a wonderful mother."

I smile, but I'm feeling nervous.

"But," she continues, "it's all pretty moot since I'm not pregnant and I can't even *start* another IVF cycle until we've saved up five thousand dollars and I'm thirty-nine and growing older every second."

Nettie is drunker than I thought, slurring on the word "second," making it sound more like "shecond." Harriet is balanced precariously on her lap and Tom, as if reading my mind, takes Harriet from her.

Ollie has finally stopped basting the turkey and is paying attention. He shoots me a panicked look. Meanwhile Diana takes a careful sip of wine then replaces her glass on the table. "So you want to be like Lucy, do you, darling?"

"Yes," Nettie says. There's a trace of defiance in her voice that has me steeling myself.

"I see." Diana's voice is calm and controlled and there's something sinister about it. "And what do you think would happen to Lucy if Ollie died?"

I open my mouth, but Nettie doesn't miss a beat.

"I imagine that Ollie has life insurance."

"Enough that Lucy doesn't have to work?" Diana laughs. "I doubt it. She has two children to feed, clothe, educate. And what kind of job will she be able to get, after taking all these years out of the workforce?"

"Mum!" Ollie says.

Diana looks around the room. "What? You all look horrified, but tell me. What would you do, Lucy?"

"Mum, that's *enough*!" Ollie says.

"Lucy hasn't even thought about it," Diana says, turning away from us all to look at Nettie. "Is that the kind of mother you want to be?"

Nettie and I rise to our feet and Tom and Ollie struggle to insert themselves between us. But they are a couple of pieces of tissue and we are bullets.

"You want to know what kind of mother I'd like to be?" Nettie screams. "The kind that *helps* her children when they come to her for help. The kind that makes them feel good about themselves, instead of like lazy, worthless spongers."

"So you'll give your children anything they want?" Diana says. Her pitch rises slightly and I can see she's starting to get flustered. "Teach them they can have something for nothing, and not have to work for anything?"

"You think I haven't *worked* for a child?" Nettie's voice is ragged, her face red. "I've been trying for three years. I've been on every fertility drug known to man. I've done two failed rounds of IVF. I've had four miscarriages."

Diana shakes her head, looking away. But as she folds her hands in her lap, I notice they're shaking. "Helping is the worst thing I could do for you, Nettie," she says.

"In that case, you've been fantastic," Patrick says from his bar stool at the end of the table. He raises his beer; a "cheers" to the room. "Merry Christmas to us, eh?"

28

Lucy

The present . . .

Patrick throws his head back and lets out a long, loud, *wrong* laugh. Gerard and Nettie and Ollie look away uncomfortably, but I can't stop looking at him. He looks . . . different. His lips move in jerky, twitchy movements, as if they can't decide whether to curve up or down. "Are you saying Diana hasn't left her children *anything?*" He presses the thumb and forefinger of his right hand to each temple and shakes his head.

Gerard looks down at the documents in front of him. "Just some personal effects." He lifts a page and places his glasses on his nose. "Photo albums, furniture from your childhood bedrooms to be retrieved at your convenience. Nettie has been left Diana's engagement ring and Ollie has been given his father's cigar collection. Lucy has been left a necklace—"

Patrick releases a spasm of air that might be a laugh or possibly a gasp. "And the cash? The properties?"

"Diana's charity business will continue operating, and a board will be appointed to oversee the running of it. The cash will support the running of the business, as well as any other ventures deemed by the board to be in the interests of the charity. The properties will be sold and the proceeds will also go to the—"

"I'm sorry," Ollie interrupts this time, holding up a hand. "Can we back up a second? We don't get *anything* aside from personal effects? No. This must be some kind of mistake."

Gerard looks somber. "I can assure you, there is no mistake. Diana made her wishes very clear."

He blinks, pauses. "Can we contest it?"

"You can," Gerard says, clearly expecting this. "But it wouldn't be a quick process."

"Would we win?"

"You might." He hesitates. "I can't be the one to advise you on this, as the executor, but I suggest you get advice once you've had a chance to think it over."

"We don't need to think about it," Ollie says. "We'll be contesting it."

"I . . . agree," Nettie says.

"So do I," Patrick says.

"Lucy?" Gerard says. "What do you think?"

I swivel in my chair and look from Patrick to Nettie to Ollie. Their faces are etched with hurt and bewilderment. But there's something else in their faces too, something ugly. So ugly, in fact, that I have to swivel my chair back again.

"It has nothing to do with me," I tell Gerard. "Nothing at all."

29

Diana

The past . . .

Apparently our house has more than thirty rooms. I still find that hard to fathom. The first time Tom brought me to look at it, I'd point-blank refused to live here. I spent my days with women who lived in homes the size of a car parking space, why should I live in a palace? But Tom, as usual, talked me into it. It's funny how quickly things become normal. Funny how morals can bend.

Tonight, Tom and I are in the den. I'm down at one end of the Chesterfield and Tom is at the other. His trousers are pushed up to the knees and I am massaging his calves. His legs have been giving him some trouble lately. ("It's the old age," he always says, when I tell him to go to the doctor.) At night, I often find him pacing around the bedroom, walking off cramps.

"Mmm," he mutters now, from behind his newspaper. "That's better."

It's been two weeks since what Tom is calling "Christmasgate" with a smile. He *can* smile, because the children are still speaking to him. It's irritating. It's easy to be popular if all you say is yes. In fact, *he's* the reason I have to be the way I am. Heaven forbid there was no bad cop. If they had two parents like Tom Goodwin, what kind of entitled brats would they be?

I haven't told Tom what had gotten me hot under the collar at Christmas. In truth, I've hardly been able to process it myself. It was a few days before Christmas when Kathy had called me out of the blue and suggested we meet up for a coffee. ("Not with the girls," she'd said. "Just the two of us.")

I'd thought it was going to be about Kathy's health—perhaps she'd found a lump or had a bad test result. That was what "news" was about when folks were our age. But as it turned out, it was nothing to do with Kathy at all.

"I was away in Daylesford for the weekend," she'd said. "And I saw something. I really shouldn't be saying anything because I'm not a hundred percent certain but . . ."

She'd been quick to point out that it may have been a misunderstanding, but she would've bet her life that it was Patrick, coming out of a restaurant, with a lady. A lady she could've sworn wasn't Nettie. His arm had been around her. It didn't look platonic.

I'd decided not to get involved. After all, Kathy wasn't sure about what she'd seen and it was none of my business. But then, at Christmas, Nettie started talking about IVF again, and I panicked. I hadn't meant to upset anyone or insult Lucy. All I wanted was to make Nettie think twice before trying to have a baby with a man who may not be faithful.

Instead I'd acted hastily and alienated them all.

The quiet since Christmas has been surprisingly loud. As someone who knew a lot of women who had very little to do (Jan, Liz and Kathy), I'd always been smug about my full life—my charity, my chores (which I did myself rather than outsourcing), drinks with the girls, the children, the grandchildren. When people talked about the elderly being lonely, I always thought: *that won't be me.* I am surrounded by people. People like me *wish* for loneliness. But it's been two weeks since Christmas, and I'm starting to feel, well, lonely.

"I noticed Ollie and Eamon were here today," I say to Tom.

Tom lowers his newspaper, revealing a guilty face.

"How much did you give them?"

I'd just driven Faizah home from the hospital with her baby when I'd returned home to find Eamon's ridiculous sports car in the driveway. It didn't take a genius to figure out what they were doing here.

"It's an investment," Tom says. "In their business."

I take Tom's sock-clad toes and bend them back toward his knee, stretching out the calf muscle. He groans.

"Are you upset with me?" he says.

"No. I'm not upset, I'm tired."

The fact is, sometimes, being a mother is impossible. From the time your children are little, you're thinking not only about whether you should let them have chocolate for breakfast *juuuuust this once,* you're also wondering if it will rot their teeth, set them up for a lifetime of bad habits, and contribute to the childhood obesity epidemic. When they're adults, it's worse. I worry about Nettie not being able to get pregnant, I also worry that she might have a baby with a man that is a philanderer. I worry about Ollie's business going under. I worry about my children expecting their parents to provide for them when they are adults.

Tom puts the newspaper down. "What would you say if I said I'd given money to Nettie too? A few months back, for IVF."

I sigh. "I'd say I'm not surprised."

"But you don't endorse it?"

I close my eyes. "No. I don't."

I feel Tom's hand on my leg. "Come on, Di. Think about what your life would have been like if your parents had supported your desire to have your baby rather than sending you away."

I shake my head. "It's different."

"It isn't," he says. "It's all about support. Whether you want to give it or not."

I open my eyes. "Actually it's about whether to give *money* or not. And that's not the same thing."

On the fourteenth day, Nettie extends the olive branch. I find her on a bar stool in the kitchen when I return from running errands. She's dressed in tailored pants and a white shirt, but she's taken off her slingbacks and is leaning over the counter on her elbows. It reminds me of when she was a teenager, lolling all over the counter after school, scavenging for something to eat.

"Nettie."

She spins on her stool so she is facing me. She's lost weight. Her eyes look more prominent in her face. And her hair has a dull look, like it hasn't been washed in a while. "Hi, Mum."

"This is a surprise."

I continue into the kitchen and Nettie swivels her stool to follow me. "I wanted to check we were okay."

I set my handbag on the kitchen counter and climb onto the stool next to hers. "I hope we are."

"I hope so too."

I nod. "Listen, I'm sorry about Christmas. I shouldn't have said what I said. I know how much you want a baby, darling."

Her eyes fill up with tears. "It feels like we've been trying forever. And I'm nearly forty, Mum. Our time is running out, at least mine is. Patrick has all the time in the world. It's not fair."

I put a hand on her back and pat gently. "How *is* everything with Patrick?"

She sniffs. "Fine."

I wonder, yet again, if I should tell her what I know about Patrick. Or at least, what I *heard* about Patrick. I could tell her to do her own investigations and see if there is any truth to it. I could just be the messenger, and stand true to the fact that it's none of my business. I can tell her that whatever she decides to do about it is fine by me. But I don't do this. Perhaps it's the fact that I know if I told Nettie what I'd heard . . . I'd lose her. She is proud, my daughter. I've already lost a lot of her—to adulthood, to Patrick. I want to hold on to the little bit I have left.

"Have you ever had a miscarriage, Mum?"

"No," I admit. "I never have. But I understand that it must be—"

Nettie presses her hands into her face and lets out a sob. "No you don't understand. You have *no idea* what it's like to have a baby inside you, to pray and beg and bargain that one day you will get to hold it and love it and raise it and be its mother."

It's funny, what the younger generation assumes we don't know.

They assume we couldn't possibly understand the agony of heart-break, or the pressure of buying a house. We couldn't understand infertility or depression or the fight for equality. If we *have* experienced any of these things, they were milder, softer versions, played out in sepia, not experiences that could compare to theirs. *You have no idea what I know,* I want to tell her. Instead I open my arms and let her lie against my shoulder and cry.

30

Diana

The past . . .

"Do you mind if I ask you something?" Ghezala asks me. She's nursing her baby girl while her serious little boy Aarash wanders around my house, looking at everything with wonderment but touching nothing. Ghezala pops by from time to time now, with Kahwah, or biscuits or cakes, and I enjoy her visits immensely.

"Go ahead," I say.

"Why do you help pregnant women? I see that you do not need to work."

Usually when someone asks me this I tell them I do it to keep myself busy, or that I like to give something back to the community. But Ghezala and I have been through too much for me to give her the standard response. The funny thing is, sometimes I find myself telling her things that I don't tell anyone . . . my friends, Nettie, even Tom.

"Because I was young and pregnant once, with no money and no one to help me. I was twenty years old, unmarried. My parents sent me away."

"I am sorry." Ghezala sits forward and places her russet hand over my own. "Where did they send you?"

I shake my head. "Oh, it wasn't that far away, even if it did feel a little like another planet. I went to a home for unwed pregnant girls, where you go to live until your baby is born."

Ghezala keeps her hand on mine. Understanding comes to her eyes. "And what happens to your baby after it is born?"

I'm not sure why, but I decide to tell her the truth.

1970

When I turned up on my father's cousin's doorstep after escaping from Orchard House, Meredith wasn't overjoyed to see me. I still remember her giving me the once-over from the doorway. Her gaze had lingered for a long time on my belly.

"So," she'd said finally, "you've been exiled too."

I almost hadn't recognized her. In a previous life, whenever I'd seen Meredith her shoulder-length hair was teased and full, her clothes freshly pressed. Now, her hair was cut stylelessly short and her clothes were rumpled, shapeless and practical.

"Well," she said after a world-weary sigh. "I suppose you'd better come in."

As it turned out, Meredith didn't just look different, she was different. As I watched her whizz about the tiny house—making me a fried egg on toast, getting out towels and sheets—I wondered if she was the same woman. The Meredith I knew was overwhelmed by guests when she lived at her magnificent home in Hawthorn, and I recall Mother saying she often had to "take to her bed" to recover from even a small afternoon tea at her house. To the contrary, now she seemed more than capable. She made me up a bed in what amounted to not much more than a shed in the backyard of her rental. The main house wasn't much more than a shed: four rooms—a bedroom, bathroom, kitchen and living.

"You can stay until you've had the baby and you're back on your feet," she said. "After that, you'll have to be on your way, I'm afraid. I can't afford to feed two more mouths."

I spent the next two weeks doing what I could to earn my keep—scrubbing Meredith's floors, fetching groceries from the store, doing the laundry. I made my way through a large pile of Meredith's clothes that needed mending, sewing on buttons or fixing hems. I organized her pantry, I mowed the lawn. If Meredith noticed any of it, she never commented. But it least it kept me busy and kept my mind off what was coming.

I still had no idea what to expect in terms of the birth, although the moans I'd heard in the hallways at Orchard House from girls in early labor did nothing to reassure me. In another life—a life in which I was married and had friends who were married—I could have asked my friends about it. A lot of the friends who had been away would be returning from Europe around now, perhaps wondering where I was. I imagined getting in touch with them, all big-bellied or with a newborn in my arms. I didn't need anyone to tell me that it wouldn't end well. Even my dearest friends—even

Cynthia—would not have been able to find a place for me in her life under these circumstances. We came from a tight-knit neighborhood, Catholic no less. It was problematic enough to give up your baby and return to your old life, but to return to it with your baby wasn't an option.

I'd written to Mother after arriving at Meredith's to tell her the decision I had made, and where I was living. For days after sending it I'd been on guard, half-expecting her to turn up on Meredith's doorstep and physically drag me back to Orchard House . . . but she'd never even written back, let alone showed up. I knew what the silence meant. I remember seeing the letters from Meredith in the garbage at home, unopened and unanswered. "There's no point keeping up correspondence with someone who isn't in our lives anymore," she'd say crisply if anyone referred to them.

Now, clearly, *I* was no longer in her life.

Two weeks after arriving at Meredith's, I woke to the feeling of something popping deep inside. It was a cold night, and moonlight streamed in the crack of the shed door, illuminating my single bed. Between my legs was wet. I gripped the cold wall to help me push myself upright. More water came when I stood, and when I walked, more still. I stuffed my feet into slippers and pulled my robe around me and made my way to the toilet that abutted the house. There was no pain yet, and I didn't see the point in waking Meredith if it was a false alarm.

I dropped my knickers and sat down. There was blood, a little of it, and a lot of clear odorless "water." As I stared at it, my abdomen pulled tight and firm. This was it.

To my extraordinary surprise, I wasn't scared.

. . .

When I returned to Meredith's house ten days later, there was a secondhand bassinette set up in the shed. Next to it, neatly folded on my single cot, was a pile of cloth diapers, two knitted jackets, knitted pants and a woolen hat. It was about as far from the scene I'd always expected to bring my first baby home to as I could possibly have imagined, and yet, it brought a tear to my eye.

"It's the bare minimum," Meredith said, "which will have to do."

Meredith didn't engage much with Ollie in the first few weeks, which surprised me as she was obviously taken with him. I often caught her peeking into his bassinette and smiling (and it was rare that Meredith smiled).

"You can hold him," I'd said to her once, but she'd immediately shaken her head.

"It's not my job to hold him."

Meredith was quite particular about my jobs. Looking after Ollie was one of them, obviously, but there were others too. When the tire on her car went flat, it was me using the jack. When the lightbulbs needed changing, or errands needed running, I did it. I cleaned the house, took care of the laundry. I did the grocery shopping, carrying Ollie down to the store in my arms, because we didn't have money for a carriage.

Meredith never thanked me for anything I did, but there was something about the way she asked me to do things. I started to look forward to the requests. ("You can fix that leaky sink, you're good at figuring things out." "Come on up to the roof and see if you can't do anything about the broken tile." "Find the cheapest place you can to repair these shoes, I know you won't let anyone rip us off.") I came to realize she was right—I was good at figuring things out, I could repair most things, and I didn't let people rip us off. A couple of months into our living arrangements, I found she hardly had to tell me what to do at all.

One morning when Ollie was about two months old, I fell asleep in the armchair when I should have been going to the grocery store. The store closed at noon on a Saturday and I'd told Meredith I'd make roast chicken for dinner. But Ollie had been awake for hours during the night, and I decided I could catch a few minutes' sleep while he napped on my chest.

When I woke, it was with a start, just before noon. I'd leaped out of my seat, transferring Ollie to my other shoulder, searching around for my purse. That's when I'd noticed Meredith sitting at the kitchen table. She'd gestured to the whole, raw chicken in front of her.

"You looked like you could use the sleep," she'd said.

Sometimes, in the evenings, Meredith and I chatted a little. I asked her what it was like, to lose her husband and her life.

"It was the worst time of my life," she'd said introspectively. "My friends wouldn't speak to me, my parents disowned me. Richard married Cindy within the year and moved her into our home while I was working in a factory six days a week."

"It's not fair," I told her.

"You haven't even gotten me started on the fact that I was only paid two-thirds of a man's wage for the very same job. And do you know why? Because they assume a wife has a husband at home to take care of her!" She laughed—a rare, wonderful treat. "But there were silver linings. I had so much to lose, back then. Now everything I have belongs to me. That's worth more than you'd think."

I was beginning to understand what she meant.

When Ollie was three months old, Meredith told me to get a job.

"But what job could I do with a baby?" I'd asked.

"If there's anyone who can figure it out, it's you, Diana."

"Maybe I could work at night," I said, after tossing and turning for three nights, trying to come up with something. I had become fond of Meredith's comments about my ingenuity and I was determined not to let her down. "Or the weekends?"

"But . . . what will you do with Ollie?" she'd asked, looking perplexed.

"Oh," I started, feeling foolish, "I thought . . . *you* would help me."

"Darling," she said. "Helping is the worst thing I could do for you."

After I finish telling Ghezala my story, nothing is off the table. I tell her how I wrote to Mother to tell her she had a grandson and still, she didn't reply. I tell her how I sent her pictures of Ollie every year. How one day I caught the train to my childhood home to check that my parents still lived there, and saw my father's car parked in the driveway, and Mother in the garden pulling weeds. I tell her how Mother looked right at me then lowered her straw hat so it covered her face and went back to weeding. I tell her how that was the last time I saw Mother before she died, four years later. That, after Mum's funeral, I never saw my father again.

"I'm sorry," Ghezala says.

"It is what it is. I moved forward with my life and started a new family. I have Tom and the children now."

"But your children are unhappy with you?"

I sigh. "Because of money. It's always about money."

"Your children want your money?"

"Naturally."

"And you don't want to give it?"

I smile. There's something so delightfully simple about the way Ghezala speaks—no double entendre, no judgment. It frees me to speak equally simply.

"Being poor and having to survive without my parents was the single most defining thing I've ever done. It showed me what I was capable of. As a mother, I think this is the most important gift you can give to your children. Unlike money, it can't be taken away or lost."

"It sounds like you have your answer," Ghezala said.

"But it's more complicated than that. Nettie wants to have a baby and she's having trouble getting pregnant. IVF is very expensive and she wants us to help her with the cost. The clock is ticking, as she's forty now. And that's not even the whole picture. I have reason to believe that her husband is unfaithful."

Ghezala's brown eyes widen. "Does she know?"

"I'm not sure. The funny thing is . . . I'm not sure she'll *want* to know. This baby thing has sent her quite mad. She's got her eye on the prize—a baby—and she's unable to see anything else."

"So . . . instead of talking to her about it, you're . . . ensuring she won't get pregnant, by withholding money?"

"As I've said, I have many reasons not to give her the money. But to be honest, yes, I'd rather not help her shackle herself to a man who is possibly unfaithful. She's already struggling. I couldn't bear for her to become pregnant, give up her livelihood and her career, only to have it thrown back in her face when he leaves her for another woman."

I look at Ghezala, waiting for some wisdom, or comment or even a question. But Ghezala doesn't say anything at all, which, I realize, is a much more powerful response.

31

Lucy

The present . . .

"No iPads," I tell the kids, to a chorus of moans. They have just gotten home from school and my front hall is full of school bags, my sink is full of lunchboxes and my couch is full of children. "Go play a game or read a book."

They proceed to go ballistic and I ask myself . . . why am I doing this? Who cares if they watch the iPad for twenty-four hours straight? Their eyeballs won't bleed or turn square, their brains won't rot. It doesn't matter a single jot. And yet, I continue my mothering on autopilot, as natural to me these days as breathing even in spite of everything going on.

Ollie came home from the will reading and immediately shut himself up in the home office. He didn't say much in the car, other than that he was still in shock and needed some time to think.

He hasn't been back to work yet since Diana died, and I'm starting to worry about that. For the past year it's been so hard to keep him away from the place—he regularly worked weekends and well into each evening. I'd hoped that by this point, four years into the business, he'd have been able to back off a little and enjoy what they'd built, but they always seemed to be hurtling toward the next target. ("When we sign this client, we'll be able to take the kids to Disneyland." "When we land this contract, champagne for everyone.") But they kept signing clients and landing contracts—and Ollie kept placing candidates—and still, profits seemed to be skinny.

A year ago, I'd suggested Ollie and Eamon get someone to look at the books, to do an inventory of incomings and outgoings. Ollie had liked that idea, and came home and reported that Eamon had hired an accountant he knew to do exactly that. But the accountant had come back with the same advice that Eamon had been giving. "More clients = more money." A good philosophy, but with Ollie as the only recruiter, and no money to hire anyone else, it had taken its toll on him. Now, to hear that his parents had disinherited him, it's got to feel like the final straw in what has been a stressful couple of years.

From the living room, I hear Ollie's phone ring, and then quickly stop. He's screening the call, probably, he's been doing that all day. I imagine him in his swivel chair, his forehead resting against the desk. Ollie and I had never talked explicitly about the fact that we would one day come into money—it always seemed to be in poor taste—but even I could admit that I'd thought about it from time to time, and it always made me feel secure to know that even if we were poor now, our retirement would be taken care of. The idea that

Diana would cut all of us out of her will had never occurred to me and it had clearly never occurred to Ollie either.

There is a sharp *bang bang* at the door. My stomach constricts. Lately, a bang at the door has always signaled bad news, and given the amount of force this person is using, it seems unlikely that this one should be any different.

I tread slowly down the hall. Through the window at the side of the door I notice the distinctive royal blue of Eamon's suit jacket. When I toss open the door, he straightens his spine, bending his lips upward in what I think is supposed to be a smile. "Hi, Luce."

"Eamon," I say. "Is everything all right?"

His expression is tight and he has a slight twitchiness about him that is unnerving. "Sure, sure. Everything's great. Fantastic."

Fantastic. Ollie had started using that word too, since being in partnership with Eamon, mostly on the phone. ("Everything is fantastic, how are things with you, Steve? *Fantastic!*" Someone must have told them in a networking course that it is highly important to be fantastic at all times.)

"Ollie home?" he says.

Ollie is already behind me; I feel him there even before I turn and see him. I take a step back and watch the men regard each other, squaring up against one another like cats in the street.

"G'day, mate," Ollie says, unsmiling.

"G'day," Eamon replies equally coolly. "Sorry to intrude. Just wanted a quick word."

Ollie turns and walks back down the hall and Eamon follows. I find myself overcome by an urge to go after them, to demand to know what on earth is going on. But Ollie closes the door.

"Muuuuum?"

I startle. It's Harriet. She appears before me looking utterly appalled. "What?"

"Archie is watching the iPad!"

"Oh." I walk into the living room. Edie has managed to turn on the television and is staring at *Play School,* open-mouthed. "Where is he?"

"He's in his bed hiding!" Harriet wails. "It's *not fair.* Muuum!"

I follow Harriet to Archie's room where she points an accusing finger at the suspicious mound in the center of the bed. I tug off the blankets and Archie looks up guiltily.

"I *said* no iPad," I say without much force. The fact is, I'm thinking of reconsidering this whole no iPad thing. I could really use the time to try and unpack my thoughts, not to mention to eavesdrop on the conversation between Ollie and Eamon.

"Now I get it for the rest of the day!" Harriet says, lunging for the iPad.

"No you don't!" Archie cries.

I grab the iPad and exit the room, and Archie and Harriet tailgate me down the hall, a swishing appendage of fury. I pause outside Ollie's office door. The volume has risen now so I don't have to strain to hear the sound of a fist hitting something: the wall? The desk? Then I hear Ollie's voice.

"How *the fuck* was I supposed to know?"

The kids freeze. I concentrate on keeping my face neutral as I circle around the kids and start pushing them toward the family room.

"This is bullshit," Eamon cries. "This is fucking *bullshit!*"

There is a terrific crash, and the kids and I pull up short at the same time as the door flies open and Eamon comes crashing out. Ollie's hands are wrapped tight around his throat.

32

Lucy

The past . . .

There is truly nothing worse than having to ask for a favor when you're trying to hold the moral high ground. It's been three months since Christmas and we're in the sweaty, summer-is-never-going-to-end period when people hang out at the supermarket in swimsuits and flip-flops, buying watermelon and ham and bread rolls and sunscreen. I'd like to be hanging out at the supermarket, too (since it's air-conditioned), but I'm too ill to even lift my head off the couch. Because I am eight weeks pregnant.

If it wasn't for Harriet, I could have coped. Archie could have watched *The Wiggles* on repeat and wouldn't have bothered me for days (except maybe for food), but Harriet, at ten months, has not yet mastered the art of solid, uninterrupted screen time. Ollie has a full day of interviews at work, but he has promised to come home as soon as he can, and my Dad is down at Portarlington for the week. I think about hiring an agency nanny, but my eyes water at the cost and Ollie has been watching the pennies lately. Finally, I realize there's nothing else for it and I ring Diana.

"Hello?" As always, she answers the phone sounding mildly inconvenienced.

I'm flat on my back on the floor with Archie on my lap and Harriet banging a toy repeatedly against my head. "Hello, Diana," I say. "How are you?"

"Lucy?" There's a short pause. "Are you ill?"

Leave it to Diana to cut to the chase.

"Actually, yes. That's why I'm calling. I have the flu and I'm . . . well, I'm feeling quite shocking."

I'd decided not to tell Diana I was pregnant until I reached the three-month mark. With my previous two pregnancies I couldn't wait to tell her—thinking she'd enjoy being in on the early secret—but both times she'd merely smiled and assured me she'd keep it to herself until we were out of the danger period. There had been no congratulations. No hug. (She did, bizarrely, drop off bags of grapes periodically, with both pregnancies.) So this time, I decided she could find out around the three-month mark like everyone else.

"And you need help with the kids."

It's not a question, nor is it an offer, though I have to respect the way she doesn't waste anyone's time. "Yes."

I hear shuffling in the background, Diana flicking through her diary perhaps. She'll have a full calendar, no doubt, but I'm holding out hope that she'll find a half-hour slot somewhere ("between two-thirty and three P.M., but it has to be a three P.M. sharp pickup because I have to take a baby carriage across town and I'd like to get back before the rush-hour traffic"). Fact is, I'm not too proud to take that half hour. I'll take anything I can get.

"I'm free," she says after a moment. "I'll come and pick them up right away."

I blink. "You'll . . . pick them up?"

"I just have to reschedule a drop-off, but that won't take long. I'll be there within the hour."

When Diana knocks on my door I'm still horizontal but I've moved to the couch. Archie is glued to the iPad and Harriet is sitting on my stomach, whining for attention. The floor is littered with cushions, the coffee table with toast crumbs, plates, mugs, and oddly, one of my wedding shoes (kids!). I don't try to conceal any of the mess. It's all I can do to answer the door.

Diana has pharmacy bags. "I stopped at the drugstore. I have Lemsip, apparently it's nothing more than acetaminophen but I always find it comforting when I'm sick. I also have cold and flu tablets. Take two right after we leave and get some sleep." Diana takes Harriet. "Right, I'll pack a bag for the kids."

Diana swishes about the place, finding a weekend bag and stuffing it full of the kids' clothes. She finds bottles and formula and a couple of jars of baby food, which she efficiently loads into the diaper bag, along with some diapers and wipes and pacifiers. I'm helpless to do anything but lie there and watch.

"All right, kids," she says, when she's filled two bags. "You're coming for a sleepover at Dido's."

This is exciting enough to tear Archie from his screen. *A sleepover?* Diana has never had the kids for a sleepover before. Not even Archie. Sleepovers at grandma's were something that only ever happened in my dreams. Also, evidently, in Archie's dreams, judging by the way he runs around in circles now. Archie adores Tom and Diana's house. The games of hide-and-seek are epic, and he is remarkably unfazed by Diana's unceasing monologue about how he isn't to touch or break anything. I do worry about the stairs—marble, of course—and Harriet, who is just starting to crawl, but right now I decide it's worth the risk.

"Be careful of Harriet on the stairs," I say to Diana as she gathers up the kids. Suddenly I realize I haven't thanked her for anything. I open my mouth to do that, but before I do, another thought jumps into my brain. "And don't let them near the pool!"

Call me crazy but I have a terror of kids and pools. Tom and Diana have an indoor swimming pool (obviously) and they have managed to get around the mandatory pool fencing laws by having high door-handles and auto-closing doors. It's all well and good except that Archie loves going into the pool area to look at the giant aquarium fish tank they have installed (of course) and if Diana got distracted by Harriet, I didn't want to think about what could happen.

"No one in the pool area," Diana agrees, and she disappears out the door with my children.

That's when I realize I never did say thank you.

I sleep. An unfathomable all-consuming *orgasm* of a sleep. Pregnancy will do that to you.

I haven't slept like this in years. My dreams are odd and ever-changing, and I rouse every few hours only to realize that my children aren't here and I can go back to sleep indefinitely. It's unthinkably luxurious. I find myself wanting to savor every second.

Around five P.M., when I rouse again, the phone is ringing. I snatch it from the bedside table and press it to my ear, eyes still closed.

"Hello?" It sounds more like "nnmmo."

"Lucy?"

I open my eyes. It's Diana, I can tell right away, even though her pitch sounds different, a note or two higher than usual. ". . . yes?"

I hear talking in the background, unfamiliar voices speaking urgently. I feel a chill slip down my spine, a sluice of ice water. I rise to my elbows.

"What is it, Diana? What's happened?"

"We're on our way to the hospital, Lucy," she says. Her voice is threaded through with fear. "You need to meet us there."

33

Lucy

The present . . .

Eamon is gone. Thankfully I didn't need to break up the fight—as soon as Ollie had seen us watching, he'd released Eamon, who'd brushed himself off and stalked out the front door. Ollie also brushed himself off, and then turned and walked back into his office without a word. I'd left him alone only long enough to get the children in front of their screens, and now I knock on the door firmly.

"Come in," he says.

Ollie is sitting in his chair, his elbows on his knees, his head in his hands. He doesn't look up.

"What's going on?" I ask.

He keeps his head down, which does nothing to ease my anxiety. I think about all the things I know about him—the way he eats his breakfast cereal dry, no milk; the fact that he sleeps naked all year round; his ferocious hatred of celery, so strong that he can tell the moment he walks in the door if it's been in the house. But clearly, there are a lot of things I *don't* know about him.

"I'm sorry," he whispers.

"Why are you sorry?"

Finally, he looks up. His face is tearstained. My mind goes to the very worst places. Actually it goes to one particular place, very quickly. An image of Ollie appears in my mind, pressing a gold-threaded cushion into his mother's face.

Was it possible? Certainly, Diana had made me do things I never thought possible.

Ollie takes a breath. "I'm sorry because we're ruined financially."

It takes a moment for the relief to come, but when it does, it is a flood. I drop to my knees in front of him and take his hands in my own. They're sweaty and warm and I kiss them. "Oh, Ollie! *No* we're not. Sure, we don't have millions upon millions of dollars coming our way but we're not ruined. We've survived so far, haven't we? And we don't need much!" A beat of silence passes. Ollie keeps his eyes on the floor. "*What?*"

"This isn't about the inheritance. Well . . . I'd hoped the inheritance would save us. But . . ." he drifts off.

My mind reels back, suddenly sticking on the bank statement I opened a few days ago. The huge number, the debt, at the bottom. A panicky feeling starts in my chest.

"The business?"

Ollie nods.

"How bad is it?"

"It's bad," Ollie says. "We sunk so much into it the first year, setting it all up. I actually have no idea how we spent so much, the money just seemed to fly out of the account."

I sit back on my haunches.

"We kept getting new contracts and I was working my ass off. And we *were* making money. But not enough, it seems. I should have kept a closer eye on the outgoings, but I thought Eamon had it in hand." He drags a hand through his hair. "When Mum died, I thought we could pay off our debts and leave the business behind once and for all. But now . . ."

". . . now, we have nothing."

Silence envelops us. I lift my hand to my temple. Now, not only are we *not* inheriting millions upon millions of dollars, we're also in extraordinary debt.

"And Eamon doesn't have any money he can . . . invest?" I ask.

"Eamon was counting on the money too. I'd talked about clearing the debt so he could keep the business operating."

I close my eyes. I hear the faint sounds of *Sesame Street* and the irritating melodic tune of one of Archie's games on the iPad. "And our savings—"

"Our savings are long gone." Ollie begins to cry—real, rolling tears. "We are in a huge amount of debt. Dad's dead. Mum's dead. There is no one to help us."

I'm furious with Ollie, but I crawl to him and put my arms around his neck. He's right, there's no one to help us now. The funny thing is, this is what Diana wanted all along.

34

Diana

The past . . .

The truth is, I'd always intended to let Archie swim. I knew what Lucy had said, but I didn't see how it could hurt. After all, I was going to watch him. Before Archie could talk and tattle me in, I used to do even more things I knew Lucy wouldn't like. I wasn't doing it to spite her or anything. It was just that she worried about a lot of things that didn't matter.

("Make sure he wears his coat," she'd always say, as I disappeared out of the house with Archie. I'd nod and agree, but when Archie flung off his coat at the park, I wasn't going to chase after him to put it back on. Natural consequences were better. If the child was cold, he'd put the coat on.

"Did he nap for two hours at one P.M.?" she'd demand.

"That sounds about right," I'd say. All this fuss about naps.

"No junk," she'd say when I was taking Archie to the movies, but what child didn't have popcorn and an ice-cream cone when they went to a film with their grandmother?

But clearly, she'd had a point. And I should have listened to her.

Archie had been begging to go in the pool all day. And why not? I enjoyed a swim myself and there was no question I wouldn't supervise him. I'd shower him afterward and he'd fall off to sleep, exhausted, and Lucy would be none the wiser. That's what I'd figured. And now, here we were. In the hospital.

I thought I'd done everything right. I'd waited for Tom to get home. Harriet was too young to swim, and besides, I wouldn't have trusted myself with both kids in the pool at once.

"Tom," I'd said, when he walked in the door. "Can you hold Harriet for me so I can swim with Archie?"

For someone who was so fond of holding his grandchildren, Tom had been surprisingly reluctant. "Oh. Can't you just put her in the stroller?"

"I think she'd prefer a cuddle from her grandfather."

Archie was already naked, running for the pool, leaving a trail of clothing in his wake. "Archie, don't run!" I called after him. The floor was limestone and slippery when wet. At one end was a giant aquarium, which I thought was over the top, but Tom insisted and the children loved it.

"Take Harriet up that end and let her look at the fish," I said.

Tom did, reluctantly. He was in a strange mood; I didn't know what was bothering him. I slid inflatable armbands onto Archie and he dive-bombed into the pool while I got in slowly via the steps. Tom carried Harriet over to the aquarium. She was a pudgy baby, shorter and much fatter than Archie had been. I watched her chunky legs kick insistently as she watched the fish swim past.

"Watch this, Dido," Archie said, and I watched him pretend to walk down the street and then accidentally fall into the pool. Funny little fellow.

I glanced at Tom at the end of the pool and noticed Tom was holding Harriet strangely, sort of using his forearms to press her against him. By the time I realized she was slipping, it was too late. I pulled myself up and out of the pool but I was still several meters away when Harriet slid from his grip and her head hit the limestone tiles with a crack.

In the ambulance, I sing "Old MacDonald Had a Farm."

"Old MacDonald had a farm. Ee ii ee ii oo."

There is blood. A lot of blood. Heads bleed a lot, I remember someone saying that once. Lots of blood vessels close to the surface of the skin or something.

"With a quack quack here, and a quack quack there . . ."

Harriet is awake, which is a good sign, but she's very distressed, has vomited twice and a sizable bruise is already coming up on the side of her head. She seems drowsy, but it *is* her nap time. My job, the paramedic said, was to keep her awake. And so, I sing.

". . . here a quack, there a quack, everywhere a quack quack . . ."

It's funny, the places the mind goes. My mind drifts from the idea that I may have permanently injured my grandchild, to the question of why Tom dropped her at all. Mostly my mind sticks on what I'm going to say to Lucy. I know what it's like being told that you might not get to keep your baby. I remember that feeling as if it were yesterday. I cannot be the reason that Lucy has to hear these words.

I run my fingers through Harriet's soft, baby hair.

"Ee ii ee ii oo."

Lucy and Ollie arrive at the hospital in a flurry. Ollie is in his work clothes, minus the suit jacket—he must have come in such a hurry he didn't stop to put it on. Lucy is still dressed in the tracksuit she wore when I picked up the kids this morning.

This morning feels like a lifetime ago.

"Lucy," I start, but she ignores me, rushing to Harriet's side. I cringe. Harriet looks terrible. Her head is bandaged but blood soaks through the gauze. Lucy rears back in horror.

"Is she . . . unconscious?"

At first I think Lucy is talking to me but then I realize there is a tired-looking doctor in the doorway. She's dressed in scrubs and glasses dangle around her neck on a chain.

"Your daughter has been sedated for an MRI," the doctor says. "We do that with young children, to make sure they'll lie still. Try not to worry."

"Why does she need an MRI?"

"It's just a precaution. She has a depressed skull fracture, which may require surgery to lift the bone to prevent it pressing against the brain. We also need to check for cerebral lacerations and contusions, which are tears and bruises to the surface of the brain," the doctor says. "This can happen when the skull is fractured. Your daughter was vomiting in the ambulance, so we want to make sure we don't miss anything. Chances are, she'll be fine, but we can't be too careful with head injuries." There is movement in the doorway—a nurse gesturing to the doctor. She nods, then looks back at Lucy. "I'm just going to check that we have everything ready here, and then we will be back to get Harriet."

Lucy turns back to Harriet. Ollie comes to stand beside her and she reaches out to grip his forearm.

"Lucy," I start, but she holds up a hand, silencing me.

"Why were you in the pool?" She doesn't even face me to ask me this.

"I'm sorry. I know you said no swimming, I just thought . . ."

". . . that you knew better?" She whirls around. Her eyes flash wild. "That you were entitled to override me in decisions about *my* children?"

"You have no idea how sorry I am, Lucy. Honestly, I am. But it's done now and I think it would be better if we could just—"

"What?" A rush of air expels from Lucy—almost a laugh, not quite. "Put it behind us?"

"Well . . ."

"Did you hear what the doctor said? Harriet needs an MRI. My daughter could have *died*, because you thought you knew better than me." She takes a step toward me. Lucy is usually hard to pin down— like a child she is in a state of perpetual movement—but right now she's eerily calm and quiet. I find myself taking a step back.

"I know we've never been close, Diana. First there was my wedding day. I thought we'd shared a moment when you gave me that necklace. Then you felt the need to remind me that I had to give it back, which I knew, by the way, but pointing it out like I was planning to steal it wasn't the best way to ingratiate yourself to me." She takes another step toward me. "You made me feel like a gold digger when we asked for money to buy a tiny worker's cottage. You know what? I didn't even *want* your money. It was Ollie's idea." Lucy's entire body pulses. "You bring me a raw chicken when I have a newborn. A raw chicken!" I can actually see the flickers in Lucy's brain, sparks, metal on metal, memory on memory. It all forms into a spinning cyclone, more powerful together than separate. "My baby might have brain damage because of you. We cannot *ever* put that behind us."

"Lucy . . ." Ollie says. I'd almost forgotten he was here. In the back of my thoughts it occurs to me that Ollie is the fruit of my womb, yet at some point he's become almost insignificant. He and Tom and Patrick are the cogs and spokes, but Lucy and Nettie and I, we are the wheels. "You need to calm down."

Lucy takes another step toward me.

A nurse appears in the doorway. "Is everything all right in here?"

"Lucy," I say, holding up my hands, "just take a breath—"

But Lucy thrusts a palm out, flat like a stop sign. It connects with my own hands and I stagger backward. I feel a sharp pain in my ankle and I go down, hard.

"We need security in here," I hear someone call.

Lucy disappears and people I don't recognize appear right up close.

"Ma'am, are you all right?"

"I need a doctor in here!"

"Are you all right, Ma'am?"

"Don't try to move her."

They're making a big fuss about nothing. I'm fine. I'm on the floor now, I believe. Color dances in front of my eyes. And then it's just . . . black.

35

Lucy

The present . . .

I wear Diana's necklace to the funeral, the one she lent me on my wedding day. She'd left it to me in her will. When I'd tipped it out of its envelope this morning, there had been a little note attached:

At least this time, you don't have to give it back.

One thing to be said about Diana, she had an unexpected sense of humor. I'd planned to wear the necklace with my hot-pink wrap dress, but instead I'd gone for a simple black shift. There was something to be said for black at funerals, and I did add a pair of hot-pink wedges.

Outside the funeral home are dozens of people who know my name and who talk about how we had met down at Sorrento, or at Tom's sixtieth birthday party or some other such event. I nod and smile and ask after their families but the small talk is achingly limited. All of the normal, day-to-day topics are off the table, being deemed too trivial for the occasion except oddly, the weather, which is freely discussed at funerals, and indeed one of the few safe topics of discussion. "The sun is shining down on Diana, today." Or even, "The sky is crying." (Interestingly though, the sun is not shining and the sky is not crying, it is merely a dull grey day. I wonder, idly, what this is supposed to say about my mother-in-law.)

Nettie is in quite a fragile state. She has dressed up at least, in a cream dress and brown leather wedges, but she looks drawn and tired. She dissolves into fresh tears periodically and I wish I could console her. But she won't even accept support from Patrick, who stands beside her uselessly, smiling politely at people who offer condolences.

The children mill about at my heels, bored and excited, pinching and pushing each other, but they quiet down when I hand them a fistful of gummy bears from the stash in my bag. Inside, the crowd is the typical upper-middle-class folk, apart from the smattering of dark-skinned faces, rare enough among these parts to assume they must be the refugee ladies that Diana worked with. I notice Eamon as we make our way to the seats at the front. There's no physical sign of his fight with Ollie that I can see, other than perhaps the expression of mild defiance on his face. I'd have wondered why he bothered coming at all if I didn't know how into appearances he was. Jones and Ahmed are there, too, which is a surprise. They wear their usual black suits, and as such should look like any other mourner, but there's something about them that screams COP. Perhaps it's that I can feel their presence, like ants crawling up my back.

The service is slow and dull, in large part because of the lack of hymns. Ollie gives a eulogy that is as heartfelt as it can possibly be, which is to say, fairly generic. Lots of *I love you*s, lots of stories about how Diana did lots of charitable work. As I listen, I can't help but think of the eulogy Ollie gave at Tom's funeral. There hadn't been a dry eye in the house. Ollie himself had become so choked up that I ended up standing behind him for most of it, with my hand on his shoulder. But today, he doesn't manage so much as a misty eye.

I try to imagine the eulogy that *I* would have given Diana, had I been given the role. I glance up at the photo of her, framed on her coffin. Her chin is raised, her eyes guarded, her lips curved into the barest smile. It is so *Diana* I can't help but feel something. It's hard to believe I won't see that guarded smile again. It's equally hard to believe that she might have exited this world on anything other than her own terms.

I become aware of a flutter in my body; a niggle at first but slowly it fills my chest like a scream. I put a hand gently to my lips but a sob escapes, excruciatingly loud. The children look at me curiously. Even Ollie pauses in his eulogy and frowns. I want to get it together, but it's like a train. I double over, all at once consumed by it. The stark emotion. The utter, inexplicable loss.

Ollie and Patrick are pallbearers, along with two friends of Tom's. The other two positions—apparently there is a requirement for six— are given to the funeral staff. I think briefly that perhaps those roles should have been offered to Nettie and myself, but no one asked me and I assume no one asked Nettie either. And so Diana is taken out and placed in the hearse, and we are forced to endure small talk for another forty-five minutes, as my children tear around the lawn like they're at a garden party. Harriet has climbed a tree and is sitting on a branch with a child I saw in the venue, a grandchild of one of Diana's friends, perhaps. The hems of their dresses are grubby with dirt.

People disappear in dribbles, most heading to the function room at the Half Moon Hotel, where we are putting out sandwiches and drinks this afternoon. But a few people who aren't heading to the Half Moon hang around to give their condolences. Condolence after condolence, in the absence of alcohol, is quite frankly, exhausting. Ollie obviously thinks so, judging by his drawn expression, so I tell him to head out and leave me to farewell the final few mourners.

"What about the kids?" he says.

"I'll handle the kids. Go."

Finally he does, catching a ride with an old friend of Tom's.

I am standing there, with Edie hanging off one leg, when another mourner approaches me. She's young, perhaps five or ten years younger than me, and her skin a beige-brown color. The man beside her looks vaguely familiar.

"You are Lucy," the woman says.

"Yes," I say. My gaze moves back to the woman. I don't think I've seen her before, but then again, there have been a lot of people here today that I haven't recognized. "Have we met?"

She smiles. "I have seen your picture at Diana's house." She's wearing a black long-sleeved dress and black boots with an emerald green headscarf. "I am Ghezala. This is my husband, Hakem."

"It's nice to meet you both. How did you know Diana?"

"I was pregnant when I came to Australia," Ghezala says. "Diana was wonderful to me. She was there when I gave birth to my son Aarash on my kitchen floor."

"That was you?" I exclaim. "I remember hearing about that." It's hard to forget the image of Diana on the floor, let alone delivering a baby.

Ghezala smiles. "She was a very good woman."

"And what do you do, Lucy?" Hakem asks.

"I'm a stay-at-home mum at present," I tell him. I've been asked this a lot today. (*What are you up to these days, Lucy? What are you doing with yourself now that you've finished having babies?*) Usually I don't care what other people think, but with our soon-to-be bankrupt status, I can't help but wonder . . . What *am* I doing with myself? I'd been so determined to be a stay-at-home mum, so keen to do as my own mother did, that I'd never questioned it. Now, suddenly, I was questioning it.

"I was a recruiter in a past life—" I start, but Hakem cuts me off.

"It must be in the family. Diana found me my job, several years ago when I couldn't get an interview in this country. Now I am an engineer again, because of Diana."

That's when I realize where I know him from. That day, at Diana's house. I remember the way he thanked her, the extent of his gratitude. I remember the way Diana had brushed it off like it was no big deal.

"Actually, just yesterday Hakem and I were invited to have seats on the board of Diana's charity," Ghezala says. "It was her wish that the board have representation from refugees."

"That doesn't surprise me," I say. "Diana was passionate about that charity."

"We will make sure her legacy is carried on. We will make her proud."

I pause, thinking about how that was all I had wanted for the longest time, to make Diana proud.

Ghezala takes my hand. "Diana was in the business of giving people chances," she says. "But maybe, she was so busy looking at the problems in the world, she forgot to give chances to those right under her nose."

I smile at Ghezala and just like that, after her death, I understand Diana a little better.

36

Diana

The past . . .

"Are you sure you're all right?" Tom says to me, as I slide out of my hospital gown.

"I'm *fine*. It was a small knock to the head. It was a lot of fussing about nothing. The hospital only kept me overnight in case I sued them for a slippery floor or something." I step into the trousers Tom brought for me.

"I still can't believe Lucy pushed you."

"She was worried about Harriet, Tom. As we all are. That should be our focus right now, not this silly bump to my head."

I slip on my blouse and start matching up the buttons.

"Are we going to pop up to the ward to see Harriet before we go?" Tom asks.

I hesitate. "I don't think I should."

"Nonsense. You're her *grandmother*."

"Lucy made it very clear—"

"Lucy was emotional. She didn't mean what she said or did. She'll probably apologize when she sees you."

Tom is the eternal optimist but I don't share his confidence. He didn't see the emotion behind Lucy's words. Since yesterday, the only news I've had was a text from Ollie, saying: *Harriet awake. MRI looked good*. I'd heard nothing at all from Lucy, despite calling three times. "I'm not sure about that, Tom."

"We'll stop by on our way to the car," he says firmly. "It will all be fine, you'll see."

When we arrive at Harriet's room, Lucy is sitting on a chair that has been pushed up to Harriet's bedside. Her back is to us. From the doorway, I can hear her humming "Twinkle Twinkle Little Star" even though Harriet appears to be sound asleep. She's a good mother, I have to admit. It occurs to me that I've never told her that.

Tom lifts his hand to knock on the door, but I grab it before it connects. "I just want to watch them," I whisper. "Let's just watch for a moment."

And so, we watch. And for the first time, I really see Lucy. Not a girl who was handed everything. A girl who knew what she wanted. A family. A girl who has stood by my son and her children, and even me, in spite of hardship. A girl a lot tougher than I gave her credit for.

I think about all my conversations with Jan and Liz and Kathy about daughters-in-law. We'd always focused on how different they are from us, how their mothering is different, their attitudes are different. We've never once focused on our similarities. As women.

As wives. As mothers. It occurs to me suddenly that there are a lot more of them.

"Let's go," I say to Tom.

He looks as though he's going to protest, but I pull him out of the doorway before he can. Lucy won't want us here today. And today, I'm thinking about her.

Tom and I drive home in silence. I assume the quiet is to allow me to process my thoughts about what happened with Lucy, but when we pull up in front of the house and Tom doesn't get out of the car straightaway . . . I realize I'd assumed wrong.

"This was all my fault," he says. "I'm the one who dropped Harriet."

"Nonsense." I release my seat belt and pivot in my seat. "It was an *accident*."

"Accidents have been happening for a while. My grip strength has been getting worse and worse."

I roll my eyes. "We're getting older, Tom. Nothing works as well as it used to."

"I went to the doctor about it, a couple of months ago."

I pause. "You did?"

"Dr. Paisley ordered some tests and told me I should see a specialist. A neurologist. So I did."

"You did what? Saw a specialist?" I'm stunned. How could this have been going on without my knowing? Tom doesn't have secrets. (Once, when the kids were little, he told them on Christmas Eve that Santa had told him he was going to bring them bikes the next day. *I just couldn't wait to see their little faces,* he'd said.)

Tom stares straight ahead, his hands on the wheel at ten and two. "I haven't seen the specialist yet. But I have an appointment tomorrow. It's with a guy who specializes in motor neuron disease. It's also known as ALS or Lou Gehrig's disease."

I stare at him.

"I didn't want to tell you until I had more information, but . . . after what happened . . . it's my fault what happened to Harriet. I should never have agreed to hold her."

My throat is dry. I try to swallow but there's nothing there. I stare at the side of Tom's face. His large, craggy face.

"I'd like you to come with me to my appointment tomorrow."

"*Of course* I'll come. I wish I had been there for all your appointments."

"I know you do," he says, and he lets go of the steering wheel and lays one hand, palm up, in my lap. We sit like that in the car for nearly an hour, staring at the windshield.

The next day, Tom and I go to the neurologist's office. We enter the waiting room, announce our arrival, and take our seats on a couple of chairs. In the space beside me, a man sits in a wheelchair, head lolling, his chin supported by a white pad, a purple travel pillow horseshoeing his neck. He is, at a glance, at least ten years younger than Tom. The woman beside him, his wife presumably, flicks through a magazine, glancing up at him every so often and smiling, or leaning forward with a tissue to wipe the corner of his mouth. Even after the lady sees me looking, I'm unable to look away.

"Tom Goodwin?" says the doctor.

"Yes," Tom says.

I keep looking at the woman. She gives me a slight frown but then her gaze slithers to Tom and understanding dawns. She gives me a small, almost indistinct nod.

"Diana? Are you coming?"

"Oh . . . yes." I break gazes with the woman and Tom and I walk into the room.

I drive home. It is one of only a handful of times I've driven while Tom was in the car. Most times have been when he'd had too much to drink—a lot too much, because often he drove anyway, we weren't as vigilant about drunk driving in our day. But there were a couple of other times. Once, when we were newly married and on a road trip to visit his cousin in Bright in the Victorian countryside. Ollie was in the backseat of the car, just a toddler, and Tom was driving far too fast for my liking so I demanded he slow down. Finally he pulled over onto the dusty side of the road, wrenched up the hand brake and said, "Fine. If you never want to get there, *you* drive." He could be dreadfully hot-headed, Tom. I'd taken the wheel, and despite Tom's lack of faith, we did make it there and in good time. He'd muttered and moaned about it for an hour or so, then calmed down like he always did. By the time we arrived we were chuckling about it. I wonder if, soon, the rest of my memories of Tom will be catalogued like this. Memories of him as a father, memories of him as a grandfather. Memories of fights, memories of joy. All of them memories, because he is gone.

"When we get home, I'll get on the phone about a second opinion," I say, my voice full of authority. And I will get a second opinion, a third one too. We'll go through the process and exhaust all the avenues. But in the end, Tom will die, somehow I know this. He won't be in his nineties, he won't even be in his seventies. He will die, and I will have to live.

"When we get home," Tom replies, "I want to go to bed."

We pull to a stop at a red traffic light and I turn to look at him properly. His eyes are shiny, the bottom lid heavy, threatening to spill. "Okay," I say. "We'll go to bed."

The tears spill as I pull out of the intersection. I leave him to it, his own personal grieving process. He doesn't need me telling him everything will be okay when we both know it won't. Instead I give his hand a firm squeeze. My role is clear to me now. I will be the strong one. I'll be good at this. I am aware of my limitations. I'm not warm, I'm not especially kind. But I can be strong. I can allow Tom to slip away knowing I will be all right. This, I can give him.

At home, Tom goes right upstairs. I do too, but while he heads for the bedroom, I tell him I need a quick shower. In the bathroom, I set the shower running and I strip off my clothes and I stand under the stream of water and cry. I cry until I don't know which is water and which is tears.

I cry until I'm dry.

By the time I get out of the shower, Tom is in bed. At first I think he is asleep, but as soon as I crawl in beside him, his eyes open.

"How are you going to live without me?" he says.

We both chuckle, even as a tear slides from the corner of Tom's eye.

"I won't," I say, and then he reaches for me and we don't talk anymore.

1971

When Ollie was four months old, I got a job at the Star Theatre in Yarraville. The Star was unusually opulent for the area, and was packed every Saturday night. Unique to the cinema was a baby room where babies were lined up in their carriages and each given a number. If a baby started crying, its number was flashed on the screen and its mother would come and collect it. Ollie was one of those babies.

Like Meredith said, I figured out how to get a job and look after Ollie at the same time. I was surprised how good it felt to be able to do that. I wasn't completely self-sufficient, I didn't pay rent at Meredith's and I still slept in her shed, but I started to contribute toward bills and food. I worked Tuesday and Saturday nights to begin with. Tuesdays were busy but Saturdays were nearly always fully booked, all one thousand seats. I roamed between the ticket box and the concession stand as the foyer swelled with people. I'd been to the Star before, as an attendee, but there was a different buzz to working there. I liked it better. I felt like I was behind the scenes on a show, or had a backstage pass to a concert. I saw people I knew from time to time, but they never saw me. I existed in a different world to them. Sometimes they looked directly at me, but still, they never saw me.

I raced around the busy theater, directing people in with a flashlight, serving popcorn. Once everyone was inside the movie, I'd often go to the baby area and look at the babies, all lined up. Seeing them, it was hard not to think about the babies of the girls at Orchard House. They would have been lined up like this in the hospital nursery before they were taken home by someone else. None of the girls thought they had a choice. I wished I could go back and tell them they did.

During the movie, if I heard a baby cry, I'd try to settle them for a few minutes before I'd run their number up to the screening room to flash over the screen. Nine times out of ten, I did settle them. Ollie always slept, even then my simple, content boy.

I was watching over the babies one night when a young man came out of the cinema, twenty minutes after the film started. I made my way to the concession stand, where he was headed.

"Just a popcorn, please," he said.

"Small, medium or large?"

The young man blinked at me, looking me full in the face. It took me a moment to place the young man as Tom Goodwin, the plumber who had visited my parents' house a couple of times. According to my father, he was "a good worker." He wasn't a handsome man, but he had clear blue eyes, a good crop of hair, a great smile. He was on the shorter side, and he did nothing to conceal his intrigue at finding me working at a candy bar in Yarraville.

"I know you," he said.

"And I know you." I smiled. "Tom, right?"

He cocked his head. I could actually see the cogs turning in his head.

"What are you doing *here*?"

"What does it look like?"

"I haven't seen you around for a while," he said eventually. I recognized it for what it was: a question. For that exact reason, my first instinct was to be vague in my response. *I've been busy* sprang to my lips as did *I was over in Europe for a while*. But I forced those words away. Suddenly I understood what Meredith had said about the freedom of having nothing to lose.

"I went away to have a baby."

I loved the way Tom didn't try to conceal his surprise. He blinked, long and slow, and then blinked again. He actually took a step back. It was, I am certain, the fact that I admitted it rather than the fact that it happened, that caused his astonishment.

"A boy," I said. "Oliver. He's over there in that basket."

"He's . . here?" To my surprise, Tom walked over to the baby area and peered into Ollie's basket. "This little fella?" He gazed down at him and his face softened. "And . . . your family—"

"They're *thrilled*."

I laughed, and Tom surprised me by laughing back. He had a great laugh. A full-bodied, hearty laugh that came from the well of his stomach and the cavern of his chest.

"So how are you supporting yourself then?"

"I live in a shed in Spotswood, in the backyard of my father's disgraced cousin. I cook and clean for her. And I'm working here for money."

He frowned. "You're kidding?"

"Afraid not. But don't worry about me, I'm doing just fine. Very well, actually."

I glanced at the clock. I'd been talking too long. I had to get things cleaned up and organized before the intermission. I grabbed a popcorn container and made Tom a large one and handed it to him. "That'll be a dollar," I said to him.

He reached into his pocket and pulled out a fistful of crumpled notes, handing the lot to me without even glancing at them.

"You'd better get back in there. You're going to miss the movie."

He jerked slightly, looking over his shoulder as if he'd forgotten where he was. Then he looked back at me and gave me the best smile I'd ever seen. "Problem is, I don't want to miss what's happening out here."

37

Lucy

Wakes are always an interesting affair. Anything that mixes family and alcohol usually is. When I arrive at the Half Moon after Diana's funeral, Ollie is looking more relaxed with a beer in hand, occasionally even chuckling at something someone has said. Football is on the television in the background, which also provides some normality to the abnormal occasion.

Nettie, too, seems more together than at the funeral. Edie takes pride of place in her lap, and Nettie offers her what appears to be a pink lemonade. I'm glad to see her issues with us haven't extended to our children. Say what you want about Nettie, but she was a devoted aunt. I have to love her for that.

Patrick has sunk at least half a dozen beers since I arrived, a good hour after everyone else, and it has to be said, he's looking a bit worse for wear. I suppose I can't blame him. I'd like to throw back a few too, but between chasing the kids around and ordering them to get up from under the tables, there isn't a lot of time. Harriet and Archie have kicked their shoes off and are scampering around on the floors, where the dirt is forming a paste with the spilled drinks. Soon, someone will break a glass, one of the kids will step on it, and we'll be all headed to the hospital. Actually, it would be a relief to get out of here.

"Hey," I say, finding Ollie at the bar. He has the glassiness of a man a few beers in, and he seems somber, but then he has just attended his mother's funeral. "Are you okay?"

Apart from the fact that it's your mum's funeral, your business is failing and the fact that we're financially ruined?

"Actually," he says, "I was just thinking about how bad my eulogy was today."

"It wasn't bad."

He cocks his head. "Come on."

I put my arms around his waist. "Listen. It's not as if she was there to critique it. Just let it go. It was fine."

He opens his mouth to respond but we are interrupted by an elderly couple, coming to say their good-byes. At the same time, Harriet comes to tell me that "Edie wet her pants and Auntie Nettie wants to know if she has spare undies."

"I'll deal with the undies," I say to Ollie.

I follow Harriet through the throng, turning sideways to squeeze past people. Harriet and I come to a clearing on the outside deck where Edie stands, naked, apart from a pair of gold sandals. Tipsy adults smile. *Sweet.* Nettie squats next to her, drying her legs with a wad of paper towels. There's something so maternal about it, it stops me short. I have to remind myself that Edie is *my* daughter, that I'm her mother.

A chink of spoon against glass steals everyone's attention and when I turn around, I see Ollie is standing on a chair. I leave Edie with Nettie and charge back inside. What on *earth*?

"Can I have everyone's attention please?" he is saying as I slip back inside.

A hush goes around the room and I feel my insides squeeze tight. Ollie isn't the type to give impromptu speeches, he is a planner, a practicer, a reader of index cards. I glance around for support, but there is only Nettie, who is still outside dealing with Edie. Patrick is over by the bar.

"Sorry to steal you away from your drinks and conversations," he starts. "I just feel that I didn't quite say everything I wanted to about Mum today."

One by one, people whisper hushed endings to their conversations and give Ollie their full attention. I grab a glass of champagne from a circling waiter and throw it back.

"The fact is, Mum wasn't the warmest and fuzziest person in the world. Actually, she was a pretty hard taskmaster. If there was ever a spider or rodent to kill, guess who we went to? I'll give you a hint, it wasn't Dad."

A gentle chorus of laughter rings through the room. It reassures me a little.

"As kids, whenever we sat down, Mum would always hand us a bag of baby clothes that had been donated and make us sort them into sizes. We'd complain, usually, and she'd tell us that she'd be happier to take away our clothes and make us accept donations from clothing houses and then see if that changed our tune on helping." At this, Ollie's voice starts to wobble. "I remember folding up a tiny white knitted jacket once and putting it on the top of a pile of new-born clothes. Mum noticed it and yanked it out of the pile, saying it was stained. I told her they'd probably still accept it and she said, 'It's not my job to give them what they would accept.'" Ollie does a pitch-perfect Diana impression. "'It's my job to give them what they deserve.'"

He glances at me, and I nod. Perfect.

"Mum could be difficult, but that was part of what made her great. And that's what made her a lifeline to some people."

"Come on, give me a break!"

The voice, coming from the back of the room, over by the bar, is booming and unapologetic. Heads whip around. It isn't hard to find Patrick, a full head and shoulders above the crowd.

"Diana wasn't a 'lifeline,'" he says, "she was a life-*sucker*."

Ollie looks startled. Like most people, he'd been so caught up in his lovely tribute he hadn't seen it coming. I, too, am startled. The crowd shifts to look at Patrick. I start toward him, but the room is full and it is like walking through sludge.

"If we're honest, we'll admit that no one is upset that she's dead, we've just come for the free food and booze. And why not?" Patrick spots me charging toward him through the crowd. "Save yourself the trouble, Lucy, I'm done." He raises his glass. "To Diana. May she rot quickly."

He tips his glass to his mouth and swallows the drink in one mouthful. I glance around for Nettie and find her standing in the corner of the room. A single tear runs down her cheek.

38

Lucy

The past . . .

I snap a photo of Harriet, asleep in her hospital cot. The morning light dapples on her and I feel hyperaware of the preciousness of it. If things had gone differently a few days ago, she may not be here, and I don't take this second chance for granted.

"How is our little angel?" Ingrid asks from the doorway.

Ingrid has been the primary nurse tending to Harriet. A grandmother, she'd proudly told me a few days ago, to a little boy named Felix who is about Harriet's age. It is, perhaps, the reason she'd gone above and beyond for us—even picking me up a latte from her local coffee store on the way in after hearing me tell Ollie I couldn't stand the hospital coffee. Then again, Ingrid seems the type to go above and beyond with everyone.

I put my phone down on the side. "She's fine. Sleeping."

"Do you want me to get a photo of the two of you?"

I think about that for a second. "Actually, I would love that."

I scoot up beside my sleeping daughter and place my head next to hers while Ingrid snaps a picture. The picture is filled with chins and you can see right up my nose and I will cherish it forever.

"Your mother-in-law phoned a moment ago," Ingrid says lightly.

Diana has phoned every day, twice a day. When I didn't answer my cell she started calling the hospital and checking in with the nurses' station. She knows Harriet is going to be okay, I made Ollie text her as soon as we knew. I'm still angry with her, but no one deserves to worry about a child for a second longer than they have to.

I feel Ingrid's eyes on me and I sigh. Ingrid knows, of course, what I did to Diana—everyone in the entire hospital knows about *the assault*. That's what the nurse who had discovered us had called it. An assault. It actually is probably an accurate description of it, though Diana had been quick to refute it, insisting, even after she was taken to emergency on a stretcher, that it was all a private family matter. I had to hand it to her, Diana Goodwin would go to any lengths to avoid making a scene.

"You're a bit of a hero around here, you know," Ingrid says, opening Harriet's chart. "Everyone's wanted to give their mother-in-law a head injury at least once in their life."

"Even you, Ingrid?"

"Especially me! And my daughter-in-law wants to give me one occasionally, I'm sure of it."

"I doubt that," I say. "If I had a mother-in-law like you, Ingrid, I'd be over the moon."

"Ah, you think that now." She smiles. "But I'd get on your nerves after a while. Everyone, given enough time, will get on your nerves if they join your family."

"Why is it that mothers-in-law and daughters-in-law always seem to have issues, and never sons-in-law and fathers-in-law?"

Ingrid scribbles something on the chart. "Sons-in-law and fathers-in-law don't care enough to have issues."

"So we have issues because we care?" I ask.

"We have issues because we care *too much*." Ingrid glances at her watch, then makes another note on her chart. Then she replaces the chart on the end of Harriet's cot. She's in the doorway, about to leave, when she pauses.

"Your mother-in-law has been calling a lot, you know."

"She loves her granddaughter," I say. "I'll give her that."

"Perhaps," Ingrid says. "But you should know that each time I've answered the phone when she's called, the first person she's asked about is you."

When Ollie arrives at the hospital half an hour later, I tell him I have to go. He doesn't ask where, and I'm sure he assumes I want to go home and shower, or change my clothes or get something for Harriet—we have been tag teaming in this way for a week. I let him assume that.

As I drive, I am thinking about what Ingrid said. *We care too much.* I wonder if it's true. If I didn't care, I could go on with my own life, accepting the mother-in-law I have. Like Patrick has. He doesn't like Diana particularly but unless she had done something to irritate him in that particular moment, he is positively undisturbed by this dislike. He doesn't pretend to get along with her, or get upset about it. It doesn't seem to affect him at all. And so, I'm going to forgive Diana. Not because I like her or because I think what she did was forgivable. I'm going to forgive her to release myself. I'm going to give up caring so much.

I pull up in front of Tom and Diana's house, behind Tom's car which is parked in the front—unusual, for a work day. I ring the bell, but no one comes. After a while, I press it again.

It takes a long time for Diana to come to the door, but finally I see her through the glass door.

"Lucy," she says.

I blink. It might be the first time I've seen Diana without any makeup. Her hair is wet and combed straight back over her small, oval head and her entire face, skin, eyelashes, lips appear to be the same wishy-washy beige color. She puts a hand to her chest. "Oh no. Is . . . it Harriet?"

"No, no," I say quickly. "Harriet's fine."

But Diana is shaking. All of her, trembling. I reach out and steady her.

"Diana, Harriet is fine," I say again.

But she continues to shake. I grasp her shoulder and bring her into the house. Something isn't right. She stares at me, her eyes wide and vulnerable. I take her other shoulder, about to ask her what's wrong, when her knees give way. I catch her and lower her to the floor.

"Tom?" I call. "Tom? Are you here?"

"I'm sorry," she says, starting to sob. "I'm sorry, Lucy . . . It's Tom. It's my darling, Tom."

· · ·

"Tom has MND," Diana says. "Motor neuron disease. It's—"

"I know what it is," I say. I remember the ice-bucket challenges a few years back, people dumping ice water over their heads to raise money and awareness for it. Clearly it was successful, as before that I'd never heard of it.

"Tom has suspected something wasn't right for a while, but he kept it to himself. It's all crystal clear in hindsight. His muscle cramps. Weakness. His handwriting is worse than Archie's. His drooling." A tear slides down her cheek, but other than that, she's regained her composure. "I always found it so adorable when he drooled. Little did we know . . ."

Diana and I are sitting in the good room. Diana holds a cushion in her lap and fiddles with the little bits of gold thread that are woven through. "The MND won't affect his intellect, but it will strip him away from his physicality until he is no longer able to express his intellect. Until people are speaking to him like he's a child and he's powerless to tell them that he's not deaf." Another tear slips down her cheek. "But I'm not going to let them do that. No one will speak to him like he's an imbecile. He will have me."

Diana brushes the tear off her cheek and gives a little nod, as if this fact pleases her. And likely, it does. She may not have any control over Tom's illness, but she has control over how he is treated and she's going to make sure he's treated well. For all of her foibles, Diana is someone you want on your side. Perhaps that's the problem. I've never felt like she has been.

"What can I do?" I ask.

Diana gives a hopeless little shrug, the saddest shrug I've ever seen. She blinks slowly, hugging the cushion in her lap to her body. She looks so fragile I want to grab a throw rug and wrap it around her shoulders. I've never wanted to do this to Diana before.

"Diana—" I start, as my phone begins to ring. It's Ollie. "Sorry, I'd better get this. It might be about Harriet."

"Don't tell him, Lucy. Please don't tell him."

Diana looks at me and it's as though her soul has returned to her body, the sharpness has returned to her eyes. She's *on*. It makes me feel sad and also strangely privileged that she let her guard down with me, even just for a few seconds.

"Okay," I say.

She turns her head away as if to give us some privacy.

"Harriet's awake," Ollie says. I hear her babbling in the background and maybe it's the news of Tom's illness but my need to have my daughter in my arms is so fierce it takes my breath away. "I thought you'd want to come."

"I do," I say. "I do want to come. I'll be right there."

"Thank you," Diana says, as I put the phone in my purse. "Tom really wants to be the one to tell the kids."

It's funny hearing her call Ollie and Nettie "kids." But then, perhaps, that's how a mother always thinks of her offspring. I wonder if, perhaps, that's at the root of all our problems.

I sit in Diana and Tom's good room, but this time I'm in on the secret. Nettie and Patrick sit side by side on the overstuffed couch, upright, at attention. Ollie and I sit in the armchairs, facing each other. Diana and Tom sit side by side opposite Patrick and Nettie.

"Can I get anyone a drink?" Diana asks and we all shake our

heads, eager to get to the point of tonight's family meeting. We haven't had a family meeting before, and I know Ollie assumes it's about what happened to Harriet. I haven't been able to tell them otherwise without admitting what Diana told me about Tom, and I don't want to do that. For one thing, I think it's Tom's right to tell his children this. For another, it's the first time I've had Diana's confidence and I'm determined to prove that I can keep it.

I watch Tom, in the armchair, looking for symptoms of his MND. As far as I can see, he is healthy. As for his gentle slur, it's something I've become fond of, and always attributed to the fact that he is usually on the scale between tipsy and drunk.

"All right I won't mince words," he says. "We all know I'm here to tell you something, and you're probably feeling like it's something bad . . . which I'm sorry to say, it is. I've been diagnosed with motor neuron disease, which you've probably heard of. It's the disease everyone was doing that ice-bucket challenge nonsense for a few years back. It's otherwise known as ALS or Lou Gehrig's disease. Anyway, it's a degenerative disease affecting the nerves in the brain and spinal cord that tell your muscles what to do. Eventually the disease will progress to the point that my muscles will weaken, stiffen and waste. I won't walk or talk properly, I won't be able to eat or drink very well, even breathing will be difficult."

Tom speaks quickly and he sounds mildly irritated, but I know it's just because he feels so off-kilter. He's always the one in the family that smooths things over, makes problems go away. It would be killing him to be the one creating problems this time.

"Anyway, it is what it is, and I'll make the best of it," he says. And then, he doesn't say anything.

Nettie's and Ollie's reactions surprise me in that they have precisely no reaction at all. No movement, no sharp intake of breath, just a rhythmic blink, a second or two out of sequence. Patrick brings a hand to his mouth, rests his chin on his thumb.

"Will you die?" Nettie asks, finally.

"I will die, yes. As will you, your brother, your mother, Lucy and Patrick . . . all of us will die. But I will likely be the first one to go. Probably in the next five years. Maybe even in the next year."

Diana reaches for Tom's hand.

"No one lives forever," Tom says, "so I'd like to make the next year count. For me that means lots of time with family. My wife, my children and their spouses . . ." His gaze finds mine. "And my grandchildren, if you'll allow it, Lucy. I am responsible for what happened to Harriet. If she hadn't recovered, I'd never have forgiven myself."

"Of course you can see the kids, Tom. As much as you'd like."

"Dad, I . . ." Ollie sits forward. He appears to wrestle with something, but finally continues. "I know this is early days, but you'll want to get your affairs in order. Your power of attorney, your medical instructions. You'll want to look at succession planning for the business, and a sale to a partner if you want to go that way."

Idly, I wonder how Ollie knows this. It rolls off the tongue, as though he were a wills and estates lawyer rather than a recruiter. Then, suddenly, he looks awkward.

"Also, you'll want to make sure your will is up to date."

"Oh, I think it is too early to start discussing that, hon," I say.

"Everything is in order," Tom says.

Ollie nods. "Can I ask what it states?"

"Ollie!" Diana and I exclaim together. I understand that bad news can bring about unusual emotions. But Ollie is being extraordinarily insensitive.

"There's no secrets to be had here," Tom says. "In the event of my death, everything goes to Diana. If we both go at once, everything goes to you kids and your partners, an even split."

I glance at Ollie. He seems appeased.

"You never expect to have to discuss these things with your family," Tom continues. "Deep down, we all think we're going to live forever. This is, I'll admit, a bit of a rude awakening." Tom tries for a laugh, but his voice cracks.

"Oh, Dad." Ollie goes to Tom's side and puts his arms around him. "I'm sorry, I'm so, so sorry."

Tom leans into Ollie and his eyes close briefly. It's a beautiful moment.

I only wish it had happened *before* they'd discussed the contents of the will.

39

Lucy

The present . . .

It's strange, being back at Tom and Diana's. Gerard gave us strict instructions that we were not permitted to remove anything other than sentimental items, but Nettie and Patrick were here yesterday and things have vanished since then. A vase that had been on display in the main room, for one thing. I can't really say I blame them. With the financial hardship we are in, I could be tempted to pick up a vase or two myself. I'm relieved, though, that Ollie hasn't suggested it. His behavior has been so strange lately—I'm glad to see he is still the man of integrity that I married.

In the library, I watch him open a photo album, flick a few pages, then put it down again without looking at it.

"We don't have to do this all today, you know."

"We have to do it sometime," he says. "Might as well be now."

I take him by the hand and walk him over to the couch and sit beside him. "Ollie. Talk to me."

He closes his eyes, massaging his forehead with thumb and forefinger. "It's just being here, in this house . . . it's weird, right? I can't believe she is gone."

"I can't either."

He opens his eyes, stares right ahead. "I have no parents. That shouldn't freak me out, in my mid-forties, but it does. On top of that, my sister doesn't want anything to do with me." He blinks several times, as if processing this. "You're all I've got, Luce. You, and the kids."

"We're not going anywhere," I tell him.

He looks at me. Nods slowly.

I try to picture what our life will be like now, our new life, now that we are financially ruined. I'll have to get a job. The big kids will have to go to before- and after-school care and Edie will have to go to full-time day care. It will be different, that's for sure. But we're not going anywhere.

Ollie looks at me. "You look different lately. Your clothes aren't so . . . wild."

I look down at my black jeans, gray T-shirt and nude ballet flats. The shirt has a bedazzled picture of the Eiffel Tower on the front, but it's a relatively plain outfit by my standards. I don't even have any hair accessories or adornments in. The only jewelry I'm wearing, in fact, is the necklace Diana left to me.

"My style is . . . evolving," I admit.

Ollie smiles. "This outfit actually reminds me of something Mum would wear."

I smile back. I don't tell him Diana didn't own a pair of jeans, and she would roll over in her grave if she heard anyone suggest that she might wear a bedazzled T-shirt. His point, that I'm favoring plainer, more practical outfits lately is a valid one. Odd as it sounds, Diana *might* have played a role in that.

We go through a few more items before we decide to call it a day. Then, as we are about to get into the car, I hear gravel crunching on the driveway.

"Lucy! Ollie."

We turn in unison. Ahmed and Jones are coming down the driveway toward us. Immediately, I go on high alert.

"Hello," I say uncertainly.

The continue walking toward us. They're not alone. Beside Ahmed is a woman in workout gear whose face is far from friendly. She plants her feet, several meters back from us.

"It was him," she says quietly to Ahmed. "*Him*. Definitely."

Ahmed remains beside the woman, and Jones continues a few paces farther up the driveway, stopping in front us.

"Can we help you?" Ollie says.

"We've just been talking with the neighbors again," Jones says, "trying to ascertain who was the last person to see your mother before she died." She glances back over her shoulder at the woman in the activewear, the woman who is looking at Ollie, but slightly south of his face, as though she's nervous to look him in the eye. Nervous to look at *Ollie*.

"It was him," the woman says again, louder now.

"What was him?" I ask her.

"I live across the road," she says. She seems happy enough to look *me* in the face. "I was headed out for a run last week, the same day

Diana was killed, and I saw *him*," she jabs a thumb at Ollie "walk through the gates."

"Were you here, Ollie?" Jones asks. "The afternoon your mother was killed?"

Ollie shakes his head, baffled-looking. "No."

"You *were*. You were . . . wearing navy trousers. And a checked shirt." The woman nods deeply, as if becoming more convinced herself. "Blue and white!"

"You must be getting him mixed up with someone else," I say. "Or maybe you saw Ollie here another day?"

Both are reasonable explanations. Besides, Ollie's not particularly distinctive looking. Tall, medium build, brown hair. It would be easy to discount this woman's account of things, and that's exactly what I do. Until a memory flashes into my mind. It's Ollie, arriving home from work the day Diana died.

He's wearing navy trousers and a blue-and-white checked shirt.

40

Lucy

The past . . .

"Shhh," I say to the kids as we enter Diana and Tom's house. Of course it doesn't make the blindest bit of difference. It's impossible to silence kids' plastic shoes against marble, and Archie and Harriet scamper loudly through the place, feet slapping as they go.

We let ourselves into the house these days. I get the feeling Diana isn't delighted about this, but her life is about practical matters now that she is caring for Tom around the clock, and it's not practical for her to be answering the door all the time.

I follow the kids, hauling baby Edie in her car seat through the main floor. Everything has been moved onto this level since Tom has been in his wheelchair. I like the house more like this actually. With the extra furniture down here, the house is filled out nicely and has a cozy feel it didn't have before. Also, everything is closer together. You can call out and pretty much anyone in the house can hear you.

"It's us," I say as we enter the back room.

Tom's wheelchair is pushed up to the table. Diana is beside him, reading the newspaper aloud, but she pauses to hug Archie and Harriet, who throw themselves at her with abandon.

"Give Papa a hug," she instructs them.

They look at her uncertainly and she nods. *Go on.* They're a little frightened of him now. His hands are gnarled and his head is bent. He can be difficult to understand, but he is determined to keep talking. I think this is wonderful but the kids get frustrated by it or lose interest, or worse, say something rude.

"Papa's spitting," Harriet will say. Or "Why is Papa's head like that?"

"Papa can hear you," I say, in a false jovial voice.

But Diana doesn't gloss over it like I do. A couple of weeks ago, she asked Archie and Harriet to imagine how frustrating it would be to want to say something to people when no one would listen. Archie came to me a few minutes later and told me he would always listen to Papa, and to his credit, he's been very patient ever since. Harriet hasn't been quite so empathetic, telling me she doesn't understand why he wouldn't just watch TV and not bother talking to anyone. I vacillate between accepting that she's just a child and feeling responsible for the fact that one day Harriet will be out there in the world, inflicting herself on anyone who'll listen.

It won't be long now. Tom has been in and out of the hospital for months, with upper respiratory tract infections, breathing difficulties, pain and discomfort. Diana is constantly in motion, feeding Tom, shifting him in his seat, giving him medication. She phones doctors and nurses, gives instructions, makes arrangements. It is as though she's become an extension of him—he just has to look at her and she's out of her chair, tending to him.

Tom's illness has put a temporary halt on the family issues. We've all been working well together as a team—taking him to appointments, dropping off meals, driving across town to pick up various pieces of equipment designed to make him a little more comfortable. But everyone is brokenhearted. I am brokenhearted. I can't fathom this family without him.

I watch Diana, intermittently wiping the corners of his mouth. She says something to him and his eyes crinkle up and his lips twist, and I know he's trying to smile. The rest of us, we'll be brokenhearted after Tom dies, but it will be worse for Diana. I'm not sure what will happen to her. I don't know how she'll go on.

41

Lucy

The present . . .

"Is Ollie under arrest?" Nettie asks me.

She's on my living room floor surrounded by Legos, while Patrick engages the kids in an epic game of tag that involves pools of lava and cushions you have to stand on to stop your feet from getting burned. When the lady in activewear identified Ollie as being at Diana's house the day she died, and Jones said she wanted to talk to Ollie back at headquarters, I called Nettie to see if she could help with the kids. (I never would have asked her a favor for myself, but I knew Nettie would be there for the kids and I certainly needed her help.)

"No, he's just answering some questions. He'll be back in a little while."

But in fact, I have no idea if this is true. Ollie wasn't under arrest when he left with Jones and Ahmed, but for all I know he is now. And I don't know if he'll be back in five minutes or five years. The only thing I *do* know is that he was wearing a blue-and-white checked shirt the day Diana died . . . and that he came home from work early even though he wasn't unwell.

Now, I'm wondering why.

Nettie's face is drawn and worried. Nettie is the younger sister, younger by six years, but she has always seemed older. And despite our issues, I know she loves her brother.

"Are you okay?" I ask her, and her eyes immediately begin to well. I sweep the Legos to the side and kneel on the floor beside her.

"I'm sorry." She produces a tissue from her shirtsleeve and dabs at her eyes. "I don't know what's wrong with me . . . there's just a lot going on."

I hover awkwardly beside her. Once I would have hugged Nettie, but as we are no longer in that place, I place a reassuring hand on her shoulder instead. I'm caught off guard when she throws her arms around my neck in response.

"Shhh," I say. "It's all right."

But it's not all right. None of it is. My heart bleeds for Nettie. Even without everything else going on . . . I still remember the rawness of losing my mother like it was yesterday. It occurs to me that Nettie and I have this in common now. She is older than I was when Mum died, obviously, but I doubt there is a loss in the universe more profound than a daughter losing her mother.

"Sorry," Nettie says, sitting back and wiping her face.

"Please. Don't apologize."

"It's just . . . being here. The kids. The toys . . . it's just hard, you know. It just reminds me of . . . what I'm not going to have."

"What you're not going to . . . ?" It takes me a moment to understand. She's not upset about her mother. She's not even upset about Ollie. She's upset about . . . her fertility.

I shift away from her.

"I thought you were upset about your mother. About Ollie being called in for questioning."

"Oh, everyone's been called in!" Nettie waves her hand dismissively. "It's no big deal."

"No big *deal*? Didn't the police tell you about the cushion? Didn't they tell you they think someone might have smothered Diana?"

Nettie starts picking up Legos, putting them into the basket absently. "At the stage of life I'm in," she says, her voice cracking, "I thought there'd be Legos all over *my* floor. Scribble on the walls. I thought I'd be spending my weekends at school carnivals and ballet lessons. You have everything I want, Lucy."

I look at her. Really look. Physically, she's right in front of me, but emotionally she is somewhere else. It occurs to me that she's been somewhere else for a while.

"I really thought you'd help me," she says, then dissolves into tears.

"Nettie . . ." I sense movement in the corner of the room and Patrick steps forward. Something gives me the idea that he's been standing there a while.

"I think I should take Nettie home," he says.

Patrick gathers up Nettie's bag and her coat and for the first time I wonder how it must be for him, living with Nettie's baby obsession. That kind of thing had to take its toll on a person.

"Why don't you both stay here a while?" I say. "I could make . . . some tea?"

Nettie gets to her feet, her gaze miles away.

"Patrick's right," she says robotically. "We should go."

42
_____

Lucy

The past . . .

"Head on inside," I say. "There are refreshments in the back room."

I stand at the grand double doors of Tom and Diana's home, ferrying mourners inside in small groups. Tom's funeral was at St. Joan of Arc, the church on the corner, so most of the guests decided to walk down to the house, even some of the elderly ones. The day is crisp and bright, with beating sunshine that everyone suggests is Tom's doing, and maybe it is. If there is an afterlife, Ollie had said in his eulogy, Tom would have certainly made an entrance, demanding the best of everything, including the sunshine.

Tom had died the previous Friday of an upper respiratory infection. He'd wanted to be at home, and Diana had fought hard for him to have his wish, but in the end they'd both had to accept that it wasn't to be. His disease had progressed quickly, faster than anyone expected, and for the last few months he'd been unable to breathe unassisted or do anything for himself. Thankfully he had Diana to do it all for him.

Edie has been on Nettie's hip most of the day, and the older kids tear around the house as though it's a birthday party rather than a wake. Even Archie, who'd been quite overcome with emotion in the church, seems more relaxed now. He's removed his tie, which he'd wanted to wear and borrowed from Ollie, and now he's chasing Harriet between the legs of the guests.

"Archie!" I shout-whisper. "Why don't you go play upstairs? You can even turn on the television, if you'd like."

Within seconds, both of them are gone.

Inside the house, waiters circulate with platters of food. Along one wall, a long table had been set up with sandwiches and soft drinks, cakes and wine. Somehow, Diana has managed to get the details exactly right, so it is welcoming but not festive, somber but not depressing. Tom would have been pleased.

My role, as handed to me by Diana, is to welcome guests as they arrive. There's not a lot to it. People come in, talking about how it was a lovely service and they say they're sorry. I welcome them and point out where they can find themselves a drink and a chicken sandwich. A year ago, I'd have assumed that Diana had given me this role to keep me out of her hair, or because I wasn't capable of much more. But today, knowing she specifically gave me this post, I feel a strong sense of commitment to it.

From my post at the door, I catch glimpses of Diana every so often, standing on the edges of circles, accepting people's condolences. She does so with the utmost composure and grace. Diana managed the funeral details single-handedly, with the exception of the eulogy, which she had delegated to Ollie and he'd done a wonderful job of it. I'd looked over at Diana during the funeral and found her sitting very still and I had a sudden urge to slide over to her in my pew, perhaps place a hand over hers. Now, I regret that I didn't.

"Come in," I say, as a new gaggle of mourners step through the gate. I take the arm of a woman who must be in her nineties and support her weight as she climbs the three steps to the house. She smiles at me and says, "Thank you, dear."

It makes me think of my mother. *Lucy, dear. Dinner's ready.* It had been a long time since someone called me dear. I'd forgotten how nice it felt to be dear to someone.

"Excuse me, ma'am."

When I turn, a waiter in a grey jacket is standing before me. "I can't seem to find Mrs. Goodwin."

I glance around. The room has filled. The hum of chatter has risen and there are small plates of half-eaten canapés on tables and mantels. Diana is nowhere to be seen. "Oh . . . well, what is it you need?"

"I'd like to check if we should start serving coffee and tea?"

"I don't see why not." I glance at the front path and decide it's safe to leave my station. "I'll see if I can find Diana."

I search the ground floor of the house. I find Nettie on the back patio, Edie still clamped to her hip.

"Lucy, where is the diaper bag? Edie is ready for a nap and I need to find her pacifier and her lambie."

"It's in the bedroom at the top of the stairs. The portacot is already set up in there. Have you seen your mum?"

Nettie shakes her head. "But Uncle Dave is looking for her, he and Auntie Rose are leaving, they want to say good-bye."

Nettie takes Edie up the stairs and I keep pushing through the crowd, scanning the faces. Ollie is in the front room, listening to his cousin Pete reenact a story that appears to involve a donkey. "Lucy!" he calls out. "Where's Mum? Everyone is asking."

"On it."

I take the stairs to the second floor without much hope—Diana and Tom haven't used this floor for a year. The door to the first bedroom—the one where I'd set up the cot for Edie—is closed so I creep past. I peer into the next room where Harriet and Archie are spread out on the bed, watching the screen, their eyes and mouths wide open. The door to the next bedroom, Tom and Diana's old bedroom, is closed too. I hesitate in front of it, then tap lightly.

"Diana?"

When there's no response, I walk inside. I haven't been inside this room before and it is, quite frankly, ridiculous. There's a hallway, a sitting room, the actual bedroom (though Tom and Diana have been sleeping downstairs for over a year now), and a bathroom the size of our old worker's cottage. Finally, behind the last door is a walk-in closet that would make Carrie Bradshaw weep, complete with shaker cabinetry and a ladder on a pulley that could slide from wall to wall. An ottoman is in the center of the room, and Diana is sitting on it, her head in her hands.

"Diana?"

She looks up. She's crying, but her face has not swelled or become

red. No eye makeup has smudged. Diana even *cries* with composure.

"Are you all right?"

There's something about her, like this, so totally vulnerable. She
gives me a pathetic excuse for a shrug, as if her shoulders were ultimately too heavy to lift. Then she sighs. "There's only so many
times you can say the same thing. *Yes, it was a lovely service. Yes, the
sun is beautiful. Yes, Tom would have loved this.* I'd reached my quota,
so I came in here, to hide."

I nod.

She looks around the space. "It's nonsensical, all of this, isn't it?
This room was Tom's idea, obviously. I barely have enough clothes
to fill that cabinet." She points to one of the dozen cabinets in the
space. "Tom was always so excessive. More is more. It's bizarre that
I didn't hate him, isn't it?" She laughs, not waiting for me to respond.
"I should probably move to a smaller place now. It makes no sense,
me staying here alone. But now that he's gone, I'm not sure I can
leave. He's part of this house. I feel him here."

"I feel him here too," I say.

Diana looks at me properly. Her lips press together and for an
excruciating moment, I think she's going to lose it. Her lips bend at
the edges, her chin puckers. But then, at the eleventh hour, she regains control. "Everyone is looking for me, I suppose," she says in a
freakishly normal voice. "Is that why you came up here? To get me?"

She doesn't move yet, but I can see she's readying herself. She'll
wipe her face and straighten her blouse and she'll go down there
and do what she needs to. That, after all, is what Diana does. But
she shouldn't have to, not today. And so I shake my head.

"No one's even noticed you weren't there," I say. "Everything is under control. You stay up here for as long as you need."

I spend the afternoon talking to people I've never met, taking donations for the MND foundations. (Diana had requested people make donations in lieu of flowers, and while I don't think she'd meant in cash, I end up with an envelope stuffed with enormous amounts of cash. I make a mental note to figure out how to donate it later.)

I sign for the caterer, and open the back gates when it's time for them to leave, and then I stand at the drinks area and act as a barmaid myself. Patrick and Nettie have had far too much to drink, and when Nettie comes back for another wine I make her a cup of tea instead, though I doubt she'll drink it.

By seven P.M., the kids are all asleep upstairs.

By eight P.M., people are hungry again and I order pizzas.

Diana is still in the walk-in closet, as far as I know. I've told everyone that she's not feeling well and headed off to bed early and while I hoped people would take this as a hint to leave, they don't seem to be getting it.

At ten P.M., I make a tray of sandwiches and send them around. Nettie is flat-out drunk and Patrick is in a similar state. Ollie is comparatively sober, and once Pete and the rest of his cousins leave, he comes to give me a hand with Nettie.

"Have a sandwich, Nettie," I tell her. "And shall I make you another cup of tea?"

She shakes her head sullenly. "I want wine."

"I think you've had enough, Nets," Ollie says. "Anyway, we're all out of wine."

"Trust Mum to cheap out on drinks at her own husband's funeral," she slurs. I try again to give her a sandwich, roast beef and horseradish, but she pushes it away. "She's not even down here talking to people! You'd think she'd be a little more respectful of Dad's memory. She'll sell the house next, just you wait. Then it will be like Dad was never here."

"I don't think she will," I try.

"She *will*," Nettie says. "I know my mother. She'll probably leave her entire estate to the Lost Dogs' Home."

I walk away from them, toward the kitchen. I need to unload the dishwasher and Nettie is in no state to talk anyway. I think of Diana up there in that huge room. I wonder if she's moved since I left her. I make her a plate of sandwiches and a cup of tea, and then I head up to her room, let myself in. She's in the bed now, but her eyes are open. She stares at the wall.

"Most people have left," I say, resting the plate and mug on her side table. "Patrick and Nettie are still here, but I'll order them an Uber. The house is tidy, more or less, but I'll come back and help you vacuum and mop tomorrow." Diana stares at me, through me. "There's a sandwich and a cup of tea here, in case you feel like it."

I wait, but she doesn't respond, so I turn and walk back down the hallway. I'm just letting myself out when I hear the faint words: "Thank you, dear."

43

Diana

The past . . .

It was Tom who insisted that Ollie never know he wasn't his father. Initially, I'd disagreed with him, but Tom had been adamant.

"I don't think we should lie to him, Tom. You shouldn't lie to children."

"People always say that. But why should it be a blanket rule? Surely it should be more of a risk/benefit analysis? By not telling Ollie, we'd be risking him finding out later and blaming us for his missing out on a relationship with his biological father who, may I add, never wanted him to exist in the first place. But what about the benefits of *not* telling him? Ollie would believe he was born into a family with two parents that loved each other and wanted him. He'd believe he had a full biological sister. He'd have all that well-adjustedness that children from two-parent families have. Why should we deny him that, just so he can't blame us later? After all, what are parents for if not to blame for your life's troubles?"

Tom had been so immovable that ultimately I'd gone along with his wishes. His logic may not have added up but if he was willing to carry the secret to his deathbed for the sake of my son's adjustment, I didn't see how I was in a position to argue. It was the decision a father would make, I figured.

So I let him make it.

Tom's not here.

I've spent so long trying not to be weak that I'd forgotten how wonderful it feels. For as long as I could remember, I've had to be strong for my family. And being strong has its payoffs. It makes you feel powerful, like you can face anything and survive. It's the reason I've lived my life the way I have, working hard, not wallowing, not accepting weakness. But power is overrated. And being weak—and wallowing—is surprisingly lovely.

Tom's not here.

I lie on the downstairs sofa and stare into the unlit fireplace. The cleaner comes and clears it out on Tuesdays and Thursdays and today is a Wednesday, which is a relief. I might cancel the cleaner. I can clean the house myself.

"Don't be ridiculous!" Tom says in my mind. But it's not ridiculous. I'd always found the cleaners to be more of a hindrance than a help, to be honest. To me, cleaner day always meant a furious whip around to ensure I wouldn't be deemed a pig, followed by a need to

make myself scarce because being home, twiddling my thumbs, while some (invariably) foreign girl worked up a sweat scrubbing unspeakable things from my husband's en suite toilet was just too awful to bear. Tom didn't share my worries about cleaners. If he was home, he'd have languished on the couch, newspaper and coffee in hand. Once, I recall watching him lift one foot, then the other, as the girl vacuumed under his boots. He winked at her and she chuckled. Only Tom could get away with that.

Tom's not here.

I'm not lonely. There are people I could call to keep me company. Ollie would come, I know that. He'd leave the office in a heartbeat and come straight over, delighting in the opportunity to do a good deed for his old mum. This is probably the reason his business is failing—his priorities are out of whack. He needs to stay at work and make a living to support his wife and family.

Nettie might come if I asked—unless she was doing something related to making a baby. My position in her food chain is high, but not highest, which is exactly as it should be. Besides, I have the feeling she has her own issues. Since the sighting of Patrick in Daylesford, I've heard more whispers. Someone spotted him in Bright, someone else in Albury. Patrick, as it turns out, is a busy man. Once, I'd have confronted him, asked him what he had to say for himself. Now, I can barely find the will to get out of bed.

I could call Kathy or Liz or Jan. They've all been calling and texting, offering to drop off meals or take me out. Liz did manage to convince me to come to the Baths for drinks a couple of days ago, but I still haven't quite recovered. The normality of it was simply too much and I am not ready for normal yet. Tom is dead. I don't care about your daughter-in-law or your fight with your husband or the funny story about your bladder-control issues and the dog park. I don't care about any of it.

Because *Tom's not here.*

I miss the feel of him. Even a week ago, when Tom was barely alive, I could still reach out and touch him. He was always physically warm, as well as the other type. His warmth was his superpower. People wanted him to lead them. Friends wanted to be around him. Our children loved him best.

I loved him best.

Mothers aren't supposed to say that. But it's the truth. I was born to love Tom Goodwin.

The doorbell rings. I ignore it. This couch feels like a life raft; the outside world is shark-infested waters. I grab the throw rug and pull it around my shoulders, hoping that sleep comes and carries me through until evening, when I can finally change into my pajamas and slide into the comforting blackness of evening. I might have some toast and a cup of tea, and put something on the television to take the edge off the silence as I rattle about in this big old place. Sometimes, at night, I pretend that Tom is still here. I pretend that I'm up and about, ready to stretch out another cramp, or give him another sip of water. Those moments we shared in the wee hours of the morning feel so unimaginably luxurious now, those stolen moments, both of us against the world.

"I'll be right there, my love," I whisper into the empty house. "You'll feel better in a moment."

The doorbell rings again.

"You get it, Tom," I whisper, and close my eyes.

44

Lucy

The present . . .

It's dark when I hear the key in the lock. Nettie and Patrick have left, the kids are asleep and I'm on the couch, listening to nothing, staring at nothing.

"Ollie? Is that you?"

I hear keys drop into the bowl and then he appears in the living room. He flops onto the sofa, rests his head back onto the cushion and closes his eyes.

"What happened?" I ask.

He keeps his eyes closed. "They questioned me."

"About what?"

"Everything."

"Ollie—"

He opens his eyes. "Honestly, they questioned me about *every-thing*. What I was doing the day Mum died, my relationship with her. They asked about my relationship with Nettie, my relationship with you. My business."

I frown. "Your *business*? Why do they care about that?"

"Well, clearly they knew things weren't going so well. They had all our profit and loss statements. Debt is a pretty big motivation to kill someone."

"But you didn't profit from her death!"

"But I didn't *know* I wouldn't profit . . . this is something Jones kindly pointed out."

"She was going to tell you."

He looks over at me. "What?"

"I mean . . . she must have been. Surely Diana would tell you something like that."

Ollie shrugs. "I honestly have no idea." A frown touches his forehead. "I saw Eamon while I was there. He was being questioned too."

"About your mother's death?"

"I guess so. Who knows?" Ollie sinks back against the couch, defeated. "Lucy, can I ask you something?"

"Yes."

"Do you think I killed Mum?"

I look at him, every part of him so achingly familiar—at the angles of his face, his devoted brown eyes, the curve of his chest. "No. But I do think you are lying about something. And I want you to tell me what it is."

45

Lucy

The past . . .

I've never been one to believe in fate, or "having a feeling," but as I drive along Beach Road, I have a sudden urge to call in on Diana. In fact, I make the decision so quickly I nearly take out a cyclist on the inside lane and end up waving profusely as he shakes his fist at me.

"Sorry," I mouth, and he gives me the finger.

I turn into Diana's driveway. She won't like me turning up unannounced like this, but ever since Tom's funeral I can't seem to get her out of my mind. She must be lonely in this big house, all alone. I'd asked Ollie to call her a couple of times, and he had. "She sounded all right," he'd reported each time. "A bit flat, maybe, but that's to be expected."

And it *was* to be expected. That didn't mean she couldn't use a friend. If that was even what I was.

I press the doorbell. When there's no movement inside I try the door and find it open. "Hello?" I call out. "Diana? It's Lucy."

I find her in the den, horizontal on the couch.

"Diana?" I say, but she doesn't so much as lift her head from the pillow.

And that's when I realize. Something is very, very wrong.

Diana stares out the passenger window of my car, trance-like. She's wearing her normal "uniform," navy slacks, white blouse, pearls— but her clothes look rumpled, like she wore them yesterday and left them on the floor before putting them on again. She's also wearing black sneakers instead of nude pumps or ballet flats, and her hair is flat on one side (presumably the side she slept on) and she hasn't bothered to fluff it up. She hasn't said a word since she got in, not even to comment on the biscuit crumbs that I wiped off the seat before she sat down.

"Are you okay, Diana?" I ask, when we stop at the traffic light. She's staring at the beach side of the road, at the kite surfers zipping along the horizon at Brighton beach, but I get the feeling she isn't seeing any of it.

"I'm fine," she says when enough time has passed that I'm about to repeat myself. I'd offered to call Ollie ("No, he'll be too busy at work") and Nettie ("All she's worried about lately is babies!") but it appears she's happy enough for me to be around. She says she's not ill, but she's clearly not well. And so I'm taking her to see her family doctor, Dr. Paisley.

But when I pull into the parking lot, Diana still doesn't move.

"All right," I say in a faux jovial voice that makes me cringe at myself. "Here we are."

Finally she moves, but slowly, like a much older woman. She goes straight to the waiting room and sits down, leaving me to report to the desk. This is not the Diana I know. She's been sad since Tom died, but today she seems almost childlike. She's much easier to deal with this way, admittedly. But I don't want to "deal" with her. It's a shock seeing someone so in control become so . . . helpless.

I report to the desk and then I sit beside her and wait. Diana takes the magazine I offer her but doesn't open it. I don't open mine either. When her name is called, a few minutes later, I turn to her. "Would you like me to come in with you?"

She shrugs, which I take as a yes.

Dr. Paisley appears to be in her midfifties, plump and smiley, dressed in a brightly colored kaftan. Apparently Diana has been seeing her for years.

"Hello," she says, sitting at her desk. She swivels her seat to face us and stretches her hand out to me. "I'm Rosie. Nice to meet you." She looks back at Diana. "I heard about Tom, Diana. I'm so sorry for your loss."

"Thank you."

"What can I do for you today?"

I look at Diana who looks at me. Finally she sighs. "Well, I haven't been feeling myself since Tom died. Which, I imagine, is to be expected. But Lucy wanted me to come and see you."

Dr. Paisley's eyes touch mine for a second. "You're right, no one feels themselves for a while after losing a partner. Sometimes a long while. But we need to be keeping an eye on your health through this period, so Lucy was right to bring you in."

Diana shrugs. "Good then."

"How has your sleep been?"

"Broken."

"Have you been doing things you normally do? Catching up with friends, seeing your grandchildren?"

"I had drinks with the girls at the Baths last week."

"And how was that?"

Diana looks out the window. "It was all right, I suppose."

As we chat, Rosie wraps a blood pressure strap around Diana's arm and the machine starts pumping it up. Diana barely notices.

"Has your mood been low in general?" Dr. Paisley asks her.

"You could say that."

"Any issues with memory?"

"I don't remember," Diana says, deadpan, and I chuckle.

Rosie asks a few more questions, nodding at each answer as though it makes perfect sense.

"Well," she says finally, "I think it might be a good idea to do some blood tests."

Diana raises an eyebrow. "Blood tests for what?"

"Several things. Anemia. Thyroid. Plus the usual standard things." She types into her computer and a blue referral paper spits out of her printer. "But from what you've said, Diana, there's no question in my mind that you're suffering from depression. And so, I have to ask . . . have you had any thoughts about suicide?"

Diana doesn't answer. After a moment, Dr. Paisley's eyes move to me.

"Would you prefer if we talked without your daughter in the room, Diana? Sometimes it's easier to be frank if—"

"I don't need to speak privately," Diana said. "No, I haven't thought about suicide."

"Good. Good."

Dr. Paisley prints out a referral for a good psychologist and prescribes some antidepressant medication, and we make an appointment to come back in a week. It's not until we get out of there that it occurs to me that the doctor called me Diana's daughter. And Diana didn't correct her.

46

Lucy

The present . . .

"Ollie," I say as the landline starts ringing. "The day your mother died. Were you at her house?"

He sits forward, resting his hands on his knees, and takes a deep breath. "I was."

"Why?" I say, a moment before the more important question comes. "And why didn't you tell me?"

"I wanted to."

"Then why didn't you?"

The phone keeps ringing, a loud, shrill interruption. I want to pull the damn thing out of the wall.

"I'll just answer it," Ollie says, walking over to the phone.

"Ollie, no! Just leave—"

But he's already snatching up the receiver. "Hello?"

I swear under my breath.

"It's Ollie." He's quiet for a moment, then his eyes find mine. "Yes. Just a minute." He holds the phone out to me. "It's Jones."

"For me?" I feel a pinch of worry as I take the phone. "Lucy speaking?"

"Lucy, it's Detective Jones. Ahmed and I need to speak to you as a matter of urgency." Jones's voice sounds clipped. "Do you think you could come down to the station?"

"What for?" I say. I want to say that I've had enough of the police calling at ridiculous hours of the night, hauling Ollie or me down to the station. I want to tell Jones that we have little children who are asleep, and that unless I'm under arrest, she'll have to wait until the morning. But I don't say any of this. Because I have a feeling my ability to be outraged may just have been compromised.

"We want to talk to you about an organization called VEI. It stands for Voluntary Euthanasia International. We've received information that indicates your mother-in-law was a member of this organization . . . and we have reason to believe that you have knowledge of this."

I tell her I'll be there as soon as I can.

47

Lucy

The past . . .

When I arrive home after Diana's doctor's appointment, Patrick and Nettie are pulling up out front.

"Hi," I say, emerging from the car. "This is a surprise."

"We called Ollie," Nettie says. "He said we could come on over."

"Oh. Well, good. Actually, I'm glad you're here."

"Us too," Nettie says, oddly chipper. Patrick, to the contrary, seems a little down. He takes his time locking up the car, then slopes up the path a few paces behind us.

"How has your day been?" Nettie asks.

I let them in with my key. "Actually it's been a little strange. Which is why I'm glad you're here. I need to talk to you about Diana."

We walk into the kitchen and living area where Ollie is standing at the fridge cracking a beer. "G'day everyone," he says. "Beer, Patrick?"

"Mum?" Nettie says to me. "What about Mum?"

"Yes, what about Mum?" Ollie says.

The kids, in front of the TV in their PJs, look up, then quickly down again.

"Have they been fed?" I ask Ollie.

"Chicken nuggets, peas and corn," he says proudly. "Wine for you, ladies?"

"Sure," I say.

"I'm fine," Nettie says.

Ollie holds out a beer to Patrick, which he accepts and opens in record time. I wonder if everything is okay with him, but I'm too preoccupied with Diana to spend too much time thinking about it.

"Why don't we go into the dining room to get away from little ears?" I suggest. "And I'll tell you what's going on with Diana."

As I clear the clutter from the dining room table, I notice Nettie giving Patrick a look—somewhere between a smile and a wince. I feel a little dance inside. She's pregnant, I realize. She must be pregnant.

"So . . . do you guys have anything to tell us?" I ask, when we're all sitting. Nettie's smile indicates that she does, but she shakes her head.

"No, no, you first. Tell us about Mum."

"Okay," I say. "Actually I dropped in to visit her today."

There's a short, loaded silence. Even Patrick stares at me like I have two heads. "You dropped in to visit *Mum*?" Ollie says.

Admittedly it is not the kind of thing I usually do. Still I'm taken aback by everyone's level of shock.

"Well . . . we've hardly seen her since Tom died, we've barely even *heard* from her. I was worried! And it turns out, I was right to be. She looks like she's been sleeping in her clothes, not eating properly. I took her to the doctor, just to get her looked at."

Ollie puts down his beer. "What did the doctor say?"

"She's had some blood tests, but she's most likely depressed. She was given a prescription for antidepressants. The doctor also recommended exercise and keeping some sort of routine. And I thought we could all take turns taking her out, bringing her food, that kind of thing."

"Good idea," Ollie says.

"Sure," Nettie says. "Yes, why not."

But Nettie seems distracted. Jittery. Her eyes bounce around the room the way the kids' eyes do when they arrive at someone's house for a playdate and they can't decide which toy to play with first. It's distracting.

"Is everything all right, Nettie?"

"Well, actually . . . Patrick and I *do* have something we'd like to discuss with you." She beams at Patrick, who smiles back a little less enthusiastically.

"You're pregnant!" Ollie exclaims.

Nettie's beam dims a little. "Well, no. Not yet. But that is what we wanted to discuss with you. The thing is, my fertility issues are multilevel. It's not just the polycystic ovaries, it's also my ovum and my uterus. Give me a fertility problem, and I have it." Her laugh is a thin, empty titter. "Our doctor told us this week that our best chance we have for conceiving a child is using a donor egg, and a surrogate."

I take a sip of my wine, drop my gaze.

"It's not how we imagined becoming parents obviously. The baby wouldn't be biologically related to me, but it would be related to Patrick and it would have been conceived to be ours. I think this is our best chance at having a baby."

"Wow," Ollie says. His expression says he doesn't know if this is good news or not. I, on the other hand, am fairly certain it is *not*. "So, you guys are going to do it? Use an egg donor and surrogate?"

"Well that's where it gets complicated." Nettie winces slightly. "We'd like to but egg donation and surrogacy is only allowed in Australia for altruistic reasons so we can't pay anyone. Someone would have to volunteer to do it—"

"Can't you go overseas?" Ollie interrupts. "I saw a documentary about people going to India to do this? Or the United States?"

"That's an option," Nettie says. "But it would be very expensive. More importantly, the baby would be so far away from us while it was in utero. We wouldn't be able to go to any scans, or check on the mother's health, maybe not even be there for the birth, if the mother goes into labor early. Also, we don't understand the health system over there. How do we know their systems are reliable?"

Patrick still hasn't said a word. Admittedly it would be hard to when Nettie is saying *so many* words.

"So what are you going to do?" Ollie asks.

Ollie still has no idea. He must be the only one. I take another very large sip of my wine and force myself to swallow.

"She wants me to do it," I say.

Nettie looks at me. She's cautiously excited but trying to keep it under wraps. She takes a clear plastic bag out of her handbag and places it on the table between us.

"I have some information here," she says. I see the words BE-COMING A SURROGATE printed on the front of a purple brochure, next to a picture of a headless, pregnant body. "It's actually a pretty straightforward process."

Ollie looks at Nettie, blinking wildly; a deer in the headlights. "You want *Lucy* to donate an egg? To be your surrogate?"

Nettie keeps her gaze on me. "I know I have no right to ask."

"You have the right to ask . . ." I say. "But—"

Nettie sits forward in her chair, her hands folded on the table in almost a businesslike fashion. I get the feeling she is prepped and ready to refute any argument I might have. I feel sweat bloom under my arms.

"Wait," Ollie says. "You do want Lucy to donate an egg? And carry the baby? So it would be Lucy's child and . . . Patrick's?"

"No," Nettie says. Her nervous energy seems to have abated now and she is oddly calm. "It would be mine and Patrick's."

"But," Ollie is stuck on this point, and for once, I agree with him, "biologically, it would be Lucy's?"

"Yes," Nettie admits, looking at me. "I don't want to put you on the spot, Lucy, but . . . can you tell me what you think about this idea?"

I push back in my chair, blinking slowly. "I mean . . . it's a little out of the blue, Nettie. Obviously I'd need to think about it."

"Of course," Nettie says, nodding. "Of course you do. But . . . maybe you could share your *initial* reaction?"

"She said she needs to think about it!" Patrick says, uncharacteristically gruff. "Give the woman a break!"

In contrast to Nettie's businesslike body language, Patrick is almost sullen looking. He sits back in his chair. His arms are crossed and his chin is lowered, almost to his chest.

"Nettie, my initial reaction is shock," I tell her. "There's a lot to think about. Ollie and I would have to talk about it—"

"So it *is* a possibility? It *is* something you would consider?" Nettie squeezes her eyes closed and pumps her fists as if making a wish.

"Honestly?" I say. "I don't think it is."

Nettie's eyes open, but her gaze remains lowered.

"I'm sorry. I've thought about this before, in a philosophical way and . . . I just couldn't do it. After all, it would be my child—"

"Half your child," Nettie corrects weakly.

"There's no such thing as half-children. It would be mine as much as Archie and Harriet and Edie are mine. I'm sorry, but I couldn't conceive a child, carry it to term and then give it away. I just couldn't. Even for you."

"You won't even think about it? For a few days? Sleep on it?"

"I could," I say. "But my answer would be the same."

Nettie rises to her feet, pushing her chair back hard enough to hit the wall behind it. "Nettie," I say. "Nettie, I'm sorry."

Patrick puts a hand to his face, smoothing it across his forehead. I can't tell if it's a gesture of sadness or relief. I can tell what the expression on Nettie's face is though, without a shadow of a doubt.

Hatred.

48

Diana

The past . . .

Ending your own life, peacefully and painlessly.

I type the words into the Google browser and hit enter. I can't remember the last time I used this damn computer, but it must have been a while ago, because the mouse has run out of batteries. Now I have to use the damn pad on the computer and it's highly irritating. I finally manage to get the cursor to hover over the first link, Lifeline Australia, a suicide prevention organization. It's not what I'm looking for, but I suppose it's quite prudent. There are probably all sorts of teens who want to end their lives over a relationship breakdown or a scandal over exposed nude photographs or something. Those kids don't know that their little crisis will pass and they will be far better off for the learning experience. One day, they will speak to their own children about how once, they thought their life wasn't worth living, but lo and behold, look at them now, a parent, a success, happy! Those people needed to find Lifeline and call the number. Not people like me. I am an old lady. I've lived a good life, been married, had my children.

I need help to die, not help to live.

I fiddle with the mouse pad again, and refine my search. *Voluntary euthanasia, Australia.* Google tells me some things that I know, such as the fact that euthanasia is illegal in Australia even though it happens routinely in hospitals for the terminally ill in their final days. Google also tells me things I *don't* know, such as the fact that it's incredibly difficult to purchase the drugs or equipment to euthanize yourself in a humane fashion. I don't qualify to go to Dignitas in Switzerland without being terminally ill, and the medical evidence they require is exhaustive and impossible to fake. Which leaves me, as far as I can see, with the internet.

I've been taking the antidepressant medication that Dr. Paisley prescribed for nearly six months now, and I think it's been effective. My sleep has been better. I'm getting more enjoyment out of things. I'm managing to get dressed, feed myself and do a bit of work. But Tom's still dead. There isn't a pill that will change that.

I find a link to an organization called Voluntary Euthanasia International (VEI). The print that pops up under the link says:

VEI PHILOSOPHY: That all adults of sound mind should have the right to end their life in a manner that is reliable, peaceful and at a time of their choosing. VEI believes control over one's life & death to be a fundamental civil right from which no one of sound mind should be excluded. VEI MISSION: To inform members & support them in their end-of-life decision-making.

I click on the link and keep reading.

49

Lucy

The present . . .

I drive myself to the police station. Ollie offered to come with me, but I told him not to be silly, someone had to stay with the kids. I didn't tell him the real reason I didn't want him to come. That I couldn't bear to see his face when he found out what I'd done.

I go to the desk to announce my arrival but before I've even had a chance to say my name, Jones appears.

"Lucy. Come on up."

In the elevator, she apologizes for calling me this late, and I tell her it's fine, no problem, happy to help, but my voice sounds funny because I'm abuzz with nerves. Ollie must have been in this elevator not more than an hour before. Nettie and Patrick have been in here. Eamon too, apparently. A joke comes to mind. How many people does it take to kill a rich old lady?

I only wish I knew.

We shuffle down the hallway and into a different interview room, that smells of cheap perfume and cigarettes. I take a seat and so does Jones. Several beats pass and she doesn't speak.

"You had some . . . questions?" I ask, finally.

"We're just waiting for Ahmed."

"Here I am," he says at precisely that moment, appearing in the doorway. It's a small room, and it feels even smaller with three of us in here. It makes me more nervous than I already was. The video recorder is in the corner, and they go through the spiel again, explaining that it is being recorded. Finally, we get down to business.

"As I said on the phone," Jones says, "the reason we called you in is we have become aware that your mother-in-law was a member of a group of proponents for voluntary euthanasia. This organization holds meetings where they provide information on how a person can humanely end their own life."

I keep my facial expression carefully blank. "Oh?"

"We have information that your mother-in-law attended one of these meetings and signed up to become a member."

"She did?"

Jones regards me head-on. "She did."

"So . . . you think she *did* kill herself?"

"We think she was thinking about it. It doesn't explain her death, because she wasn't found with any poison in her system . . . but it is an interesting development."

I don't know what to say to this, and so I say nothing.

"Can you tell me about your professional background, Lucy?" Jones says after nearly a minute's silence.

I find a hangnail and pick at it. "I'm a stay-at-home mother."

"And before that?"

"I was a recruiter."

"A recruiter?" Jones glances at Ahmed and doesn't try to conceal her smirk. "In which industry?"

I hesitate. "Information technology."

"And your university degree was in IT and data analytics, is that correct?"

"It is."

"So if someone asked you about how to encrypt email addresses, you'd know how to do it?" It's a question, ostensibly, but Jones makes it clear that it's actually a statement.

"I . . ."

"You could figure it out?" Jones suggests.

"Probably," I admit.

"Do you know what bitcoins are?" Jones's questions are coming faster and I wonder if it's a technique to discombobulate me. If so, it's working.

"Yes . . . I think so . . . why?"

They stare at me, a knowing look in their eyes.

"Am I under arrest?" I ask, flustered. "Because it's late. I really need to get home to my kids."

"Just one more question, Lucy," Jones says, "and then you can go home. But I want you to think about this one before answering, okay? Really think about it."

"Okay," I say.

"Do you know that assisting someone to commit suicide is a crime in Australia? Punishable with up to twenty-five years in prison."

5o

Diana

The past . . .

There are protesters out in front of the library, which I hadn't expected. They are not the silent type. They have placards and cruci-
fixes and are chanting about God being the only one who could
choose when a person can die. Clearly not, I think to myself, or
they'd have nothing to protest about.

I wish I'd brought a book along. Then I could have held it up,
and they'd have left me alone. *Just returning a book,* I'd say. Instead,
someone carrying a fluorescent yellow sign with the words SUICIDE
IS A CRY FOR HELP, NOT A REQUEST TO DIE comes up to me with an
offer to pray for my soul. A mother with a stroller and a couple of
young Asian student-types with laptops enter at the same time as
me and are not approached.

It was relatively easy to book a ticket. The guidelines said you had to be over age fifty or seriously ill with documentation to prove it, and I quite plainly meet the first criterion. I'm not sure what I expected. Some sort of secret handshake and a dingy back room perhaps. But the meeting is taking place in Toorak, of all places, one of if not *the* most affluent area of Melbourne. Leave it to the affluent to want to dictate the circumstances of their own death.

The meeting is in a large room in the basement of the library. A man and a woman stand at the door, the woman holding a clipboard, the man, judging by his size and the fact that he appears to be serving no specific purpose, is a security guard. I haven't been to the Toorak library before but it seems unusually busy for a Thursday afternoon. I wonder if this meeting is responsible for the bustle.

I approach the woman with the clipboard. "My name is Diana Goodwin. I booked a ticked online." I produce my folded ticket, which I printed off that morning, and the woman checks it against her list. Online it said that attendees may be required to present identification, and I have mine ready, but after giving me a long look, she doesn't ask. Still, she is thorough. As she peers at me, I'm reminded of standing at immigration, being surveyed, questioned, required to be a convincing version of exactly who you are. Eventually, I pass the test, and I'm allowed in.

The room is underwhelming—mottled blue/grey carpet, black steel chairs with burgundy fabric seats arranged in rows—twenty rows at a guess—six and six with an aisle in between. There's an old-school whiteboard at the front with markers. I sit in the second row from the back, trying to make myself invisible. A few seats down from me another woman, around my vintage, is clearly trying to do the same. In front of us sits a woman a good deal younger than fifty, alongside an elderly wheelchair-bound man, her father perhaps. He is hooked up to a plethora of tubes that meet up at an oxygen tank that sits on the back of his chair like golf clubs on a buggy, and I can't help thinking of my dear Tom. The rest of the people in the room are in varying levels of health—two wearing oxygen masks, three suspiciously bald. A seventyish man holds the hand of his wife who is clearly suffering some sort of mental condition and is muttering constantly under her breath, and I hear her utter a few of the very worst curses. Only a couple of people sit boldly at the front—they look to be a husband and wife couple, silver haired but straight-backed. Proud, paid-up members of VEI if ever I saw them. The man wears a shirt with his collar popped under a navy woolen sweater and he sits back with his arms folded and an ankle balanced on the opposite foot. The woman wears a white blouse, a forest-green sweater and a string of pearls, and she is half turned around, talking to another woman, bizarrely, about herb gardens and the difficulty the other woman is having with her basil. The woman in green seems to know a lot about growing basil. I feel a pang of something looking at her, and I suspect it is to do with the proximity of her husband beside her. To the casual observer he appears to be in fine health, but the casual eye doesn't see everything: of this I am all too aware.

After five or so minutes, the door closes and the lady with the clipboard comes to the front of the room, leaving the large man stationed outside the door. I understand then that the woman is running the meeting. I knew the meeting would be led by a doctor—it might be sexist of me to have assumed it would be a man. If Tom had made the same assumption I'd have given him hell for it.

"Good afternoon," she says. "Thank you all for being here. I see some familiar faces and I see some new ones. My name is Dr. Hannah Fischer."

Dr. Fischer is warm, bright and efficient, and delivers a talk she is clearly familiar with. Indeed, she has dedicated her life's work to this talk and her belief in assisted suicide and voluntary euthanasia. She talks generally about the history of voluntary euthanasia, the current legalities of what we can and cannot do, and preparing a last will and testament. She talks about the importance of being clear about your intentions. "If you are going to take your own life," she says, "you need to be clear that this was your intention. It is important to be as clear as possible to avoid any of your loved ones being held responsible and sent to jail. We recommend writing a letter making your intentions clear and leaving it in a prominent place. In the past we have seen charges brought against family members. If you have a large estate, it might be worth donating it to charity to avoid your loved ones being seen to have a motivation to assist you with your death."

I think of my estate. There is no doubt it is large. I imagine Ollie's and Nettie's faces if they were to find out they'd been disinherited. It would be slightly less horrifying, I decide, than being found to have a possible motivation for my murder.

We are given a handbook called "The Serene End," which sets out specific approaches to euthanasia, including how to obtain the required materials through the internet. "How do I purchase the drug you have recommended? The . . . Latuben?" the woman sitting next to maybe-her-father asks.

"We're going to talk about that in a moment," Dr. Fischer says. "And you'd better have your notepads ready. I can tell you of an effective way to end your life, but getting your hands on this drug is going to take some effort and commitment from you."

I sit forward, my notepad and pen ready. Finally, the information I came for.

51

Diana

The past . . .

"Aarash! Put that down."

The little boy turns around, holding my blue-and-white vase in his sticky hands. Tom had purchased the vase in Paris many years ago. Even then, it cost over ten thousand euros. A ridiculous amount of money, though I'd always been fond of the vase.

"Just leave him, Ghezala," I say. "It doesn't matter."

I'm actually rather pleased to see Aarash wandering around my house like he owns the place. His sister, Aziza, looks just as comfortable here. They remind me very much of my own grandchildren, burrowing under furniture and finding little crannies to hide in and fragile things to touch. And why not? What's it all for if not for children to play with? That's what Tom would have said anyway.

"How is Hakem?" I ask.

"Working hard," Ghezala says. "He's just employed two more people for his project. One of them from Afghanistan, one from Sudan."

"That's wonderful." I try for a smile. I'm more comfortable with Ghezala than many other people, but still, smiles don't come naturally these days.

"We have many friends here from Afghanistan now. Hakem's sister and her husband are here."

"That's wonderful," I say, and now a smile does come, a real one. "Are they working?"

"They're looking. But they've been looking a while."

"What kind of work did they do back home?"

"Different things. Some sales, some IT. Aarash, put that down!"

Aarash is holding the vase again, peering into the hole at the top as if it's a telescope. But hearing his mother's voice he sets it down hard on the floor. It doesn't break but Ghezala puts her hand to her heart and closes her eyes.

"Pick it up," I tell him. "It's fine. Play with it."

I cannot find jobs for all of Ghezla's friends, unfortunately. Even if Tom was alive, I couldn't. I can, however, let Aarash and his sister play with my priceless vase. I can let them hold it or break it or use it as a telescope. And so I will let them.

"Where are your friends living?" I ask.

"In an apartment near us," she says. "They know they are lucky.

They're just not as lucky as us. Not everyone has someone like you, Diana, to take them under their wing—" We hear a sharp crack and Ghezala's hands form a tent over her mouth. "Aarash! Oh no."

We look over. The vase is broken into three large pieces on the parquetry flooring. The children stare at it, stunned and terrified.

I just laugh and laugh.

52

Diana

The past . . .

"I have something to tell you," I say to Lucy, the week after my meeting at VEI. She is standing at my sink, hand-washing dishes. Edie is at her feet, playing with Tupperware containers and lids. I want to tell Lucy to leave the dishes—that I can do it myself, but I'm not sure I can. I feel bone-tired, weighed down, like I could lay my head on the kitchen counter and never lift it up again. Besides that, the fact is I'm enjoying being looked after. It doesn't come close to filling the gap that Tom left. But it fills it a little.

"What is it?" Lucy asks.

"I saw Dr. Paisley last week."

Lucy wipes a hair out of her face with a gloved hand. "I didn't know you had a doctor's appointment."

"It was a follow-up appointment. To get some test results."

She gives me a funny look. "Test results for what?"

"Mammogram and ultrasound. My regular two yearly appointments."

"Oh." Lucy picks up a dish towel. "You should have told me, I would have driven you."

"I'm not an invalid, I can drive myself."

Lucy looks hurt. "I didn't say you were an invalid."

"I'm sorry," I say quickly. "That was rude. You've been a great help to me these past few months."

Now she looks touched. How easily words can affect this one. It almost makes me regret what I'm about to say.

"I have breast cancer, Lucy. Quite advanced."

She freezes, a plate in her hand. Dishwater drips from the fingertips down onto the floor. "Diana, no."

"I haven't told the children yet. I will, of course. But I wanted to tell you first. Actually, I was hoping you could help me—"

"Of course I will help you." Lucy puts the plate down. "I can be here, when you tell them. I will help support them . . . and you—"

"No," I interrupt. "That's not what I meant." I search around for the words I'd planned, but they don't come to me. All of this is harder than I thought. "I need help with . . . something else."

Lucy removes her gloves. "What do you need help with?"

"I need to buy some things. Online. But, you see . . . I need an encrypted email address and bitcoins. I thought you might know how to get these."

Lucy blinks. At first she is confused, but slowly I see it morph into suspicion.

"Have you been taking your medication, Diana?"

"Yes."

"And you're feeling better?"

I shrug. "Tom's still dead. No drug is going to change that."

We drift into silence, apart from Edie playing happily on the floor. I watch as understanding comes to Lucy's face.

"And now," she says slowly, "you've discovered you're sick and you want to buy something online that requires an encrypted email address and bitcoins?"

"Yes."

It's funny. For so long I've felt at such a disconnect with her. And yet, it's amazing what I've been able to communicate with her, without saying a single word.

"If I tell you any more, Lucy, I will be exposing you to trouble so please don't ask. I'm going to write a letter which will make my intentions clear. No one will ever know you were involved. Not Ollie. Not anyone."

She closes her eyes. "Diana—"

"Do this for me, Lucy. Please. You're the only one I can ask."

It's the truth. Ollie and Nettie would never help me. I'm their mother, which means in our relationship they will always be children, and will only see things from their own perspectives. They won't want me to die, and that will be the end of that. But Lucy sees me differently. Like a mother-in-law, yes. But also as a woman.

Which means, for this, a daughter-in-law is perfect.

53

Lucy

The present . . .

I take the long way home from the police headquarters. As I drive, questions circle in my head. *Is this what you wanted, Diana? For me to go to jail? Was involving me all part of your elaborate plan? Or did your plan go horribly wrong somewhere along the line?* My mind swirls with all the possibilities and the worst part is that I can't ask her.

I left the police station after claiming no knowledge. Now I am going to have to get in touch with a lawyer. Not Gerard, we can't afford him. Actually, we can't afford anyone. We're going to have to declare bankruptcy, we have no inheritance coming our way. I'll probably have to find someone from Legal Aid.

I look at all the pieces of my life that have fallen apart in recent weeks. My husband's business has failed. My formerly pleasant relationship with my sister-in-law has soured. And my mother-in-law is dead. The funny thing is, until recently, news of my mother-in-law's death wouldn't have been devastating (beyond the obvious feelings of sympathy for my husband and children). But now, the loss cuts surprisingly deep.

It's quiet when I let myself into the house. Then I hear Ollie.

"Lucy?" he whispers.

I drop the keys into the bowl and follow his voice to the bedroom. The side lamp is on and Ollie is sitting on the edge of the bed in his boxer shorts, his elbows on his knees, his head in his hands. He glances up when I enter.

"Are you okay?" I ask.

"Not really," he says. "I want to explain why I was at Mum's the day she died."

Why I was at Mum's the day she died. It takes me a minute to understand what he is talking about, but then I remember. Before I went to the police station, Ollie had admitted he was at Diana's house the day she died. That conversation seems like a million years ago.

"Okay." I sit beside him on the bed and flick on the bedside lamp. "Explain."

"I dropped in for a visit," he says. "I wanted to tell her about my business troubles."

"But . . . why didn't you tell me that?" I ask, frustrated. "I've known for a week about your business troubles."

Ollie looks down and suddenly I'm afraid of his answer. I don't think Ollie is capable of hurting his mother, but obviously something happened during that meeting. Something he didn't want me to know. I don't think I can take another shock, another betrayal. But judging by the look of determination in Ollie's face, it looks like I'm not going to have a choice.

"Because a long time ago," he says, dropping his head into his hands, "you made me promise I'd never ask Mum for money again."

54

Diana

The past . . .

I meet Nettie at a café, at her suggestion. Nettie and I don't usually meet at cafés, but nothing is normal lately.

I'd told the children that I had breast cancer a couple of weeks earlier. Ollie had gone through the motions of shock and sadness, which I expected. Nettie's reaction was less expected. I'd thought she'd have a controlled but concerned reaction—asking for information, statistics, names of doctors. But she hadn't asked a single question. Her mind had been elsewhere, even then.

Since Tom died, I'd noticed her behavior had become increasingly odd. Every so often she'd come to the house, but rather than speaking to me, she'd just wander about searching for Tom in the folds of the curtains and the creases of the sofa. She never said that was what she was doing, but I knew, because I did it too. Once, just a few weeks after Tom's death, I came home and found her curled up on his side of the bed. I left her there, and snuck away and she never knew that I saw her. Sometimes we need to grieve together, and sometimes we need to grieve alone.

As I approach the café, I notice a playground across the road full of mothers bundled in puffer jackets pushing babies in strollers or shouting up at older kids who have climbed to the top of a climbing frame to come down for morning tea. I am wondering if I should find us a table inside, away from it all—after all, why make it worse for Nettie?—when I see her sitting at a table out in front.

"Mum!"

I nearly don't recognize her. She's thinner than she's ever been and her skin is sallow and pale . . . and yet at the same time, she looks slightly more alive than the last time I saw her. The idea flickers through my mind that she might be pregnant. I can't decide if that would be good news or not.

"Hello, darling." I kiss her cheek and sit opposite her on a cold metal chair. There are mushroom heaters dotted about and woolen blankets on the backs of the chairs, but it doesn't replace the shelter of four walls, in my opinion. "Isn't it a little cold out here?"

"I'm fine." Nettie smiles.

Nettie comes across, I'm assured from most people I meet, as a happy, cheery person who never has a bad word to say about anyone. And she is, indeed, smiley, at least she used to be. But there are some things only a mother can tell. This smile, for instance, is not indicative of happiness. It is a smile of strategy; a smile of digging her heels in. It's a smile that says, *We're sitting outside. If you don't want to, you're going to have to be the one to rock the boat.* Every one of Nettie's smiles means something.

"If you're fine," I say, with a smile of my own, "we'll stay."

It occurs to me that I should be taking every opportunity to be outside. I should be breathing in fresh air, walking in the mountains and working my way through my bucket list. But my bucket list is fairly short, fairly uninspiring. In fact, the only thing on my bucket list is to spend time with my family, and to make sure they are going to be okay after I leave them behind.

"The website you need for the email address is here," Lucy had said a couple of weeks earlier, thrusting a piece of paper at me. She'd arrived at my house unannounced again, and started talking double time as if she'd chicken out if she didn't. "Regarding bitcoins, the first thing you need to do is get a bitcoin wallet. There's an app you can download to your phone. Then you need to buy some bitcoins. You should be able to do this directly from the app."

I stared at her. She might as well have been speaking Chinese. She'd watched me for a second or two, then sighed and reached for my phone.

Now I have two bottles of the drug, the Latuben, in my fridge door, ready to drink. (It is tasteless, apparently, and should be drunk alone, though you could follow it with a glass of wine if you wished.) I've written the letter. I need to see Gerard about the will—I'll leave every cent to the charity to ensure that none of my family can be seen to benefit from my death. I'll let the children know what I've done. And then I'll go and see Tom, wherever he was.

The waitress arrives and Nettie and I both order tea.

"How are you?" I ask Nettie, when the waitress is gone.

"I'm good," she says, and then there's a few beats of silence. "I mean, I'm not pregnant, if that's what you're asking."

"I did wonder. I'm sorry, darling."

"Yes, well, it's what I wanted to talk to you about. At the last IVF appointment Dr. Sheldon said there were two problems, my eggs and my uterus. She said my best chance would be to use a donor egg and a surrogate."

"I know what you're thinking," she says, after a moment or two.

"Really? *I* don't even know what I'm thinking."

The waitress returns with our drinks, and places them on the table. I pick up my mug and lift it to my mouth.

"Listen, I get it," Nettie says. "It took me a while to process it too. I mean . . . it wouldn't be biologically my child, I wouldn't carry it in my body. At first I wasn't really on board. Then I started thinking . . . it would be a child created *by* us, *for* us. I would be able to be part of the pregnancy, I would be there at the birth. I would still be a mother. And Mum, that is the most important thing to me."

"What about adoption?" I ask, and Nettie's face falls. I realize that this had been the part where I was supposed to get swept up in excitement.

"Do you know how many adoptions took place in Victoria last year?" she says. "Six. *Six!* Four of which were inter-family. Adopting is nearly impossible in Australia."

"And surrogacy? That's possible in Australia?"

"There is altruistic surrogacy in Australia. Where a friend or family member offers to do it. I asked Lucy if she'd do it, but she wasn't open to the idea." Nettie is speaking quickly, almost maniacally. Her hands, I notice, are shaking. "And it's illegal to be a surrogate for financial gain. The most common way, and the route our doctor suggested, was to source a donor egg from India, and pay a surrogate in the U.S.A. The thing is . . . it's not cheap. The process, including the eggs, the insemination, the surrogate's medical expenses and fees, . . . it will all come to well over a hundred thousand."

She finally pauses, takes a breath.

"A hundred thousand *dollars*?" I stare at her. "Can you afford that?"

Nettie holds my gaze. "No. But you can."

I put my tea back in its saucer. Suddenly I understand the purpose of the visit. I feel a little foolish that it's taken me this long.

"You wouldn't even miss the money," she says, already countering my yet-to-vocalize arguments. "And it would be a grandchild!"

"But what if it didn't work? What if we found a surrogate and you implanted an embryo and it didn't . . . take? What then?"

"We'd try again."

"How many times, Nettie? At a hundred thousand dollars per go?"

She shrugs as if it's a minor detail, something that can be ironed out later. "As many as it takes, I guess."

How had I not seen this? I knew she was desperate to have a baby, I'd suspected she might have even been depressed over it. But today, I wonder if it's more than that. If it's the beginning—or middle—of a descent into madness.

"So what you're really asking me for," I say carefully, "is access to unlimited funds."

"This is my last chance. I need you, Mum."

All at once, I'm back at Orchard House, sitting opposite my mother, begging. Begging for my baby. I close my eyes, take a breath.

"I'll think about it, okay?"

55

Diana

The past . . .

I'm standing in the dining room sorting through donations of baby clothes when I hear the distinct sound of footsteps on the parquetry floor. I go very still. The footsteps are heavier than Nettie's, less precise and careful. It is in moments like these that I see my vulnerability—an elderly-ish woman alone in a huge, cavernous house. I creep a few steps toward the double doors and catch a glimpse of a huge, lumbering shadow.

"Oh." I find my heart. "Patrick."

"Sorry to sneak up on you," he says. "The door was unlocked."

Patrick doesn't often drop by for a visit. In fact, I'm not sure he *ever* has without Nettie.

"I need to talk to you about Nettie," he says.

He pulls out the chair closest to me and sits. I remain standing.

"What's wrong with Nettie?" I ask.

Patrick raises an eyebrow. "Are you seriously asking what is wrong with Nettie?"

As I recover from my surprise, irritation kicks in. Patrick has a nerve coming here, speaking to me like this, when everyone in the world knows he's messing around on my daughter. "This is about the surrogacy?" I upend a new bag of baby clothes onto the table.

"What else?" Absently, Patrick picks up a tiny knitted jacket. "I'm assuming Nettie has her wires crossed because she says you're thinking about paying for it."

I frown. "And you've come to plead your case?"

"Actually I've come to plead the opposite."

This catches me off guard. "You're coming to me because you *don't* want money?"

I admit, I'm lost. In the many visits I've had from my children and their spouses, never has anyone asked me *not* to give money.

"Nettie would kill me if she knew I was here obviously." Patrick looks out the window, onto the garden. "She's on a mission for a baby. She's obsessed by it."

"You think I don't know that?"

"You don't know *anything.*" He raises his voice, cutting through any pretense of decorum between us. "It's like she's possessed. Some days I'll be talking to her and it's like she's not even there! Her legs and stomach are covered in bruises from injecting herself with hormones. She spends her entire life on the internet reading stories from people who managed to conceive after years of trying. She trawls through forums of people who have done IUI or IVF or lately, surrogacy. She doesn't talk about anything else. *Nothing* else."

He tosses the little jacket back onto the table.

For a moment, I'm taken aback. Only a moment. "That must have been awful for you," I say quietly. "No wonder you had to find multiple girlfriends to ease your burden."

Patrick stares at me.

"You'll need to go a little farther away than country Victoria if you don't want to keep a secret around these parts, Patrick."

Patrick has the decency to look ashamed, which is something, I suppose.

I study him. "So . . . you don't want a baby, is that it? You don't want to be shackled to Nettie?"

"No, that's not it. I *do* want a baby. At least I did. But I accepted it wasn't going to happen a few years back. Nettie didn't. And now I . . . I don't know how to help her. She's either a walking zombie or she's totally manic from her latest fertility idea. She's not the same person I married."

He looks so sad I rein in my anger.

"So what do you want from me, Patrick?"

"I don't want anything. That's exactly my point."

"Actually you do want something. You want me to withhold money from my daughter so you can avoid having a conversation with her that you need to have."

Patrick opens his mouth but I get in first.

"—and what happens next? Once Nettie gives up on her baby dream? You give up your girlfriends and you all live happily ever after?"

He exhales. "I don't know, okay?"

But he does know. And suddenly I do too. There are age restrictions around surrogacy in Australia, even for intended parents. In a few years, Nettie and Patrick will be too old to become parents. Which means, Patrick just has to ride out Nettie's craziness for another year or two. And with my recent "cancer" diagnosis, in two or three years he'll be able to enjoy a comfortable, childless life. A life with all the little extras he's enjoyed with us over the years. Whisky, cigars, homes by the beach. Now that it's within his reach, he's not going to give it up.

"Well," I say. "Regardless of whether I give Nettie this money for surrogacy, you need to talk to her. You need to tell her about the other women, and you need to tell her you no longer want a baby."

Patrick shakes his head. This has not gone the way he wanted. He thought he could come here and form some alliance with me, I realize. Him and me against my daughter. The idea makes me sick to my stomach.

"Diana I really don't think—"

"If you don't, Patrick . . . I will."

Patrick's eyes flash as he rises to his feet. He smiles, a horrible mean smile. "Look at you, acting all concerned about your daughter. Nettie's spent her whole life vying for your attention, and you've never given her the time of day. You've spent more time worrying about your refugee women than your own children. And now you're acting holier-than-thou. Who do you think you are?"

"I think I'm her mother."

"Some mother."

He squares up against me, but I'm not scared. If Patrick wants me to change my mind, he's going to have to kill me.

56

Diana

The past . . .

After his pathetic attempt of trying to intimidate me, Patrick finally leaves. I finish sorting the baby clothes and then go into the study. I sit in Tom's old study chair, running my fingers over the surface of the desk, picking up pens and notepads, touching the things that he touched. It's been a year since he died and he's started to disappear from other rooms, which have been cleaned numerous times, but I still feel him in here.

I remember that conversation we had a few years back, about the kids and money. *It's about support,* Tom had said. *Whether to give it or not.* Patrick doesn't want me to give them money for the surrogacy. Nettie does. One way or another, Nettie has a rough time ahead of her and she'll need someone to support her.

I hear a key in the door and a moment later: "Diana? Are you home?"

It's Lucy's voice.

I sit up straight. Lucy hasn't been here since the night she came to encrypt my email address and show me how to use bitcoins. I didn't know if I *would* see her again after that. But here she is rounding the corner, dressed in jeans and a white T-shirt and hot-pink ballet flats and a zebra scarf around her neck. Still fashionable, but a little more subtle these days. It's as though she's maturing, coming into herself, figuring out who she really is.

"I'm sorry I haven't been by," she says.

"Don't apologize. I understand."

I do understand. It's a tall order visiting someone after you have helped them to procure drugs illegally to end their life. What would we talk about? The future was off-limits, obviously, as were plans for Christmas, or upcoming holidays. There was simply nothing left to discuss. Still I can't deny the fact that I feel . . . happy to see Lucy. Over the past few months I've become accustomed to having her around, making food or doing the dishes or booking my appointments. It had made it feel all the more quiet when she wasn't here. I'd been surprised, even humbled, by her devotion. Perhaps the biggest surprise was that, while I know she doesn't want me to take my own life, she's never, not once, tried to talk me out of it. It reminds me of the way she supports Ollie. Suddenly I see it for what it is: a gift.

"What are you doing here in the study?" she asks.

I look around the room. It feels empty, even filled with furniture. "Looking for Tom," I admit with a smile.

A soft smile crosses her face. "It's lovely, the way you love him."

"Funny, I was just thinking the same about the way you love Ollie."

The thing about death is that it puts things into perspective. I know what I care about now. I care about my children and my grandchildren. I care about my charity continuing to operate. I care about people getting a fair go.

And I care about Lucy.

Lucy presses her lips together, swallows. "You . . . you've never said that to me before."

"No. But I should have. I'm sorry I didn't."

She crosses the room and puts her arms around me. "I'm going to miss you," she says. She begins to sob in my arms, keening.

"Shhh." I pat her back. "It's all right, dear."

Holding her, I feel myself soften. I can't remember anyone holding me like this since . . . Tom. It brings tears to my own eyes.

"I'm not going to do it, Lucy," I whisper into her ear.

Lucy stills, but remains where she is for a moment. When she finally lifts her head I feel a surprising sense of loss, a coldness where her warm head had just been.

"Really?"

"I can't leave Nettie with everything that's going on right now," I say. "I can't leave Ollie and my grandchildren. I can't leave my charity." Lucy's hair has gone all static, fanning around her face like a mane. I pat it down, tuck it behind her eyes. "And I can't leave you, Luc—"

Before I can finish, Lucy throws her arms around me again with such force that it takes my breath away.

"I love you, Diana," she says.

I smile. "I love you too."

And then, we stand there in the center of the room, holding each other, and crying.

57

Diana

The past . . .

They say little boys love their mothers, and I think there is something to it. Little girls love their mothers, too, of course, but a little boy's love for his mother is pure, untainted. Boys see their mothers in the most primal way, a protector, devotee, a disciple. Sons bask in their mothers' love rather than questioning it or testing it.

What I like best about the mother-son relationship is the simplicity of it. When Ollie was a toddler, when times were really tight, I had fleeting pangs of guilt that I wasn't able to give him things. I remember asking him what he wanted for his birthday and he replied, "I'd like to go to the beach and then eat vegemite sandwiches for dinner." It was, perhaps, the only thing we could afford. For a moment I thought that's why he'd said it, but then I realized he was too young for that. Sandwiches at the beach was simply his idea of a perfect day.

So today, when Ollie calls to suggest a visit, I don't read into it. I expect that's all he wants, a visit. Ollie is committed to Lucy, and his family comes first, but I like to think there's still a part of his heart that is reserved for his dear old mum. But when he appears at the door, it is immediately apparent that he is not, in fact, here for a visit. He looks upset and he doesn't try to hide it—he is in his work clothes, but looks scruffy, as if he's slept at the office.

"What is it, darling?" I ask him.

He closes his eyes, shakes his head. "Can we talk inside?"

We go into the den and Ollie declines my offer for tea or coffee. Instead he drops onto the sofa. I sit opposite him and his face drops into my lap. I put a hand into the thick dark hair he didn't get from me or Tom, and run my fingers through it like I used to when he was a little boy. Now, he is a forty-eight-year-old little boy.

"What is it?" I repeat.

"My business is going under. We're not going to make our loan repayment," he says. "And the bank is calling in our debt."

My hand freezes in his hair. "Oh no. Ollie . . . I had no idea."

"Honestly neither did I. I've been working my ass off for this business for years, and I can't seem to make any headway. I honestly don't know where the money goes."

"Probably into Eamon's pocket," I mutter. I've never thought of it before, but suddenly it seems like the obvious answer.

Ollie stares at me.

"I might be wrong," I say, "but I'm betting I'm not."

Ollie blinks into the middle distance, perhaps processing this. Then he sits up. "No. Eamon wouldn't—"

"Wouldn't what? Go to any length to line his pockets?"

Ollie shakes his head. "God, I don't know. I haven't even spoken to him properly in months."

"Have you tried?"

"Of course I have. He says everything is fine and we can talk later."

"You need to insist."

He laughs blackly. "Even if I did, Mum, there's nothing to talk about now. It's over. The business is worthless."

He presses his fingers into his eye sockets. I've never seen him look more broken.

"Not if you make your loan payment," I say, after a moment or two.

Ollie frowns. "But . . . how . . . ?"

"I might be able to come on board as a silent partner. At least, I might, if Eamon had nothing to do with it. As a matter of fact, I have an idea for your business. It would be a bit of a departure from what you're doing now."

"What kind of . . . departure?"

When I tell Ollie my idea, he looks so surprised and impressed I have to try hard not to be offended. *That's right,* I want to say. *Your father wasn't the only one with business ideas.* He rests his chin in his hand, taking it all in and he reminds me so much of Tom, I find it impossible to believe they weren't biologically related. We live on, I realize. We live on through our children.

"You know what," he says finally. "That is a business I could really throw myself into."

58

Lucy

The present . . .

The phone is ringing in the background again. The darn thing won't stop. But neither Ollie nor I look at it, or even acknowledge it.

"You asked Diana for money? For your business?"

"Yes."

"Why didn't you tell me?"

Ollie pinches the top of his nose between his thumb and fore-finger. "You said it was a deal breaker."

I blink at him. "What?"

"A deal breaker. You said that. If I ever asked Mum for money. I couldn't lose you on top of everything else."

I sigh. "Jesus, Ollie. You're not going to lose me." I close my eyes.

"The weirdest thing was that she agreed," he says. "I never expected her to."

"Then why did you ask?"

"I don't know. Maybe I . . . just wanted to talk to my mum. You probably won't believe this, but she could be . . . very wise."

I chuckle a little. "Actually I do believe that."

The landline phone stops ringing and for a moment we are surrounded by pure silence. But it lasts only a second or two before Ollie's mobile starts up. I open my eyes. I want to throw it against the wall.

"She was different," Ollie says, frowning as if recalling it. "She didn't tell me to make my own way, or to figure it out myself. She told me she had my back. She said we'd pay off Eamon and go into business together."

"She wanted to go into business with you?"

"She had a really interesting idea actually. A recruitment agency for highly skilled refugees. Engineers, doctors, IT professionals. A full-service agency that helped to get candidates' qualifications recognized in Australia and giving them all the tools they needed to transition into good jobs, across all fields. It was a really good idea. She thought you might want to be involved too."

"She did?"

"A family business, she said." Ollie's chin puckers. "But then she killed herself. Why would she say all of that . . . and then kill herself, less than an hour later?"

Obviously I have no idea. When Diana told me she'd changed her mind about killing herself, I'd believed her. Why would she say that if it wasn't true? And even if she had changed her mind back again, it didn't explain the letter in the drawer, or the thread in her hands. It didn't explain the missing pillow.

"There's only one explanation I can think of," I say to Ollie. "Someone must have gotten there after you left."

59

Diana

The past . . .

After Ollie leaves, I go to Tom's study and pull out my letter. I look down at it.

> *I could have written more, but in the end, there's really only two pieces of wisdom worth leaving behind. I worked hard for everything I ever cared about. And nothing I ever cared about cost a single cent.*
>
> *Mum*

I'd never been a woman of many words. I could have crafted a letter to my children explaining why I'd chosen to end my life, or about how much I loved them . . . but that wasn't my style. Besides, how would it help them? Sentiment had a way of diluting truth, and if I was going to leave a last few words of wisdom for my children, I wanted them to be clear.

Now, of course, I won't be needing any letter. At first I think about burning it. Then I wonder if I should keep it as a reminder of how I felt this past year. Perhaps it's a good thing, to remember. I tuck the letter into the office drawer and head down the stairs and am just walking past the front room when Nettie lets herself in.

"Hi Mum," she says. "Can we talk?"

Nettie walks into the small front room. I follow her, sit beside her. She picks up one of the cushions and begins fiddling with the gold tassels nervously. "I'm here about the money, obviously," she says, not wasting any time on small talk. "For the surrogacy. I've been talking to the agency, and I'm going to need to pay the deposit soon. I'm sorry to pressure you, but this is my . . ."

". . . last chance."

"Yes."

My mind drifts to Patrick. His flashing eyes. *She's on a mission for a baby. She's obsessed by it.*

It's like she's possessed.

"And Patrick is . . . on board?" I ask lightly. "About the surrogacy?"

"Of course." She avoids my gaze, the way she did when she was little and didn't want to talk about something. "Of course he is."

"How are things with Patrick, Nettie?" I ask. "Is your relationship . . . solid?"

She shrugs. "Sure it is."

"Really?"

Nettie looks up, takes in my skeptical expression and becomes guarded. "*What?*" She sounds almost angry.

"You know Patrick has been unfaithful, don't you?" I say. "You must know, Antoinette."

The expression on Nettie's face—a kind of bewildered rage—is so jarring that for a moment, I wonder if it's possible that she *doesn't* know. Then she laughs. "*Of course* I know. Everyone knows."

I hesitate a moment, thrown by the bizarre laugh, but decide to plough on. If I'm going to help my daughter, I need to understand her, see her side of things. "Then w*hy* would you want to bring a baby into a relationship like that? Tell me, darling."

She rolls her eyes. "It's not about Patrick, don't you see that? It's about *me*."

Nettie stands up, starts pacing. She goes back and forth several times.

"Nettie, I'm worried about you," I say. "You're not in a fit state to go into surrogacy. I think you need to see someone, get some professional help."

Her pacing stops abruptly. Her eyes lock on mine. "Does this mean you won't help me?"

"It depends what you mean by help. I'll help you find a psychologist to speak to. I'll help support you if you decide to leave Patrick, and I'll help support you if you decide to stay with him. But I won't be funding your egg donor and surrogate plan, no. Not right now."

Nettie hovers over me, her hands shaking with rage. She shifts from foot to foot in front of me. I remain still, as if trying not to spook a frightened animal. "Do you have *any idea* what it's like to have the one thing you want taken away from you?" Her voice grows in volume and intensity as she speaks.

"Yes. *Tom* was taken away from me."

"Did it make you question your own life? Your purpose?"

"It did."

"I don't believe you. If you knew what I was talking about, you would never do this to me."

"Believe me, Nettie, I know," I say. "I understand what it's like to feel that your entire purpose is wrapped up in one thing, one person." I hadn't intended to tell Nettie about my planned suicide, but suddenly it feels like the one thing that might bring her to her senses. "After your father died, I contemplated suicide. I researched it, I bought poison online—it's still in the door of the damn fridge! But it was madness, the whole thing. I loved Tom, but he wasn't my entire life. I have you and Ollie and Lucy. I have my grandchildren. My friends. My charity. And Nettie, you may not see it now but your life isn't about having a baby." I stand so we are eye to eye. "Forget about babies. Take your life in a different direction. You could do anything you want!"

"So you won't give me the money?" she says, when I'm finished.

"Nettie! Have you heard *anything* I've said?"

Nettie turns her back to me and for a moment, there is total silence. But after a few seconds a curious noise begins, thin and reedy, like the ragged edge of a tin can. It takes me a moment to realize the noise is coming from Nettie. I reach for her shoulder but before I grasp it, she spins around and lunges at me like a force. Her elbow catches my nose and I career backward, landing hard on my tailbone. As I cry out, Nettie appears over me, gripping the cushion so tight the veins in her hands pop out.

"Nettie. Darli . . ."

I fall silent. The expression on her face is pure and unadulterated *hate.* I think of Ollie's visit a few minutes ago and I see the juxtaposi-tion, suddenly, of sons and daughters. Sons see the best parts of you, but daughters really *see* you. They see your flaws and your weak-nesses. They see everything they don't want to be. They see you for exactly who you are . . . and they hate you for it.

"This is over, Mum," Nettie says, and I'm not sure what she means until she presses the pillow into my face and holds it there with a resolve that tells me she is not letting go. I feel her weight on my chest. I grab hold of her wrists and squeeze hard, but she just pushes the pillow harder into my face. I can't take a breath. My lungs burn. And as the edges fade to black I think to myself . . . she got that resolve from me.

60

Nettie

The past . . .

Mum's legs stop moving first. She didn't go down without a fight, but that was classic Mum. And it worked in my favor, each kick had only served to tire her out faster. Now I sit astride her chest, the same way Ollie used to sit on me when I was a kid and he wanted to interrogate me for snooping in his bedroom. Slowly her viselike grip on my wrists weakens until she lets go entirely, but I keep holding the pillow down until she's been still for several minutes. Finally I stand, leaving the pillow over her face.

Mum is dead. Her legs have fallen to the sides so her shoes point in opposite directions. Looking at them, I'm reminded of the Wicked Witch of the East when Dorothy's house falls on her. Mum took me to see *The Wizard of Oz* at the Grand Theatre for my ninth birthday and even gave me a pair of ruby slippers to wear as a present. I missed most of the show because I was admiring the way my footwear sparkled in the theater lights. I wore those slippers every day after until the soles were thin as paper and I could feel the rocks and dirt under my feet. It was one of only a handful of times that Mum had gotten it right with me.

My brain wades through all the information at hand as I try to figure out what to do next. Mum's left arm is bent up over her head. Her nails are painted an awful flesh-colored pink, and on her ring finger is her cluster of rings, all modest, yellow gold. I'd never seen her without those rings. They are like a bizarre knuckle, a living part of her. Or, now, a dead part of her.

I'm slowly becoming aware of the trouble I'm in. I killed my mother. Killed her, as they said in the movies, with my bare hands. And yet, as I look down at her, so still and quiet, all I feel is peace. Not the untethered, free-falling terror I felt when Dad died. *Peace.* It's funny, in theory, a mother and a father do the same thing. They nurture you, protect you, try to form you into a reasonable human being. If they do it right, they will keep your feet on the ground. If they do it wrong, they'll stop you from flying. The difference is subtle, yet vast.

For me, it was Dad's way that gave me life.

Dad. His name pops into my mouth and I breathe it out. It occurs to me that it's the first time I've had a problem, a real problem, and he hasn't been here for me.

It is just a problem, Antoinette, he would probably have said, *and a problem is only a problem until you solve it.*

I massage my right wrist gently, then my left. For someone so skinny Mum was surprisingly strong. And determined.

After your father died, I contemplated suicide. I researched it, I bought poison online—it's still in the door of the damn fridge!

She had said that, hadn't she? Or had I imagined it?

I walk to the kitchen and hold the fridge door open with my hip. A half-empty carton of milk is wedged in beside an unopened bottle of tonic water and two brown glass bottles with white labels covered in medical gibberish. I squat down to examine the labels. In square green and red letters the name LATUBEN is spelled out.

An idea starts to form in my mind.

I slide my hands into a pair of washing-up gloves and carry both bottles back into the front room. When I remove the pillow from Mum's face, I only look at her long enough to see that she doesn't look serene. Her face is frozen in a haunting grimace, an angry bitter cry. I put down one of the bottles and remove the lid of the other, and I focus on tipping the contents into her mouth. Most of it spills down her cheeks and collects in her mouth, so I tip the last of it into the fireplace and leave the empty bottle beside her limp hand. There doesn't seem to be a lot of point in using the other, so I shove it into my handbag. It's not a great plan, but it's all I've got.

As I turn to leave, I rub my wrists. They're going to be bruised tomorrow.

61

Lucy

The present . . .

Ollie's phone stops ringing, finally. But when my phone starts to ring immediately afterward, it sends an odd alert through me.

"We should answer that," I say.

Ollie nods as if he's just realized the same thing. My phone is next to him on the couch and he presses it to his ear.

"Hello? Yes?" His eyes find mine. "What do you mean?" His eyebrows shoot skyward. "No."

"What is it?" I ask, but Ollie holds a palm up.

"Are you sure?" he says into the phone, and then he is silent for the longest time. I can't tell if he's listening, or processing, or what. His eyes close, hard, his face crumples. I don't dare speak. I hardly dare to breathe.

"Yes," he says after an eternity. "Okay. We'll be right there."

"What is it?" I ask, when he hangs up the phone.

"It's Nettie," he says. "She's dead."

62

Nettie

The past . . .

Who are we after we're gone? I wonder. It's a good question to ponder. Most people can't come up with an answer right away. They frown, consider it for a minute. Maybe even sleep on it. Then the answers start to come.

We're our children. Our grandchildren. Our great-grandchildren. We're all the people who will go on to live, because we lived. We are our wisdom, our intellect, our beauty, filtered through generations, continuing to spill into the world and make a difference.

Most people end up with some version of this. Then they will nod, satisfied and secure in their contribution, certain that their lives will not be void of meaning.

Of course, there are plenty of ways to give your life meaning beyond having children. Everyone says this. Some people believe it. But in the end it doesn't matter because *I* don't believe it. And this is, after all, my life.

The problem is, Patrick came home at exactly the wrong time. I was sitting up in bed, in my pajamas. After extensive googling to ensure that one bottle of Latuben would be enough to kill me, I'd poured it into a coffee mug. It was on my bedside table. On my lap was a notepad and a pen. I had just put pen to paper when I saw Patrick's car pull into the driveway.

I planned to write a note, explaining everything to Patrick, absolving him from blame and guilt and responsibility. I wanted to give him that. Even after all that's happened, I had affection for Patrick. He tried his best. If I had only become pregnant easily, Patrick and I would probably still have been happy. People underestimate the role fate plays in our lives. Silly them.

And so, when I see his car, I lift the mug to my lips and drink it down in one almighty gulp. Then I lie back and close my eyes. I'm out.

63

Lucy

The present . . .

Dad arrives early on the morning of Nettie's funeral with a bag of donuts for the kids. He stays to help Ollie and I as we roll about the house like marbles, searching for missing socks and neckties (for Archie, who now, he tells us, has a funeral uniform). The photographers are outside again today. They'd arrived two days after Nettie's death, when the whole twisted story had hit the press. "MONEY, GREED AND FAMILY: INSIDE THE SOCIETY FAMILY MURDER-SUICIDE." The article didn't have much in the way of facts, but the police had warned us that more would likely come out. There was something about the uber-wealthy falling from grace—people were insatiable for information, and the more sordid, the better. The police had also warned us that photographers would almost certainly be outside the funeral, trying to get a shot of us crying. (Yesterday Harriet had given the photographer the peace sign and trout pout lips as she hoofed her way out to the car. It was probably today's cover story, but I didn't have the heart to look.)

"How are you holding up?" Dad asks me. I am ironing Edie's only clean dress. She will have to wear it with odd socks because I can't find a pair that match. In light of everything else that's happened, I can't find a reason to care.

"Honestly? I feel like nothing will ever be the same."

"It doesn't last forever, honey."

I look up from the ironing board, blinking back the tears that come to my eyes with such ease these days. "How do you know?" I ask, a childish question, but then again, he is my Dad.

"I know because . . . I've been there."

Even as an adult, it's easy to forget that your parents are people. Now, it occurs to me that *of course* he's been there. My mother's death had come right on the heels of Dad's mother, my nana. It's not something I'd thought much about back then, after all, my dad had been a grown-up and I was just a kid. And Nana, as far as I was concerned, had been *old* (sixty-one). But it was only a year later, almost to the day, when Papa, Dad's dad, dropped dead of a heart attack. He had been sixty-seven.

It was a lot of people to lose in just over a year.

I put down the iron. "How long *does* it last?"

He offers me a sad smile. "It lasts . . . awhile."

"Muuuuuuuuuuuum," Harriet calls. "Archie's watching the iPad!"

"I'll go," Dad says.

The kids are sad about Aunt Nettie's death. All of them have cried, multiple times, even Edie, but their grief is wonderfully fickle—here one moment, gone the next. This, too, I'm becoming familiar with.

"How do I look?" Ollie says.

He stands in the doorway of the laundry room in what I think of as his "Eamon suit." It's tight-fitting, navy blue. A recruitment suit. He looks handsome in it.

"I'm going to sell it tomorrow," he says. "On eBay."

There's no point in telling him not to worry about it now, or that we could talk about it in a week or two. Ever since Nettie's death, Ollie has been on a mission to do anything he can to make money, save money or reclaim money. We've sold our watches, all of my jewelry, a handful of other items that have value. It's got a frenzied, *avoidance-of-grief* type feel to it, but at the same time, I find myself comforted by it. As though he's recommitting to his role in the family, showing us the kind of person he wants to be.

"Actually there's a Facebook page for people who want to buy secondhand Hugo Boss suits," I say. "You'd probably get a better price for it. I can post it on there if you like."

"That would be great," he says. "Or just tell me the site and I'll do it."

I would be hard-pressed to find an upside to the whole tragedy of Nettie's death, but if I was really trying, I'd say it was the new harmony between Ollie and me. Somehow, we have found ourselves perfectly aligned on the goals of our family and we are absolute partners. It never suited Ollie being the full-time breadwinner, and the funny thing was, I always knew that. Now, working as a team, I realize we are playing to our strengths again. I don't know what is going to happen tomorrow after this funeral. I don't know if we can afford to keep our house. I have no idea what's ahead for us. I know it's likely to be bad for . . . a while. But I'm hoping it won't be bad forever.

"It's nearly time to go," I say.

I turn off the iron and peel Edie's dress off the ironing board. Ollie appears right beside me and gently tugs at my necklace. "That was Mum's, wasn't it?"

I nod. I'd been wearing it every day since Diana died. Ollie turns it over in his fingers. "I remember seeing it around Mum's neck when I was little. She said it symbolized strength."

We both look down at it. "It's a shame she didn't give it to Nettie."

We're quiet for a moment, staring down at the necklace. Then Ollie lets it fall back to my chest. "Maybe she knew Nettie wasn't strong enough to wear it."

64

Lucy

Ten years later . . .

"Lucy? Abdul Javid is here for his interview. Is Ollie here?"

I glance at my watch. "He must be running late, Ghezala. I'll come out."

"Okay. I'm going home now. Have a good evening."

I hang up the phone and pull on my suit jacket. When I don't have interviews on I often wear leggings and a T-shirt around the office, part of the perks of running your own business—but today Ollie and I have had back-to-back interviews all day. Our office is a short drive from our home, in a run-down old town house not far from where Ghezala used to live. A lot of new refugees settle in this area, which makes it convenient for them and cheap for us. Ollie and I each have offices (formerly bedrooms) and Ghezala's office is in the old living room. On the days Ghezala comes in, she brings in food for us to share in the living room. She has a playpen set up as well, for those days when her youngest isn't in day care.

Ghezala has five children now. Hakem is making enough money that she doesn't need to work anymore, but as well as being on the board of Diana's charity she comes in to help us all the time—translating, making the candidates comfortable, helping explain cultural differences. She was the one who approached us a few months after Diana's death. She'd heard about the business we wanted to start and she was aware of a sizable pool of money that Diana had bequeathed that was designated for "ventures deemed by the board to be in the interests of the charity."

Our business fits this criteria.

I step into the hallway and shake the hand of a very tall man, his skin as black as burnt wood.

"Mr. Javid?" I say.

"Mrs. Goodwin?"

"Please. Call me Lucy."

"Then you must call me Abdul."

Abdul smiles a brilliant white smile. Apart from the trouser legs of his suit, which are several inches too short, he is very presentable. Abdul was a project manager for a major construction group in Afghanistan. He arrived in Australia four months ago and has been working as a night cleaner at the local hospital while trying to find work.

"Come in, Abdul. Ollie, my partner, will join us in a moment."

"Did someone say my name?"

Ollie clambers through the back door, dressed in a shirt with jeans. The days of his shiny tight suits are long gone. Now, Ollie does a lot of his interviews via Skype so he can be found dressed smartly from the waist up and wearing God-knows-what from the waist down. He works hard, harder even than he did for Eamon. He is always running late, his paperwork is never done, but he's also more alive than I've ever seen him. He spends hours with the candidates, doing whatever it takes to get them ready for an interview.

I do most of the work with our organizations, finding jobs where there aren't any, and opening the minds of decision makers at big companies, making them take on someone who perhaps doesn't fit their ideal.

"Just give them an interview," has become my catch cry. "*One* interview." More often than not, that one interview gets our client the job. Like Ollie, I live for that now. As a team, we've become passionate about making sure everyone gets a go. I like to think that we get that from Diana, and that she would be proud of us.

Ollie and Eamon's business declared bankruptcy shortly after Diana's death. Eamon was investigated for misappropriating company funds, and was found guilty of fraud. Ollie never regained any of the money Eamon had stolen from him but he had taken some satisfaction from the fact that Eamon spent six months in prison (and that Eamon's young girlfriend Bella had left him for an Iron Man, and last we heard they were writing a Paleo cookbook together).

We take a seat at the round table, and Abdul tells us about his time in Australia. He explains the difficulties he's had finding work. Some has to do with his English, and Ollie jumps in to say that we'll help him with that.

"We can help you with anything," he says. "English lessons, intercultural relations, mentoring."

After Nettie's death, Ollie threw himself into the business with such vigor I wondered if it was healthy. He'd lost his parents and his sister all within a year and he needed to heal. It took me a while to see how healing this business actually was for him.

We don't see Patrick anymore. We sent Christmas cards for the first couple of years but once he remarried (apparently to a woman who is the heiress to a very nice fortune stemming from her late father's packaging business) and became the father of twin boys, we let the contact drop. Ollie still found it especially difficult.

"It's not fair. All Nettie wanted was to be a mother. If she hadn't had fertility issues, she—and Mum—would still be alive."

Maybe that was true, maybe it wasn't. The fact was, the kids and I were his family and honestly, being around each other all day long, it had never felt more true.

"Okay," I say to Abdul. "Why don't you tell us a little about yourself?"

The agency has been a huge success, in terms of the candidates we've been able to place, particularly with organizations that formerly would never have looked at candidates without Australian experience. And yet, we may never again own a house. We live in a rental not far from our office, near the industrial part of town. The kids' school is rough, diverse and wonderful, with people from all walks of life. Every day after school, the kids are here at the office doing their homework or playing with Ghezala's kids. Diana would have loved every bit of it (and how Tom would have been befuddled). I think that is what fuels Ollie's drive for the whole thing. Everyone, no matter how old they are, wants their mother's approval. And EVERYONE, no matter who they are, wants their mother-in-law's.

I glance up at Diana's final letter. Once the investigation into Diana's death was over, the police had handed it over to us. Now it was framed on the wall of my office, one of my most cherished possesions.

I could have written more, but in the end, there's really only two pieces of wisdom worth leaving behind. I worked hard for everything I ever cared about. And nothing I ever cared about cost a single cent.

Mum

Such lessons are hard-learned. But now, we've learned them.

LAKE COUNTY PUBLIC LIBRARY

3 3113 03529 6716

X HEPW
Hepworth, Sally,
The mother-in-law

AP - - '19